THE
SLAYER PRINCE

THE
SLAYER PRINCE

ELIZABETH BROCKIE

Black Lyon Publishing, LLC

THE SLAYER PRINCE
Copyright © 2013 by Orlena Beth Brockie

Our books may be ordered through your local bookstore or by
visiting the publisher:

BlackLyonPublishing.com

Black Lyon Publishing, LLC
PO Box 567
Baker City, OR 97814

This is a work of fiction. All of the characters, names, events,
organizations and conversations in this novel are either the products
of the author's vivid imagination or are used in a fictitious way for the
purposes of this story.

ISBN-10:   1-934912-58-1
ISBN-13: 978-1-934912-58-4
Library of Congress Control Number: 2013948562

Cover Model: Jason Aaron Baca
Photographer: Portia Shao

Published and printed in
the United States of America.

Black Lyon Paranormal Romance

For David, my loving husband, for his support and patience in all those late night hours at the laptop.
For all my friends and family, with love.

A special thank you to Daniel, for his unfailing encouragement.

1.

Normally, James Lauren would enjoy a night like this—rain beading against the mullioned window panes, embers snapping in the ebbing fireplace logs, a hint of autumn behind the last of the flames. Normally, he would enjoy a night like this with a soft woman and a cold beer …

Normally.

Tonight he was alone, his lean, muscled form recessed into the shadows of a high-back leather desk chair behind a twin pedestal desk. The waning fire sketched the room in subdued hues of red—tall bookcases sweeping the ceiling, an oak fireplace mantel, a Grandfather clock that needed winding and the rolling carry-on and backpack on the floor beside him.

James pulled his black, all-weather jacket closer around him, becoming barely visible in the fading firelight. Just a shadowy outline in pale crimson. But the black sapphire on his ring shone out from the shadows like midnight captured in a star.

Leaning back and resting the heels of his Timberlands on the edge of the desk, James crossed his ankles and slowly turned his gold and sapphire birth curse between his fingers.

In the glow of the reddening fire, the gold in the band was as rich as a setting sun. And the Greek key of life traveled around the "stone sacred to Saturn" in an orbital path of red and gold eternity, embellishing the burnished setting.

Tiny blue flames flickered within the depths of the sapphire's facets. Reflections mirrored from the hearth? Or erupting from the very caves that had given the jewel birth?

The ring was hypnotic, mesmerizing.

A vampyre's ring.

James' eyes did not move from the fire in the gem's gleam until his employer's silhouette appeared in the library doorway.

The master slayer stepped into the room, and the shadow cast on the wall behind him towered above his five foot eight inches, making him seem larger than life.

In some ways, he was. The mysterious, wiry little man was Yoda—with a stake.

"Your ride is here," he said, his French accent serrated with edges of emotion.

Andre DuPre was not only the master of this house of slayers, he was James' long-time friend, and this was not an easy parting. James knew he would die by Andre's weapons if he came back more hungry than human from the journey he was about to take.

Sliding the ring on his finger, James rose from the desk chair.

The corded muscles in the twenty-six-year-old slayer's shoulders and arms rippled, honed by a lifelong love affair with baseball, and four years of stringing a crossbow. James stretched his back, and picked up his pack.

Andre glanced inquisitively at the thick shock of dark brown hair trailing the top of those broad shoulders. Yesterday James' crowning glory had been long and slicked into a pony tail to mid-back. "Somebody get to that pony tail with a kukri knife?" Andre commented with a chuckle.

An easygoing curve flashed around James' grin. "Trying to move into a new look," he said. "And it wasn't easy to let go."

"I can see. It could use trimming up a bit. Or a lot." Andre laughed good-naturedly.

His laugh was brook water, to soften a difficult goodbye. This farewell might be permanent. James knew that. In a few days, he might become twenty-six forever, and forever would chain his heart to a darkness that dissolved remembrances and farewells.

Andre dropped into an overstuffed chair near the fire and gazed into the dwindling licks of flame. "What in the hell were we thinking, James? We can't send you into a bed of vampyres. In the end, you're probably going to get bitten. You know that, don't you? You're going to get bitten and be resurrected with that damned Dracula owning your soul."

"I don't plan on that becoming part of my game plan," James assured him.

He lifted his silver cross from his neck and placed in on the desk.

Worry crosschecked the face of the older slayer.

"I'll be fine," James said. But they both knew that was a lie.

His chest suddenly felt bare, unprotected, lost without the jewel of faith. He would have no protection in the lurid, soulless places he was about to enter.

"If you are lost to us in this quest, you know what must follow," Andre said quietly.

Though his tone was even, Andre's deep set eyes were crisp, crystal hard in their warning. And James' cooler earth-brown eyes received the message well.

And in that inescapable moment, James realized that in friendship, there could also be pain—

That oversized, gnarled, wicked stake Andre could throw like a javelin would hurt like hell.

The taxi was honking. The older man rose from the chair and swiftly hugged him goodbye, the quick crush of friend to friend. James pulled his backpack straps over his shoulders, grasped the handle of the carry-on, and rolled the luggage out the front door.

Within moments, the luggage was in the trunk, his seat belt was buckled, and the cab's tires were slinging mud toward the train station. Briefly, James glanced back, but a black outline of cedars was already hiding the Shadows' two-story mansion behind a wet wall of branches.

Even so, James knew Andre's band of slayers, the warrior troupe that for all intents and purposes had been his family for the last four years, would be standing at the upstairs windows, looking out into the rain to silently wish him Godspeed and a thimbleful of luck. They could not go with him. He could no longer be seen with them. He could no longer be part of them. He was on a solitary journey to become the enemy.

You're right, Andre, he thought. *Whatever in hell were we thinking?*

Traffic was a steady stream in the rain, and the taxi was late getting to the station. Hunkering under his jacket collar to ward off the cold raindrops, James made a mad dash for the train already hissing diesel-drenched steam out from under its wheels, ready to roll. With a quick leap to the boarding steps of the last coach car, he lifted his bag ahead of him and bounded to the left through the metal door to make his way down the aisle to his two seats. James had purchased the window seat—and the aisle seat. Not for comfort. From force of habit. If he had to leap and slay, he didn't need a body in the way, living or dead.

He slung his carry-on into the overhead baggage hold and took the window seat. The car creaked. The train rolled forward.

Shortly, the conductor came down the aisle, hole-punching tickets. Night closed in over the train, and the rain was left behind. Landscape tracings in black on black swept past the window; stretches of ranchland, belts of creeks ribbed by ropes of trees, a few knots of hills …

And something … two glowing red slants in a black shadow in the rain. *Is that a friggin' vampyre hovering in a distant field and looking toward the train?*

James rubbed his eyes, then looked again.

The shadow and the red slits were gone.

Great. Other people think they see gas clouds and UFOs in the dark following along with them. I see vamps.

Obviously, the brief red points could have been a reflection in the window from within the train—someone's watch, a cell phone or laptop.

The train chugged along at an easy pace. James' thoughts became drowsy, drifting with memories of other train trips—trips with his adoptive father to Little League state championship games. They would share hot dogs and nachos from the snack car. He would gaze out the window, his ever-present ball and glove in his hand.

Usually, he would be thinking that maybe today would be the day he would hit a grand slam, or at least a home run—a high drive to deep right field maybe.

"Keep your eyes on the ball, your mind on the game, and watch out for change-ups from the pitcher," Dan Lauren would tell him between munches of chips and melty cheese. "Better to be walked than lose the mental game and strike out."

It was a philosophy James still carried with him. *Keep your eyes on the vampyre coming at you like a fast ball, keep your mind in the game, and watch out for change ups from the sons of—*

Absently, James rubbed the burn scar on his inner left arm. Had

Jane Weston been telling him the truth? That the college laboratory fire deemed an accident so long ago had been set deliberately? By the man whose boot prints of wisdom he had cherished, the man he had called father?

The Lady Jane Weston was, after all, known for her lies—a vampyre distrusted even in the Realm.

Nevertheless, her words were like a hot branding iron on his heart. His past was now punctuated with question marks.

James glanced at the ring, and his strong brow furrowed. Had Dan Lauren actually tried to murder him? Because he believed his adopted son to be a bad seed? That he carried evil in his blood? And would pass that on to his children?

Or was there another deeper reason known only to himself?

A sorrow, swelling into physical pain, pricked the crossbow slayer—youth lost, memories tainted.

He closed his eyes to shut down the pain. For the moment, he had no choice but to relegate the questions haunting him to the ravines in his heart. He would climb down there later to find the answers and resolve the past in his own way, in his own time.

Right now, he had a job to do.

James turned from the window to sit sideways and stretch his legs out across the adjoining seat.

"Holy—" He jerked back as though he'd been stung, and his feet went flat to the floor. "Where did you come from?"

An all-too-familiar ghost sat in the seat next to him looking like he wore a Victorian Halloween costume—top hat, gray suit, silver tipped walking cane—and holding that blasted umbrella across his knees.

Sticking to the Shadow troupe like a post-it note while they were in England, he—if you could call it a he—had chilled the air with his riddles and warnings in a frosty breath not easily dismissed or forgotten.

And apparently, he was still sticking around. This time to James.

The haunt was sitting comfortably in the extra seat—James' bought-and-paid-for seat.

Damned cemetery reject.

"What are you doing here?" James asked pointedly, his irritation plain.

The ghost simply tipped his top hat in greeting and smiled, his pallid lips forming a crescent moon.

Spooky. He gave James the freakies. "I thought you did your time, and went on to Heaven or something. Why are you back?"

"I am not in restitution," the ghostly voice breathed toward him in an icy froth.

"Then how about you get your transparent, icy butt off my seat and off this train at the next stop?" James said in a calm tone of terror. "Or better yet, right now. Here's a great window. You can slide right through and right on out into the night. Or wherever it is you go."

The ghost's dead, gray eyes moved languorously into his. "You should desist from discourse with an empty seat, Mr. Lauren. People will think you are—unbalanced."

"They'll just think I'm talking into my Bluetooth," James said with a shrug.

"Ah, modern inventions. I can remember, let's see, when I was alive of course, the excitement generated by the erection of the first gas street light on my block. Quite a night."

"I can imagine." James smirked. "So where you headed, Englishman?"

"With you," the frosty breath traveled across him in answer.

"Oooh, no," James protested avidly, shaking off the shivers the breath had caused in his chest. "This is a one-man outfit. I don't need your cold butt on my heels every time I turn a corner." He waved his hand at the ghost as if to shoo him away, mimicking Jimmy Stewart's famous mannerisms and voice. "Now, you, you just go on, Mr. Ghost, and help someone else. That young girl sitting right over there, for instance. Yeah, that's the one. Just up the aisle. Now she, she looks like she could use some help. You just go on over and sit by her. She looks like she just lost her best friend. She could probably use a good ghost or two."

As if on cue, the young woman rose from her seat, and a pair of curvy legs beneath a short, black skirt edged into the aisle.

Enjoyably, that wonderfully tangy, tart deliciousness in the groin erupted within James.

Open-toed sandals in red completed the tantalizing vision, complementing strong ankles and calves.

And the rest of her wasn't bad either.

She began weaving her way to the back of the swaying car. The train was rocking at a good pace now along the steel tracks, the coach car rocking right along with it, making steps unsteady. She clutched the corners of headrests to try to stay balanced while she inched down the aisle. Locks of sable hair tumbled around her cheeks and down her shoulders.

The engine picked up speed. More clutching of headrest corners to keep her footing as she drew near, more swaying of the tiny skirt, more determination to hold her own against a train intent on capsizing anyone in the aisle into the nearest unsuspecting lap of some hapless aisle side passenger.

In retrospect, James wished he had picked the aisle seat. The ghost could have the friggin' window seat.

The young woman caught his gaze and smiled, a winsome, slightly shy smile from full lips tinted cherry red that made his throat go dry.

She seemed tall.

James wanted to stand up, and stand next to her to see if she was tall—hell, he wanted to crush her to him, look down into her baby blues, and see if she was tall enough to accommodate him.

The train lurched, braking in the wake of an upcoming curve.

She lost her footing.

"Oh!" she gasped, and landed smack dab, spread eagle in the ghost's lap.

And you are pretty in pink, James thought as the skirt previewed every good thing in life. He helped her untangle her legs and get back on her feet.

She *was* tall. A slender tall. A sensual tall. Just tall enough.

Regaining her foothold, she straightened her blouse, one of those trendy little sleeveless flurries of shreddy ruffles, a seductively red flurry that had gone askew in the tumble.

Pretty in pink and red, and matching lacy bra, James thought with another enjoyable inward smile.

"I am so sorry!" she sputtered as her hand went through the ghost's shoulder to grab the headrest and steady herself so she would not topple again.

"No problem. I've never minded rescuing a damsel in distress," James smiled, a smile he knew was too deep, too—happy.

She worked her way on down the aisle, and went into the club car.

"You would be the one who gets the quickie lap dance," James tossed at the ghost.

"The one sitting with her is a vampyre," the ghost said, and vanished.

For a moment, James' thoughts went blank. Then cleared. All too lucidly.

Crap.

Looked like he was going dragon slaying tonight, and he didn't even have a feather from a crossbow bolt, much less his crossbow.

Pretty in Pink and Red returned to her seat.

And as she passed by him, James now saw—as all slayers sense and see when in the presence of the beings who haunt the night—a wing tip. Black as an oil slick at midnight.

Crap navigated into a more definitive expletive.

2.

Daelyn Bakerville sat stiffly in her train seat, staring straight ahead, her fists tucked tightly into her lap so she would not be tempted to whirl around, screech in fury, and claw the face of the vampyre guard sitting next to her.

Her third attempt at escape had just failed.

Her passageway to freedom, the club car, the last car on the train, had seemed like the perfect avenue of escape. Just flash past the drinkers, cell phones and laptops, roll open the door and fly, fly, fly.

Only that didn't happen.

She sighed. Her plan had been so carefully concocted.

While it hadn't been easy, she had finally convinced the goon sitting next to her that she needed a little wine or else she was going to bite the next human who happened along, and create a ruckus. The guard had released her, and she had hurried to the club car, to leap out the back and fly away. As far away as she could get, as fast as she could get there.

The Great Getaway. The thought of it had almost made her giddy, had made her want to laugh out loud hysterically, it had seemed so simple.

No one would have even noticed her.

The whole vampyre Realm could come flying through the club car, screeching and yowling, and biting everyone in sight, and the cell phone texting addicts would never look up. Facebook fans would be buried in posts, and beer and whiskey would be satisfactorily numbing the rest. Freedom, freedom from an imprisonment imposed on her because she was a mistake, would be hers. She could revel in the black crystalline sky and be on her way to a mountain resort in some faraway shady valley, or a swanky hotel on some foggy coast—she had enough money—or a cabin in a delightful, drippy wet rainforest. Hell, she'd even settle for the Bayou and alligators.

Of course, she hadn't expected another goon to be sitting at the last club car table by the door, to block her.

Pensively, Daelyn's fingers twisted at the thick bracelet she was required to wear. Whips of diamonds studded the black band, shining under the overhead train lights like a myriad of stars on her wrist. Exquisite, beautiful—

A shackle.

"Fix your wrist band," the vampyre next to her commanded in a frozen tone without turning to her, without emerging from the gray hood that hid his molten eyes.

The anxious motion of twisting and turning had pushed the bracelet up her arm, revealing the small tattoo on the inside of her wrist, the tat that branded her and now revealed her as a fugitive.

A black rose.

She eased the wristlet back into place.

She had been a Rose. And was never earmarked to become a vamp. She was—an "unfortunate incident," they called her.

Well, this unfortunate incident is going to find a way to gain her liberty, come hell or the hanging rope, she thought with an indomitable toss of her head. Her sable waves rolled from her shoulders to her back, and her blue eyes blazed with determination.

"If you're thinking about shapeshifting," her companion warned from within the hood, "don't."

Her eyes became downcast under their long black lashes, and glistened with moisture.

How long had it been since that fated walk on the beach? she thought unhappily.

A year? Not much more than that, she was sure. She struggled to lock in on a timeline. Her past seemed to be gradually becoming a smear in her thoughts, events fading into formlessness. Places and people who had existed in her life seemed—planetary.

"I was just taking a walk on the beach," she murmured to herself. "Just a walk on the beach ..."

I had a nice little apartment in Santa Monica. With a great Cal-king bed, nice balcony. Nice furniture, nice cat.

Nice. Expensive.

Then she took in the Nightmare on Elm Street as her roommate.

A little sparrow looking thing in Garment District clothes, Jodi
Limon rarely washed her hands, or cleaned her bathroom or bedroom. And she constantly left her cooking pots on the stove for
days, sometimes weeks. The girl was exasperating. She could have
tried the patience of a priest. She was just plain dirty. The food left
in the bottoms of the pans caked, cracked, withered, hardened, and
could have competed with toxic waste as being labeled hazardous
material. When Daelyn dared mention wash them, *please*, she left
them longer to spite her. Common courtesy seemed to be foreign
to her, but spite was, apparently, second nature. She was dirty and
devious.

Daelyn moved her own dishes and utensils to separate cabinets,
just for hygiene's sake. A couple of plates went missing. She found
them much later under her roommate's bed, stuck together with a
glue of green macaroni and cheese. Washing them was not even an
option. She threw them out with the kitchen garbage the girl had
left in a box by the front door.

Smells began to grow from Jodi's side of the refrigerator, from
things, things wrapped in plastic baggies, little things that looked
like rat bones and small birds.

The floor turned black before she would mop when it was her
month for house chores. Crumbs of quick breads and bits of things
that looked like—yep, they were fly wings—littered the counter
tops. Dishes sat in the sink unwashed. The cat disappeared.

The girl had never been much for conversation, but as the situation worsened, she rarely spoke at all, spending more and more
time in her room. Her locked room.

Of course, Daelyn did not know she was a vampyre's minion,
just that cleanliness was apparently not next to godliness on her
list of priorities. Pleasing the emaciated looking dude with dark,
slightly sunken eyes who began coming around every night was her
priority. Her only priority.

His name was Lem, and he smelled like he had lived with
wolves, and walked and talked like he had lived with hillbillies,
with his brains hanging where his balls should have been.

But sometimes, as he smiled at her when she opened the door

to his knock, he was like looking at a fire through a haze of smoke. His presence was disturbing, and left her more than a little frightened, though she could not identify why, except that she wanted to run whenever he entered a room.

And run hard.

At first, for several weeks, he spent most of his time in her roommate's room behind a door they kept locked when she was present in the apartment.

Then he found out Daelyn was a precog.

"Sweetsie says you're a precog and a Baskerville. You got any relatives in Europe?" he asked brightly one night, coming out of the bedroom and casually slinging a butter fat arm across the back of the couch as he plopped down with "Sweetsie." He grinned at Daelyn like the cat who was about to snatch the canary. "Of noble blood?"

"Noble?" Daelyn almost laughed.

His eyes were blue, but confusingly became dark rising pools as he gazed at her, pulling her own blue depths into the vortices, and she could not ignore them or move away easily once he turned them on her.

"I'm related to the Danburys. But they're not ... My name isn't—"

But she had lost her thought. Something strange had entered the portals of her mind like a whip of white lightning.

"Well now, if you ain't a fine looking little wench princess," he said. "Can you really read the past and such in objects you touch? Sweetsie here tells me you have a hefty dose of the real thing."

He nicknamed her Gypsy, questioning her relentlessly about her precognitive powers, and the one time "Sweetsie" pouted and sulked and wriggled onto his lap to compete for his attention, he swatted her away like a gnat.

Daelyn tried to avoid them and stay away whenever he was around, until she felt like she was becoming a stranger in her own home.

Her frustration with "Sweetsie" grew like a silent volcano. The girl's personal habits reached new heights of filth, and crunchy things on the kitchen counter reached the haz-mat stage.

Daelyn finally donned her favorite wind jacket and headed for the beach to breathe in the evening's clean marine air and consider her options.

Taking off her sandals, she pressed her bare feet into the clean, white, soft sand, the grainy warmth left from the day, and walked the beach until the marine layer began to purloin the night.

Her only option, she decided, was to move. Absently plucking a few stray shells from the sand near some boulders, she turned to leave, resolute in her decision.

She almost didn't see it, the shoeless foot sticking out from behind the rocks, bluish and very dead—and wreathed in seaweed.

A body had washed up on the shore fully clothed.

Lem.

She hurried over and knelt down in the sand to check his pulse and see if he was alive.

The eyes behind the bloated, blue eyelids popped open.

And her life as she knew it was over.

His fist met her face, her face met the sand—and she felt, and saw, and heard nothing else.

She woke up drugged, barely able to stand as he pushed and pulled her through an eerie darkness lit only by kerosene oil lamps and wrought iron wall sconces.

After a hot shower in a stone-walled chamber to "decontaminate" her, he said, she was ushered into gold robes and into a dark bed in a luxurious boudoir deep in the earth. She was to be pampered and become fodder for the Count's two descendent human nephews who would come courting. Tweedle-Dum and Tweedle-Dee wanted to vie for Father of the Year for sperming the first Precog Child of the Realm. A royal precog.

Thanks to Lem, her abductors erroneously believed she was a Black Rose, one of the last coveted females in royal bloodlines. She had been abducted, stolen, to "enhance" the royal vampyre bloodlines.

Human trafficking, vampyre style. To birth male mortal babies who would be "transformed" into vampyres on their eighteenth birthdays—powerful vampyres each with a special "gift" inherited through the mother's genes.

Taking a hard look at where the truth could land her, basically a hole in the ground, Daelyn did what any woman would do to stay alive. She played the royal card. Better to be a live Baskerville than a dead Bakerville.

The Dopey Duo never got the chance to bring chocolates and flowers to her stone room in the Realm caves, however. The Precog Child of the Realm was never to be conceived. Some fool who didn't know she was a royal abduction, bit her.

He was hauled off in chains to God knows where—and the bitten became the biter.

She was hauled off to a castle, she knew not where, to join the party vamps, soon relishing the goblets at the table of the Royals as she became the favorite of some master vampyre named Henri De LaCroix—until the bad-ass took off to chase after some mortal or something.

She wanted to take off, too. Ex-Roses who knew too much didn't get out much. In fact, not at all. Especially one who had become the favorite and confidant of the most feared and revered vampyre in the Realm.

The Count guarded her closely, pampering her, but keeping her locked away, to emerge only at his command.

He kept her for the pleasure of her company—more for pleasure, less for company.

"I'm hungry," Daelyn pouted impatiently toward her guard.

"Look around and pick someone. Who do you want?" he said, his voice clearly reflecting he was irritated she had bothered him. "The train will be stopping soon. There's a depot not far ahead en route. The station's a renovation of an eighteenth-century stop. With souvenirs and such inside. Everyone will be getting off to stretch and take a short sight-seeing break for about thirty minutes. Should be easy for you, as wild and wanton as you are."

Daelyn cast a short, furtive glance toward the back of the car. Toward the young human male with the wonderful shoulders and powerful, well-defined arms.

The slayer.

She had known what he was as soon as she felt those arms of iron.

A slayer who was weaponless, unprotected. His belt had touched her briefly, and she had read the leather that was worn away slightly where a utility pack full of stakes and holy water should have hung from its strap. The belt told her he had left the pouch behind, and darkness surrounded the leaving of it, but she'd had no time to read more.

"Him," she said.

3.

The train to Texas never made it to the vintage prairie depot.

The coach car that had been clipping along the rails at a good pace slowed unexpectedly.

Daelyn leaned her elbow on the armrest and her blue eyes blazed as they pierced the blackness outside the window. "Where in the middle of this forsaken nowhere are we? The train seems to be slowing to a stop!"

Not now! she thought. *Keep this crate moving!* She was only two miles to freedom—if Obi-Wan Kenobi the Younger Years back there taking up two seats didn't blow it for her, take her head off or something.

She risked another quick glimpse in his direction. He was easy on the eyes—full, warm lips instead of the cold blue zippers she was used to seeing, a brown gaze holding mystery in their centers like a tiger's eyes, and a strong, focused jawline. Good looks were poured across that face like water. He sure as hell needed to revisit that haircut, though …

He seemed—pre-occupied.

With her, she quickly realized.

His gaze was intense, hard and defined as he met her glance. The tiger wanted to strike.

He knew what she was.

Are you thinking you could smash the window, break off a chunk of glass and come barreling down the aisle to stake me? she thought with an uplift of her chin as she smiled in challenge directly into those incisive, excellent eyes. *You would certainly scare the bajee-bies out of the passengers.*

She slowly edged her smile with a silky tongue. A luscious

"come hither and get me, slayer."

The eyebrows above the brown eyes burning down the aisle toward her arched appreciatively.

She deepened the dare. Licked her lips in a slow draw. Let her eyes flash a little more fire. *Come on down, Hero. You have to get past the guard to get to me. And while you two are busy playing Bite N' Slay, I'm outa here. I'll become a tiny little something or other, and run down the aisle and through the people and out the door.*

I would shape-shift into a cockroach if I thought it would get me out of here ...

The train car jerked forward suddenly, and the train came to a full stop. The coach lights dimmed, the air conditioning wavered.

A ballpoint pen rolled against Daelyn's foot from somewhere under the seat in front of her.

A slight tingling sensation traveled up her leg. She bent over and picked up the pen in curiosity. The same sensation, like the sting from a lit match, tunneled up her hand and through her arm.

The pen was silver.

Real silver. With the name of some insurance company stamped on the side and the words, *Million Dollar Club.*

Though it stung like a bee, she curled the pen into her hand and secretly slipped it into her shoulder bag. You never knew when a pure silver, Million Dollar Club ink pen might come in handy.

The train inched forward, the lights brightened, cool wafts traveled across the backs of the seats again.

The porter pushed through the coach car door, and amiably explained that "ole" engine number nine was breaking down. Just couldn't handle the load any longer, he said, and would probably be put out to pasture, but don't worry folks, another engine was on the way.

Then he left.

Another jerk, the car rolled backward slightly. Moved forward a few yards, backed up again, halted dead on the tracks. The air conditioning stopped, the lights in the car went out, and the vampyre next to her became a pile of ash on the floor—

She quickly scooped up the silver pen she had smashed into his heart in the dark, lightly blew away the bit of lingering ash with a smile of satisfaction, and slipped it back into her bag.

Folding her hands pristinely in her lap, Daelyn kept her gaze locked straight ahead as though no one had ever been sitting by her.

The phosphorescent aisle strips began to glow neon green in the dark, casting a pale mint essence across the floor and the vampyre dust.

Disembodied outlines of faces began to float through the car as the glow of cell phone screens offered patches of light.

Those faces silhouetted in the dark did not look happy with their situation. Frowning, and more than a little frightened at being on a rail car abandoned to nothing but miles and miles of pampas grass, pastures and moonless night, the train travelers began to grumble in four letter word increments about being "stuck on the slow train to nowhere" on an uncommonly warm, autumn night in Texas.

From her window, Daelyn had a clear view of the rails rounding a hillside up ahead—and the front half of the train curling around the curve without them.

The coach car and the club car had been detached, left stranded on the track in the middle of nowhere, waiting to be switched to a new engine while the rest of the train went merrily on ahead.

The porter came through sweeping a flashlight beam across the backs of the seats, pitifully pleasant.

"Not too long, folks. About forty-five minutes. Step out and get a breath of fresh air if you'd like. But don't wander or dawdle too long. The sidewinders like to lay on the warm tracks after dark, and the coyotes and wolves come down to the crick yonder for a drink. Anyone who wants to have a smoke, please congregate at the rear beyond the club car so as not to spread second-hand smoke to the non-nicotine passengers."

Daelyn quickly rose and cut her way into the press of bodies in the aisle to keep the slayer in sight. He could help her. Rescue her. There was still another guard hanging around somewhere, possibly more.

Hurrying through the metal door and down the boarding steps, Daelyn did not notice that the boarding stepping stool normally placed in the space between the last step and the ground, was missing. She stepped down into dead air, and tumbled—right into the arms of the slayer.

Involuntarily, her arms went around his neck as she tried to catch her balance, and his delicious warmth was suddenly all over her.

And she could feel—and hear—his pulse. Her impulses surged within her.

Don't bite him. Don't bite him. He's your ticket out.

"Seems like I'm always catching your fall," he said, his voice even, controlled, but no longer as friendly.

More like a chunk of dry ice.

He was guarded.

She regained her balance, made a movement to ease out of his grasp.

He refused to relinquish her, holding on to her with those arms like a mesh of steel.

"Let go of me," she said in a lowered voice, trying to discreetly pull free of him as passengers filed past. "Or I'll scream."

"Scream," he challenged. "And it will be the last scream you'll ever scream."

Was the slayer bluffing? She could not tell.

A normal mortal she could have pushed away easily and thrown into the nearest tree—but this one, this one was a slayer. They carried that quintessential power against vampyres. Besides, being held by him was, well, kind of nice. In fact, really nice.

She acquiesced, let her body relax against his hard-muscled chest.

The movement drove fire into his eyes.

Sweet.

Grasping her tightly around the waist, he walked her away from the crowd.

Once they were out of earshot, he planted her flat in front of him. "Why did you snuff the vamp?"

His tone, though hard as mortar and brick, was edged with interest.

"Aren't you afraid I'll mesmerize you?" she tried coyly, tilting her head provocatively and gazing into his tantalizing pools of shining brown. But the only one being mesmerized was her, she realized. His eyes were deep, earthy, and held desires she wanted to call to.

"Answer me," he persisted, his smooth, strong hands holding her shoulders firmly. His hands were deft, the fingers well-formed and straight.

She deepened her blue gaze, let her glistening pupils become crystal waters, tried to throw threads of confusion across his thoughts, shackle him with her eyes.

She failed. "You're powerful," she breathed.

"No. I'm just hot and tired and was expecting a nice, cool, peaceful train ride," he said.

This was a slayer to reckon with, she swiftly realized. And she also swiftly realized how desperately she needed him.

"Help me," she pleaded suddenly in anguish. "Please! I don't want to go back there!"

Carefully, slowly, watching her for any sudden movement, he eased his hands from her shoulders and released her. "Back to where?"

"That damned, drunken castle!"

Tears began to pour down her cheeks.

His eyes widened in surprise as he stared at the streams. Then the gaze narrowed. "How old are you?"

"Twenty-three," she sniffled into a tissue she pulled from her shoulder bag.

"No. How old are you?"

"Oh. A year, I think." She shrugged. "Maybe a year and a half?"

"Damn," he murmured, sorrow rinsing his tone as he gazed at her.

He drew his fingertips across the watery trails, wiping them away.

Daelyn felt a new rush of surprise at the warmth in his fingertips as they touched her cool cheeks. And a strange sensation pelted her. She wanted to press his hand against her face, lean her cheek into his palm. She wanted to bask in the mortal's touch, the warmth she missed so badly.

His hand moved away. Reluctantly, it seemed to her.

She swept both his hands into hers. "You're the only hope I have!" she sobbed passionately. "I don't want to go back! Don't let them take me back. Please."

"Them? How many are there?"

"There's at least one left. Probably more." She gripped his hands tightly, desperately, fearful if she let go he would dissipate like a desperate dream, a lost wish.

"You're crushing my hands, darlin'," he said calmly, but firmly.

"Oh!" she said, dropping his hands quickly. "I'm sorry. Sometimes my strength just kind of—surges."

"Yeah, well, it surged," he winced, rubbing his fingers to get the circulation back. "Look, I couldn't take you with me even if you were a mortal. And while I should be sending you into eternity right now, this is your lucky night. I'm on a tight schedule, and slaying hasn't been calendared in. I have to be on a plane to New York City at 2:00 AM—if we ever get to Dallas." He glanced into the distance, at the empty rails. "Looks like I may be walking, or hitch-hiking."

"Take me with you! We can hide in the woods. I'll protect you. You can protect me." She took hold of his arms slightly above his wrists, to be more careful this time. She had to try to make him understand. She kept her touch light, to make sure she didn't hurt him again. His arms were wonderful, arms that could make a mate feel safe—or sexy, depending. "I won't be any trouble," she promised, her voice edging on the verge of panic.

She released her grip on his right arm, and he disengaged her fingers from his left. The gentleness in his touch surprised her. He was being gentle. He was a slayer, and he was being gentle with her. As he took her hand away, however, the bracelet slid, exposing a petal of the rose tattoo, and his fingers were suddenly wrapping around her wrist tightly, his eyes flashing more than surprise as they became riveted on the petal. He pushed the bracelet further down. "Holy Hell. You would be more trouble than you can imagine."

She pulled her arm from his grasp roughly, and shoved the oppressive diamond yoke back in place. "Stinking albatross," she muttered unhappily.

"Any vamp who spots you with that tat would know you've been a Rose, and are on the run," he said.

"H'lo, folks," a friendly, slightly drunken voice swaggered through the night air.

A chubby man with a beard and chipmunk cheeks, in a worn business suit ambled up behind them, his arms loaded with beer.

"Compliments of the Railroad," he said, offering the slayer a beer. "From the club car. Restitution. In apology for all our pain and suffering tonight. Might be a tad warm, but it's wet."

His eyes ran across Daelyn's low cut, red blouse. "And what

would the little lady like?"

You, little man, she thought, her own eyes slanting toward his throat in a reckless blaze.

"She probably prefers wine," the slayer said quickly, his eyes dead on hers. "Doesn't mean I couldn't calendar it in," he warned in a lowered voice.

"Well, never say this snack cart is empty!" the man laughed around his beard, pulling a bottle of red wine from his right suit coat pocket.

He dipped his hand into his left, and pulled out a glass.

"Thank you," Daelyn said, taking them gratefully.

As he meandered on to take his wares to the next traveler, she tossed the glass under the train, pulled out the wine stopper with a red tipped fingernail, lifted the bottle to her lips, and guzzled.

"Oookaay," the slayer said, taking a swig of warm beer and watching her closely, guardedly, as she lowered the bottle and wiped the red residue from her mouth with the back of her hand.

She tossed the bottle under the train with the shattered glass and exhaled.

"You still have breath!" he exclaimed, stunned.

"I guess," she shrugged.

Daelyn stepped close to him, to try again to make him lose himself in her, so she could convince him to flee into the woods with her.

A movement. In the darkness. Behind them, behind him. Something or someone was coming close. Fast. Her gaze ripped away from his eyes, over his shoulder into the piercing night beyond.

She gasped.

Catching her wide-eyed, startled stare, the slayer turned around to see what had rifled her.

His forehead met the broad end of a piece of railroad tie.

And all hell broke loose.

4.

From where he lay, semi-conscious, knocked to the ground near a giant steel wheel, James could vaguely see the outline of a vampira in a flurry of red shreddy ruffles flying across the ground, scream-ing in a rage. Her wings were out. Her fangs had dropped.

Someone was about to get his comeuppance.

Through the blur of her wings, as though he was gazing through bees' wings, James could see a man running for his life, running away from her. Skinny, all legs and flailing arms, he resembled a running stick. James tried to call to her, to stop her. His throat would not cooperate.

A second vampyre, hidden crouched in the dark on top of the train car, suddenly swooped toward her. People began to yell and run. Women screamed and grabbed shocked husbands, hauling them onto the two train cars even as they kept looking back in terror-laced fascination at the gorgeous vampiress on a rampage.

Shoes ran past James, stumbled, ran on. Kicked dirt in his face. More shoes. Tennis shoes, leather slip-ons, flip flops, high heels, cowboy boots, running past the body on the ground. The body of James. Oblivious to him.

Some brave soul briefly leaned over him, asked him if he was all right.

I'm fine. I'm lying down here in the dirt because I like it down here in the dirt with the bugs and the creepy, crawly things that live in gravel and grass.

A coyote appeared at his feet, stared at him briefly, then ran be-tween the cars and on into the brush on the other side of the tracks. The brave soul skedaddled.

Someone was running across the rails behind the club car.

More screams. They had stepped on a sidewinder. The snake sidled across the ground like a loose whip into James' vision, stopped, stared James eye slit to eye, then angled across his chest and on into the grass.

His heart stopped in those moments, he was sure.

He was also sure he must have passed out for a few seconds, because the next thing he saw was the runaway vamp ripping open the man's throat, and taking him like a Slurpy before she tossed him to the ground. Wiping her mouth with the back of her hand, she turned to face the male vampyre. And fight him.

If I was that vampyre, James thought, *I think I'd politely nod good night, and go on home now.*

James tried to move, tried to get up, go help her. Though he had no idea why. It was not his fight.

It was just the sad and sorry way she had said, "that damned, drunken castle." When he had looked into her eyes with their oceans of tears, she had mesmerized him, and hell, he had wanted her to get away from that "damned, drunken castle," too. Damned vampyre brothel.

I need a beer, James thought. *I'm not thinking straight ...*

Slowly, James realized she had gotten to him. She was knee deep in trouble and he felt sorry for her. This wasn't a prison break. She was trying to escape the Realm.

And she still had breath. Not enough notches on her belt yet to take the last of her mortality. But as James thought of the man she had just ripped into, literally, he knew that taste of breath wouldn't last long. Not at the rate she was going.

The two unearthly beings faced off. Then the night hissed and screamed with a flurry of wings, fangs, rolls of fog and something that, oddly, resembled fairie dust as they flew at one another, one fighting to be free, the other determined she should not be.

She was furiously battling, but cried out in pain each time she was flung to the ground by the stronger, older vampyre.

Terrified passengers were staring through the windows at the vamp fight, their eyes wide as saucers, shocked, but unable to look away.

A pair of white training shoes with blue trim and sweat pants appeared in James's sight, blocking the view of the train windows. Hands picked him up by his legs, another pair of hands grabbed his wrists.

Then he was being hurriedly hauled on board the coach car through swirling dirt filled with faerie dust. Fighting vampyres.

"Hell of a night," he murmured.

"Hope to hell there's a sunrise soon," one of his bearers said. "'Cause it ain't over yet."

The hands lugged him down the aisle and sprawled him across his bought-and-paid-for seats, where he figured he must have passed out again because when he opened his eyes, starlight was streaming in through the train window, the coach car was moving, and the air conditioning was pitching cool drafts across the seats.

They were moving on, rounding the bend and not looking back, pretending it hadn't happened, reading magazines so their eyes wouldn't wander to the empty seats. And they were snacking on liquor—lots of it. They were leaving the strange occurrence that had defied logic back behind them with the sidewinders.

Except one. A college student with a wide smile, forearms like the Hulk, a shaggy haircut and a red University of Oklahoma hoodie, was showing the whole train car a cell phone snapshot of "shadows" vaguely resembling a woman with wings—if you stretched your imagination several feet past impossible.

As James pulled himself up and gingerly felt around on the knot that had been his forehead, the student offered him a water bottle. James took the electrolyte water, and thanked him. "Were you part of my air lift team?"

"Yeah. Me and Jake. We were thick in the middle of it, man. Scaariee."

James thanked him again, this time for getting him out of harm's way.

"So. Were you her lover?" the kid asked, way too enthusiastically.

"Not hardly," James said. "Just talked when we got off to get a breath of fresh air."

Disappointment clouded the kid's big smile. "Oh." Then his voice became animated again. "I'm going to sell this snap to one of those mad rags—you know, alien sightings, Elvis is back in the building, ghosts, one of those 'we'll print anything' magazines. Or maybe I'll throw it out on YouTube to see how many hits I get. Then do some major pub crawls."

"Did you see what happened to her?" James asked, leaning over and holding his throbbing head in his hands.

"Yeah. We all did. It was too sad, man. Three of them took her down like a grounded bomber. Then she killed one, broke free, and flew like a wild eagle. The other two took off after her, caught her in mid-air, and that's the last we saw of her. Too dark to see where they flew with her." He paused. "So vampyres are real as folk, huh?"

"Not quite," James sighed, wondering if this kid knew just how much his life had suddenly changed and would never be the same. Had he wrapped his brain around the reality yet? "What's your major, Boomer Sooner?"

"Football. Quarterback." He grinned. "And quantum physics."

"Interesting mix," James said thoughtfully.

The train was slowing, pulling into the city station. James rose from his seat a little unsteadily, but managed to get his bag and backpack from the overhead.

People began filing out. He turned and, leaning down, handed the kid a business card with a logo of a crossbow bolt and a website address. "In case you want a summer job," he said.

"Thanks!" the kid responded, but his gaze was puzzled as he studied the barebones card.

"What? You think we're gonna advertise we stomp vamps?" James grinned, weaving, still a little woozy.

The card went missing quickly, deeply pocketed in the kid's sweatshirt.

James hurried from the train to grab a taxi as quickly as his reluctant feet would carry him with a head pulsing with pain, stinted vision and scrambled equilibrium. He hoped he was not too late for the airbus to New York.

Visions of the vampira with the face of a lost angel haunted him, but there was nothing he could do. She was gone, and he had to be on that plane.

The airport check-in line was long, but just when James thought he was home free, the security check was delayed when the conveyor belt broke. In the end he was running like an insane raptor through the airport terminal, and waving his backpack to the boarding gate attendant to not close the door to the boarding dock.

She waited amicably, her little gray and blue kerchief tied impeccably at her throat, her practiced television commercial smile firmly in place as he came to a whirlwind halt in front of her, his chop job hair in a mess.

"Thanks!" he said, catching his breath as he slapped at his shirt pockets and his pants pockets, searching for his boarding pass.

"It's here somewhere," he muttered at her with a weak smile, sliding his backpack from his shoulder.

Outside backpack zipper pocket. Okay. I'm in.

"You must be pretty special," the agent smiled at him as she scanned his pass. "The sky marshals had the flight held for you."

His mouth dropped open. And closed. *Great. I coulda grabbed a coffee as I ran past Starbucks.*

New jabs of pain stabbed at his head as he worked his way down the cramped aisle of the plane's small cabin. He put his bags away, and collapsed into his seat at the back of the plane.

Just enough head room to keep from bumping the overhead compartment, just enough leg room to sit like a zombie.

Airbuses must have been invented to transport munchkins to Oz and back, he decided.

But at least the air conditioning was working, and he wasn't getting cold-cocked by a railroad tie.

And he could drink.

Bring on those little bottles, madam. I am so ready.

The flight attendant brought James a bloody Mary and a sandwich and chips. "Compliments of your boss," she smiled.

God bless that man, he thought, and dug in. He hadn't eaten in many, many hours.

A little pillow and blanket followed—then James did the unthinkable. For a slayer.

In a plane full of vampyres—he fell asleep.

He had known beforehand, of course, there would be vampyres on the plane. His informant had not failed him. But even though the slayer's senses within him also picked up something else, something recently familiar near him, he closed his eyes.

A cramp in his leg woke James abruptly. He checked his watch, it had been only twenty minutes.

Almost time.

He rose and stretched the cramp out of his leg, then went to the bathroom.

From behind the locked door he heard a commotion in the cabin. Muffled voices, loud orders. The vamps had taken the plane. He felt the jet turn, felt the loss of altitude, heard the heavy bay doors open beneath him and the wheels drop. He held on to the walls as tires met tarmac, and the plane came to a brake grinding stop.

People protested, cried, pled for their lives while they were ushered out into the night into a desolate field next to an abandoned air strip. Controlling his impulse to leap out and slay the bastards herding the people off the plane like cows, James held his anger at bay and waited.

Finally, there was only dead silence beyond the restroom door. He opened it a slit and peered out.

The cabin was empty.

He entered the aisle carefully.

From the front of the plane, the other bathroom door was opening. A woman emerged just as cautiously. "Are they—gone?"

"Probably not for long," he said.

She hurried down the aisle with frantic steps. "Quickly then. It must be clear to the Realm that you are my find, that I caught what I thought was a passenger trying to escape, and discovered who was inadvertently on a targeted flight."

She ran toward him, stood in front of him, put out her hand—

She dissolved into dust at his feet.

"Son of a …!" he exclaimed, jumping back.

The vampira runaway from the train rose from between the seats across from him, a shadowy vision in khaki Saks Fifth Avenue man pants, blue peep-toe shoes, and a flutter-sleeved blue silk blouse. An expensive get-up. Someone kept this mistress of the dark well dressed.

"She was going to kill you," she said, pointing to the floor. "Look! Look what she had in her hand!"

James picked up the syringe covered with ash and a silver pen, and sighed, exasperated. "You just killed six and a half months of hard-ass work."

She stared at him incredulously, in disbelief she had done anything wrong. "I—saved you …" She started trembling, and the baby blues started to water.

He sighed again. "What are you doing here?"

"You said you were taking the 2:00 AM to JFK …"

Reminding himself to be more careful in the future in dishing out personal information in mesmerizing moments, James pulled his backpack from the overhead and, looping the straps over his shoulders, headed quickly toward an emergency exit.

"Where—are you going?" she called after him.

"To deplane. I'm going to grab the egress rope and get out of here as fast as I can. And I'd suggest you do the same."

"What—about the people?"

He halted abruptly, surprised at her tone as though she—cared. "The sky marshals on this particular flight were trained to run interference if it was needed."

He shoved the door open.

She ran down the aisle and leaped from the exit passage behind him, swooping to the ground.

"Well, see ya," he said, shifting the backpack as he began taking swift, long strides away from the plane.

But as he left her, James heard a single, heartbreaking sob behind him, a sob that seemed to collapse the very stars in the sky. He stopped, and for a seasoned slayer made what he knew could be a potentially fatal mistake.

He looked back.

She was standing at the plane's wing watching him go, her arms tucked over her breasts, her shoulders slumping dejectedly under her Saks silk blouse. A windy little pile of autumn leaves in pale gold and brown swirled around her peep toes.

Her baby blues spilled over.

Aww, hell.

Exhaling in a sigh, he held out his hand to her. "One condition. Control that temper of yours—and those fangs—or this partnership is dissolved."

She grabbed his hand.

And they ran.

5.

How long the slayer hauled her through the woods and thickets, Daelyn didn't know. Loons called from an unseen, distant lake somewhere. A barn owl hooted in a tree. Coyotes, running in a pack, yelped and barked, their cries close, then diminishing as their voices became lost in the grasslands. A tearing sprint across a meadow, a shotgun run down a cow path. His pace was insane. He ran like a madman.

This slayer didn't want to give a stray vamp even the ghost of a chance of catching up with them. He wanted to be long gone in a hurry.

"I can run better barefoot," Daelyn said, slowing to yank her heels off. She tossed her shoes away into the brush.

He stopped abruptly and retrieved them. "This would be like leaving a blood trail," he said, pulling them from grassy tangles. He started to hand them to her, but his eyebrows drew together in a hard line as he studied the left shoe. "Where's the little glittery thing?"

"You mean the rosette?" she said, and shrugged unconcernedly. "It must have fallen off while we were running. Why?"

Tapping the shoe in his palm pensively, the slayer looked back toward the woods and the path.

"Is anything wrong?" she asked.

"We'd better get going," he said.

"Where are we going?" Daelyn asked as he handed her the shoes and they began to sprint again.

"Hanged if I know," he said. "I have to play this by ear now."

"I said I was sorry. Play what by ear? Maybe I can help."

He slowed momentarily, and looked straight into her gaze,

studying her as though considering the truth in her offer. But she could see that delving into her eyes threw him off balance and into the edges of her eternity.

Sweet. A powerful slayer was being mesmerized by her a little. She let her blue orbs blaze, the siren's song she knew they could sing.

"Damn, your eyes are some scary beautiful," he said. "I feel like I'm being turned upside down and poured into a blue heaven. Are you trying to take me down, Blues?"

He was admitting to her that he was faltering a little, slipping like a sloop into the sea in her eyes. Couldn't tell the truth from a lie.

A strange, sudden excitement rose within her.

And behind it, the abhorrent darkness. Salient, volcanic, de-manding. Want gripped her deadening chambers with merciless tenacity.

She could hear his pulse, beating in her head, beating through the cavity of her heart …

She pushed away the demon dream. "Don't look at them," she warned. "Look at—I dunno—the trees or something." She needed him alive, not bled out on the ground.

He stopped and took her gingerly by the shoulders. "You may turn me upside down, but not inside out, Blues," he said with a curvy smile.

"Whoa," she murmured, her eyes half-closing, moistening. A warmth was spreading through her body from his touch like a summer storm. And she found herself wishing like crazy he would pull her closer. What was this wild warmth?

"I'm not going to sink into those sky wells," he continued. "And if you sink your fangs, you may find you won't like the aftertaste. It will kill you."

"Kill me?" she asked in surprise, her eyes widening.

He dropped his hands, releasing her. "I've been injected with a potion. To keep me alive. And make you very dead if you bite me."

"You carry a weapon after all," she murmured and stepped back from him.

They ran again until the slayer sank to the ground below a leafy sycamore tree to rest. A splashy little creek trickled past the tree, and he leaned over and drenched his face.

As he wiped the water from his jaw, he gazed into the creek water oddly, then looked up at her as though something in the water had puzzled him. "You have a reflection. Eclipsed, but still mirrored."

She shrugged, not knowing what that was.

"Your heart is refusing to follow your soul into hell," he said. "You're caught between two doors."

He pulled his backpack from his shoulders, unzipped the bag and pulled out a granola bar. Ripping the paper away, he tore off a chunk with his teeth while he studied her.

Dazzling white teeth, straight, well flossed, Daelyn thought, her lips parting unconsciously.

"So what's your story?" he asked as he moved his backpack a little closer to him to use as an arm rest.

She sat on a pile of leaves and twigs near him, but not too near. She could see the shadows on his face cast by the shade. He was still by all definitions, a slayer, and his trade was etched in those shadows, especially around the eyes, lion-like and iron-hard as he remained wary of her while he munched the bar.

"I don't have a story. I just want out. Why did you leave your carry-on behind?" she asked. "I could have easily carried it for you."

"Didn't think of that, to tell you the truth, since you weren't exactly in my plans at that moment." He paused. "What about the stick who board slapped me?"

"A minion. You were a nuisance, a fly the guards ordered him to swat out of the way so they could take me."

As he finished the energy bar, the slayer glanced at the sky through the sycamore branches above him. "Gonna be dawn soon. We need to find you a motel or empty house or shed or something."

"Why?"

He stared at her incredulously, impatiently. "Why? Gee, I don't know. You want to just dig a hole in the dirt?"

A tinge of gray sky began losing its coverlet of stars. "I love the dawn," she murmured winsomely.

"Does the dawn love you?" he asked pointedly.

"I can tolerate the morning and late afternoon. Midday is the fryer." Then her eyes lit up elatedly. "You were worried about me! You were afraid I would—" She searched for the word.

"Self-combust," he said drily.

"Yeah," she said, her tone becoming subdued. "Burst into flame." She drew her hand down her arm. It was smooth, cool, without blemish. Perfect. She definitely didn't want to bubble up and start frying in the sun like an egg on a hot sidewalk, then self-combust.

"I'm Daelyn," she ventured, her gaze returning to him, stealing to the black jacket he unzipped to relax. The open jacket gave her a renewed peek at the strong shoulders she was craving to explore—if he ever let her get close enough again—and the arms comfortably filling out the sleeves of a rust-colored sweatshirt.

He crossed his legs and the muscles in his lean thighs pressed against his jeans.

"I guess we should exchange names," he said. "Apparently, we're going to be joined at the hip for awhile. James Lauren."

Her eyes flew to his ring and she jumped up and back like he had bitten her. "You're the slayer prince!"

His eyebrows arched, but only briefly. Entwining his fingers comfortably behind his neck, he leaned back against the trunk of the tree. "Is that what they call me? Okay, so we know who I am. Who are you?"

Cautiously, she returned to her pine and leaf seat on the ground, drawing her knees up to her chin and tucking her toes into her hands. "I'm a precog. Ex-Rose. Gypsy Vamp. Half-vamp. Castle Coquet. The Count's—plaything." She smiled coyly at him. "And more recently—Blues ..."

"The Count's plaything?" His eyes suddenly reflected a more avid interest, like the hound who's picked up the scent of a fox. *Why?* she wondered.

"I'm his favored. That's why they were taking me back. To hang me on his arm again. I get the joy of attending all the boring 'Royals only' meetings, and midnight monster bashes, private balls, the whole blood enchilada." She paused and gazed down at the soft earth cradling her toes and hands. "I used to sink my toes deep into the warm beach sand and watch the sailboats ..." Her voice trailed off.

"We need to get you to a motel," James said, suddenly rising. "Morning won't last long."

His eyes had become deep and busy. His thoughts were grinding, she could tell, gears and cogs grinding behind that clock face. He was forming a plan for something.

A plan that might not include her. That might mean leaving her behind.

She tried not to appear anxious as she rose to fall in beside him and stay abreast of his long strides.

"What happens when I wake up?" she asked slowly.

"You'll be hungry as hell. But I'm not breakfast. Remember that."

"Then you'll be there?" She knew her voice faltered, but she couldn't help it. She was vastly alone—had no friends and nowhere to land.

"What happened to you, Daelyn, with them?" he asked, his brow furrowing with an unreadable emotion.

"Maybe we could talk about it later? Over wine?" she coaxed.

Please don't leave me.

Please.

A vision of what it would be like to wake up to a silent, sterile motel room, devoid of his presence with nothing left but a few lingering vapors of his rugged scent, threw stones in her heart.

The mysterious, sensual slayer terrified her but at the same time drove her with desire.

She feared James Lauren, and that fear imprisoned her. Fear, fear to her very core. Instinctive. All vampyres were in this prison of fear, an innate fear of being discovered, of being burned, of being staked, by men like James. He was dangerous to her. But he excited her and he was powerful and strong and she could feel within her the beginnings of the flame called desire.

He gazed at her and a smile traveled across his lips. "Actually, I'm a beer man. I could use a Bud and a steak. Just have to figure out where we are, and where the nearest town is."

Before he could look for a tall tree to climb, or a hillock for a vantage point, her wings were out and she was in the air, sailing upward. She hovered, a little higher than the tops of the trees, then grinned down at him, and pointed to the north. "Just over the next rise, Cap'n," she said. "Do we use impulse power, or Warp 9?"

She glided down, hovering in front of him, close, a few feet above the ground. "Come fly with me," she tempted, her lips only a few tantalizing inches from his own.

He drew his fingertips down the cheek that was soft as cool satin. "There are vampyres in the sky, darlin', who could see you flying. Best we keep to the woods."

She pressed his hand to her cheek, and basked in its warmth—She could feel the pulse in his wrist, like the pulsing of water through a dam. She could hear it.

With effort, Daelyn took his hand away and quietly landed. "You should flee from me."

"I know," he said.

Daelyn could feel the wet heat rising from his skin, heating the air as his temperature soared from desire for her.

His intensified scent intrigued her, mystified her.

What would it be like to have a human? she wondered.

6.

More than one hundred, eighty ancient quarry tunnels lay beneath the streets of the City of Light. Dating back centuries, the maze of tunneling was vast, knitted with hidden rooms and endless caverns. The webs of mining corridors first interlaced the city's underground when Parisians discovered that a valuable resource, limestone, was lying right under their footsteps.

After the miners left, the labyrinth of passageways remained to become corridors of the dead, a solution to burials as the city's graveyards overflowed. Drafts now whistled through the chambers of an underground graveyard—catacombs.

Adventure seekers, cataphiles, emphatically explored the Parisian arterial underground, the souterrain, as well as a loose group that included tourists and residents. But they had been solidly discouraged from delving too far into the low-ceilinged, unstable quarry corridors. The fragile, cavernous underbelly of Paris was legally off-limits.

Vampyres slipped in anyway.

Nicholai Petronovich swept his cape around him and left the emptying meeting hall of the Realm Royals with his smile in a tight, blue line.

He had pissed off the Realm.

As he stormed through the long, farthermost gray tunnels, Nicholai's anger was compounded by the knowledge the vanguards loyal to him must now remain loyal in secret. A hell of a note.

True, he probably should have kept his mouth shut. But he had taken all of their blabber he could take.

Speaking his mind in Council had of course put a quick end to the already shaky floor he walked on with the New Royals. Telling them the world of mortals would fight with their last breath to defend themselves against subjugation had fallen on deaf ears. But his words had caused quite a few frowns and questions as to his allegiance.

The current "old order" they liked to call it, was already under close scrutiny. The old order was being evaluated by the new order of Royals under the direction of the Count himself. Force reduction, reassignment, dissolution of titles and territory, confiscation of riches—it was all coming. Nicholai could see the writing in blood on the wall. First the lower level humans, then the vampyre minions, and finally the vanguards and anyone else the new order decided they didn't like—all would become defunct. But suddenly, no one wanted to talk about it. No one wanted to say no. Everyone was becoming afraid. Afraid of their power, afraid of their might … and afraid, as always, of the Count. Dracula was held in awe. Would always be held in awe. He was the Godfather of the Realm.

And he never died because no one had the guts to off him.

Nicholai's large hands curled into cold fists. There had been no one by his side, no one to walk beside him from Senatorial Council. Any vanguards standing up for him would be watched, viewed as subservient, dissidents, disturbers.

The New Royals, he thought with scorn. They had laughed at him and drank blood from golden bowls and talked of their mighty plans to subjugate humans, to make them slaves of the Realm, to be kept on farms and milked like cows. Ushered into stalls at night, they were to be chained and terrorized to keep them from any plots of subterfuge or attempts at uprisings. Law would rule them, the law of the New Realm.

Dissension would result in nothing less than death.

Royal Fools, he thought hotly. They had grown up in caves like Neanderthals and knew nothing of reality, only their own silly, vain imaginings of inheriting a world of riches and blood as they were given pompous, meaningless "ceremonies" to induct them into the Realm as vampyres.

Golden, gilded robes do not a smart vampyre make.

Nicholai took a private helicopter to his French castle at the edge of the German border and stood in the middle of his bedroom, fuming. Finally, he slammed the drapes shut to his window and howled at the walls.

He would've howled at the moon—but there wasn't one.

The night was as black as his anger—a boiling rage contained in darkness, encased in a silent well—deep, seething.

If he was going to act, he had to act quickly. Before those who still stood with him as their Captain in secret against the Realm, against the plot to put him out to pasture, fell away fearful of Dracula. Others he had thought loyal were shunning all the vanguards.

How could they? How could they shun the soldiers who had held the Realm intact and protected vampyres from slayers for eons of time?

They were kissing the feet of the new breed of nonlife birthed from the Black Roses. Birthed to terrorize the world into submission by their power, their "gifts." And their claim to royal lineage assured them a round table chair with the Count.

He would be watched now, he knew. He would have to be careful, vigilant.

Spies, spies everywhere, waiting to throw his head in the drink the moment he voiced a politically incorrect word in the wrong crowd, or on the wrong street corner, or in the wrong alley.

Perhaps he would be better off, he thought, to return to his isolated castle in Russia, where he could simply creep out at night, feed and return to daysleep unknown and unfettered.

His life would work well for him as long as poachers and fat city fathers did not discover he was not exactly as he seemed. If they did, he would be cursed to move on. Or taste the stake in his daysleep.

Cursed to move on for eternity.

He had always hated it when it was time to move on in the days of old, days when he ran with the French vampyre, Henri De Lacroix, and Jane Weston, days before the Realm controlled the underground.

No! he decided vehemently. *No more!* He would gather what few loyalists were left to him, those he knew he could trust, and he would find a way to keep from being ousted by the Count's court bastards, jesters parading as Royals.

And Jane would be with him, or else. Else he would kill her. He had chosen her to sit at his table, and it was humiliating to have her in such open rebellion, to have to watch her sitting beside Dracula swilling goblets of blood and sitting viciously happy in the seat vacated by that mistake from Santa Monica, the "favored one." Every time she escaped into the world of mortals, Jane ran shamelessly to grab her place.

Nicholai turned to his desk and rummaged through the stack of writs and documents stamped with the Realm seal.

Another tiresome warrant was in issue to find the renegade vampiress and haul her lovely little ass back—again.

You would think Jane would learn.

She was last seen, supposedly, somewhere in Texas. On a train. Unverified. None of the vanguards who had gone after her had reported back to verify the account.

Nicholai swore under his breath that he would not be relegated to the insulting position of being nothing more than a warrant server, rounding up strays, runaway serviles and rebellious ex-Roses. He pushed the warrant aside, shuffled the rest of the meaningless decrees and dung … This paper pile was just another diversion for the Count, a schoolyard pastime he had created to amuse himself for a few decades, then he would move on and the "New Royals" would be left high and dry.

Dry as dust.

Only Nicholai and others like him who knew how to move through the darkness, who knew how to hide, and had hidden in the mists for eons, only they would survive …

He picked up the papers to toss them in the trash … a computer printout of a plane's passenger list with a thick red line under one name assaulted his eyes. The red marker had pressed so hard with rage that the ink had bled through to the back of the paper.

A two-word note written in angry red was scripted across the printout, a commission from the Count himself. "Find him."

Intriguing. The crossbow slayer had been on a hard target plane. In Texas.

Nicholai's eyes moved to the warrant for the vampiress, then back to the list. Threading, he ordered three of the most skilled hunters in his castle to his rooms and handed them the warrant. "Find out where she was last seen—" He handed them the passenger list—"and find out if he was on that train."

Odds to even if they found her, they would find him.

He rubbed his chin with his hand. "Don't apprehend them. Report back to me. And me only."

Their gray eyes widened in curiosity, but they said nothing. With a short bow, they turned and left.

Opening his window, Nicholai sat on the ledge and looked out over the thick forest covering mountains that seemed to go on forever, a never-ending, jagged horizon of rise and fall. The Black Forest. Gazing at one of the most beautiful, mysterious forests in the world, still enveloped in undiscovered secrets, had always given the Russian vampyre a measure of peace.

A slight hint of perfume, floral, very French, wafted through the room and out onto the ledge.

Swirls of smoke rolled across the floor like an incoming fog, and the Lady Jane Weston rose out of the gray and stood by the window.

She touched his shoulder lightly, no more than the brush of a feather, but he felt it all the way to his soul.

"A crown full of gold for your thoughts," she said softly, sensuously.

He turned, and her wickedly beautiful, violet eyes cast their usual spell over him. He could deny her nothing. Swinging his legs over the window sill, he came back into the room. Standing in front of her, he twined the fingers of his right hand in the silky, black tresses cascading down her arms—perfect arms without a single blemish, and jerked her head back by her hair.

"I was thinking you will become subject to me, or die," he said, as though swearing an oath. He pulled her roughly against him, then just as roughly, pushed her back. She was wearing a jade silk gown and nothing else.

Jane Weston knew how to tease him, make him lose himself in the eternity in her eyes and her ruby lips.

"I will not be made a fool of, Janey. I am the Captain of the Vanguards," he said proudly between clenched teeth.

"A Vanguard the Shadow slayers forgot to behead." She smiled up at him, unafraid.

Even the worst tirades of the Vanguard had never placed terror within her. Just the opposite. They excited her, made her insane to be near him.

When she wasn't with the Count.

"Andre DuPre knew a master vampyre could come back to life, but his control was dismantled when he suddenly became entangled at the time with one far more heinous." She laughed, light, sweet. Wicked. Then she stroked his face. "Fortunately for my Nicholai."

"Those slayers of his ran out into the night leaving the job unfinished, and left me for dead in that nasty little room, left me to rot," he said in bitter tones, turning to look back outside, his desire for vengeance burning holes in the wooden window frame. "But my flesh slept the Sleep, and I returned."

"With your magnificent power magnified by second life," she cooed, excitement glittering in her eyes. "Men and beast alike now fear you! With good reason."

"And what would that reason be?" he said with a twisted smile.

"You show no mercy," she said liltingly.

"Mercy is for the weak." His fangs dropped, and he let out a low, guttural growl as she stroked his chest. "And when I see the crossbow slayer again, there will be no mercy. He will beg for mercy as he feels the holes from my bolts, but there will be none."

"You are worth more than to be a mere Captain," she whispered. "You are worthy to be King!"

"Is that so?" he responded coldly. "Is that what you want? Is that what you are thinking when you're offering the Count sweet diversions in his bed? That I should be King?"

Her rose lips turned down in a pout. "You want to shame me. All right, shame me." She pushed a set of intertwining jade straps from her shoulders, and let the gown fall to the floor.

He gazed at her freely. At her softly curving hips, generous breasts with nipples that rose before him in hard, pearly peaks.

She was forever twenty-six years old.

And forever in heat.

"It is you who shows no mercy," he said, picking her up, and carrying her to his bed. Tossing her into the pillows, he straddled her, and looked down at her with hard, flaming eyes. "Is this what you want? An endless stream of pleasure between your legs, from the Captain of the Vanguards, the Captain who would be King? And what of the Count who would be Emperor? Shall we both be slaves to the Queen of the Vanguards and Empress of the Realm?"

"I want only you, Nicholai," she said in a small voice, lifting her arms to him.

He saw no reason to refuse her.

Or himself.

7.

By the time the sun was angling high over the treetops, James had sequestered Daelyn into a motel room near the Texas-Arkansas border, bought a bottle of wine from the twenty-four-hour liquor store next door, takeout from a café across the street, and was munching from a Styrofoam box at a small writing table while she guzzled cabernet.

He caught her studying him oddly as she sat on the edge of the bed.

"What?" he said, chewing on a piece of wood-fire smoked steak.

"You have puncture scars on the side of your neck."

"Hazards of the job," he said simply.

He rubbed the small scars lightly.

Thoughts of Jane Weston puncturing his neck, the infamous vampyre who was feared even by her own, put tight wads in his gut. He had questioned his soul on more than one occasion after being pierced by her.

She was supposed to be dead.

But the jury was still out on that one.

There was no way he believed she was ash—and she wanted him.

He finished the last bite of steak, and washed it down with a draught of beer.

The Realm runaway finished her wine, wrapped herself in her wings, and fell out on the floor.

In moments, she was still and did not move again.

She was used to sleeping anywhere and everywhere, James realized sadly.

He leaned back in the chair at the table, sipped his beer quietly, and gazed at the cheerleader legs and slim, lovely arms tucked beneath soft feathers—

Damn!

She was cold! That's why she was curled into her wings with her hands tucked under her!

A vampyre who was experiencing the chill in the fall air.

How many nights had she shivered on the cold ground, he wondered, curled up like this, trying to stay warm while she clung to her fading humanity on the run from her abductors?

Taking the comforter from the bed, he placed it across her body and pulled it up around her shoulders. His hands brushed against her hair, soft as sable mink. And scented with perfume.

He pulled his cell phone from his backpack and sent a hefty text to Andre. The game plan had changed.

Within moments, James' phone chirped and a very unhappy Andre DuPre stated in no uncertain terms it was against his better judgment to send "nectar" for the "butterfly who had hitchhiked into town on James' shoulder." But he agreed.

His text had ended simply, "I hope you know what you're doing."

So do I, James thought.

Within the hour there was a knock at the door.

With a quick glance through the window in case there were curious eyes in the parking lot, James opened the door, grabbed the dark green backpack leaning against the doorway, yanked it inside, and closed the door quickly.

Resting the pack on a chair, he turned to his own black pack and pulled out a long, slender, silver chain and handcuffs, then pulled the chain taut to be sure the links were strong.

It was going to be hard to chain her. He felt wretched about it. She had a desperation about her, the driving desperation of the fugitive innocent of any crime.

She also had a savage, but innocent wantonness that drove nails of desire into him and his control as a hunter. Cold control kept his crossbow loose, his aim steady. Mind over emotion. His doctrine. Being in control of the situation instead of being controlled by it. But this vamp was doing a number on him.

She was throwing him off balance. Why did she have to smell so darn nice? And have those big blue eyes she kept turning on him with "the look?" And those rear view mirror curves that would keep a man looking back? And the power to seductively mesmerize.

Reminding himself forcefully the lovely Daelyn was not human, exactly, and that he would be big-time dead, and so would she tonight, if he didn't chain her, James pulled the comforter away, cuffed her hands behind her back, then slid his arm under her shoulders and lifted her toward him. She was limp in his arms, too new to vampirism to sense him, sense the silver danger to her. He wrapped the chain around her shoulders then strapped her wings and arms to her waist, and pulled silver lengths across and under her legs. Thought would not rule her when she awakened. Instinct would rule. Need would rule. The scent of his blood would be all over the room. Mindless need would numb any remembrance of the warning he had given her, that she would die. As soon as she woke up, she would feel only the intense, insatiable hunger that chained her more than these bits of silver, and react.

Hopefully, the silver would scald and paralyze, and the chain would hold.

James laid down on the bed and slept for several hours, then took up his vigil at the table again in late afternoon.

When the lowering sun signaled the coming of evening, Daelyn jerked forward, her nostrils immediately flaring at the scent of blood.

Within seconds, she had knocked away the blanket with her body and was twisting violently against the chain to leap at him, fangs extended with the need to strike and feed. Pits of fire burned away her pupils, and she hissed like hell for the want of human blood.

When she realized she could not rise beyond a sitting position, she screamed and screeched, her eyes darting, scared, a wild thing caught in an unknown trap. She was pinned by something that refused to yield to her strength or her command and was burning her. She fought the links, trying to break them or slide out of their hold, and her hands were straining against the handcuffs.

"Daelyn," James said quietly. "Daelyn. Look at me. Did you forget what I told you? Remember. Force your body into control and your mind to remember."

She looked up at him, inhaling and exhaling in rapid, angry, hungry breaths, her forehead wrinkled, her brows creased hard as mental will battled instinctive need, the need to survive.

Her eyes cleared. "Some damned African leaf would kill me, you said," she uttered bitterly.

"Close enough," he said.

Bending her knees and sitting sideways on her tucked legs, she hung her head, sobbing. Her hair fell across her face in limp, burnished tassels. "Never free," she sobbed, heartbroken, resigning herself to the chains. "Never free."

She's been in chains before, James thought painfully, and probably not a very pleasant chaining on her part, and probably more than once. He felt a wrenching in his gut, in his heart. One year. One year ago. And no one had been there to save her.

He opened the backpack that had been left at the door.

Her head jerked up and she gazed in intense curiosity at the twelve-ounce plastic cup sealed with a tinfoil lid that he pulled from the zippered compartment. "I want that but I don't know why," she said in a whispery voice, staring at it in wonderment. She sniffed the air. "It smells—interesting."

"You calm yet?" he asked drily, shaking the cup like a milk shake.

"Yes," she promised, looking hungrily at the cup.

He punched a straw into the center of the lid. Red liquid seeped around the edges of the hole. Her fangs dropped instinctively. He shook his head at her and waited. They receded. Reluctantly.

"As you get used to this little bite of breakfast, you'll want to use your fangs, but right now, not such a good idea," James said. Then his mouth curved in a little twist of smile. "Just suck it with the same aplomb you use on a wine bottle."

He walked to her and knelt down on his haunches in front of her with her breakfast. "Now," he said, setting the cup on the floor, "I'm going to take you out of those handcuffs, but if you fly at me, I'm going to slam you back and knock you out cold, do you understand?"

She nodded, and turned to let him release her hands.

He unlocked the cuffs, slid them from her wrists, and handed her the cup.

Trembling with anticipation, she took a small sip. Her eyes lit up with elated surprise, and she polished it off.

He went back to the table and pulled a second, smaller container, about the size of a two-ounce, take-out sauce cup, from the backpack and tore back the tinfoil lid. "This is a little heavier experience," he said, and handed her the clear, gelatinous substance. "It—umm, works better if you …"

She was already working the edges with her tongue, then dipping, slowly, curling her tongue into the depths, relishing the taste. "What is this?"

"Plasma. With a few added ingredients to calm that wild hunger streak," he said. He hoped his voice sounded normal, and not as dry as his throat felt. It was hard to watch a woman, any woman, using her tongue like that, and not want in on it.

She licked the tiny container clean with a couple more slow, enjoyable, well-placed licks.

He tried hard not to imagine what it would feel like to have that beautiful tongue slowly working him the way she was working that cup.

He was experiencing a wild hunger streak of his own.

"We—umm need to go," he said, handing her the backpack. And trying to breathe normally. "This one's yours. Strap it on and grab your shoes and let's go see if we can find a rental car somewhere before the town shuts down for the night."

The car rental place didn't offer much. An economy car that offered great mileage and not much else.

It was after five, the clerk said with tight firmness. Most of what few cars they had, had been farmed out.

He was a skinny kid, a college night class type who seemed terrified he might lose his job if James even suggested the Jeep sitting outside.

James suggested the Jeep.

Nervously, the kid drew up the paperwork. James signed the rental agreement, and the Jeep was soon jostling a country highway that cut through an alfalfa field adjacent to a horse ranch toward a horizon that kept succumbing into nowhere.

"I guess you know where you're headed," Daelyn said.

"I know where I'm going," he answered.

"Are we going to die, James, you and I?" she asked in a small voice.

"Not if I can help it."

They drove in silence for a while before she ventured quietly, "I guess not knowing where I'm going is better than knowing where I've been."

"Where have you been, Blues?"

She gazed out the window, toward a vastness of pale dusk deepening into dark, and her look seemed far away. And sad. "I've been alive. And I've been a virgin." She rested her hands in her lap. "There are no memories within me to even remember what a kiss was like as a mortal."

James felt his heart go weak, and break anew. "Why did they want you?"

She shrugged, the sadness dissolved somewhat. "I'm a precog, and some rockabilly vampyre named Lem thought I was related to some royal family in Europe. He got the spelling wrong, or the name, or something, I don't remember now which it was."

She seemed unaware her mortal memories would fade more and more to the background with each passing day. James was tender, stricken for her, but swallowed hard, knowing that could also be his own fate.

"I tried to tell him I wasn't of 'noble blood,' as he kept calling it," she continued, "but he—stole me and took me to them. To the Realm of Royals."

"How much are you involved with them?"

"I was in the inner circle once my Rose days were over," she said. "They would bring me things to read precognitively so they would have information on other vamps and humans to use for what they called, 'opportunities.'"

"Opportunities. What kinds of opportunities?" James probed, but carefully, handling her trust with kid gloves or she could fly out the window and be gone.

Her eyes suddenly widened toward the road in front of them. "Look out!" she cried. She grabbed the steering wheel, and was giving it a hard turn to the right before James could stop her. The car—Flipped.

All he saw before the roll was an armadillo that had ambled into the path of the Jeep, and her body, as she threw herself across him, placing herself between him and the steering wheel, protecting him as the car pitched and rolled and careened down an embankment.

The Jeep crunched to a stop, nose down, smack against a wall of dirt and rock, the front pleated like an accordion.

Steam poured out from around the crumpled hood.

"Are you all right?" she asked shakily, leaning back a little as the shock of the impact subsided.

"You make one hell of an air bag," he managed to smile.

"I'm—glad you're all right." She pressed his hair back from his forehead, then suddenly placed her lips on his, and gave him a long, slow kiss.

"Daelyn, don't," he said, fighting the shimmer in her eyes and drawing back.

She smoothed her hands across his tight shoulders, relaxing the muscles. "Let go, James. I won't hurt you. I just want to pleasure you."

James gazed at her incredulously. The vampyre seemed to be completely oblivious to the fact they were sitting in a hunk of mangled metal in a ditch and could have been mangled with the car. Or at least one of them would have been mangled.

He didn't like to think about that.

"Daelyn, we need to get out," he said. "In case the fuel is leaking? You know. Fire?"

She moved away swiftly.

He tried to open his door, but it was mashed inward, pinning him in.

"Let me get that door for you, sir," she said with a valet smile.

She punched a hole in the roof, climbed out, dropped in front of his window, ripped the door off, and tossed it away. "Guess that kid's going to lose his job over this, huh?"

As James worked his way out past the smashed metal of the door frame, Daelyn moved away, keeping a little distance between them. By the uncertainty in her eyes, he figured it was in case he wasn't happy with her. Again.

8.

Daelyn pulled a bit of torn silk blouse over a badly bruised shoulder, and James could see she was in pretty bad shape. Her shoes and ripped pants were dirty and bearing oil and blood smears from the impact. Patches of blood and lacerations showed through the jangled tears in her clothes like thicket vines had whipped her.

She had taken the hits for him.

"You know, the next time you want to save an armadillo, you might want to just consider joining an environmental protection group," he said, his tone mellow.

"Armadillo?" She gazed at him, confused. "It—wasn't the armadillo. It was—the man."

His eyes registered his shock. "A man?"

"He was twirling a cane and standing in the road. In the middle of the freakin' road, and you weren't slowing down ..."

"Oh, my God! The ghost! Why would he do that?" James exclaimed, his eyes flying to the road as he stammered, "I didn't see him!"

"He just kept smiling and didn't get out of the way. I thought he wanted to—commit suicide." She paused. "A ghost?"

"It's a long story." He climbed to the top of the gulch and studied the road swinging off into a winding horizon of trees. "There must be a reason he didn't want us going on."

"So he was going to kill us in a car wreck?" she cried, astonished, as she came climbing out of the ditch.

James cast a soft glance at her. "I think he knew you wouldn't let that happen."

The smile, the innocence in her return gaze capsized him, but the vampyre behind those innocent blue skies was pure sensual heat, and James remained guarded. She had instinctively saved him. Her vampyre instincts had erupted on her lips in her kiss.

She was a complicated creature, this vamp caught between two doors—each time he moved into her gaze, he moved with caution. He was not usually in contact with vampyres this closely or for this long unless they were in atonement. Close proximity was to plunge a stake into their hearts and send them into dust.

Other than that incident with The Lady Jane Weston.

"Well, looks like we're walking again," he said, and started down the road.

She turned and ran back down the embankment to the car.

"What are you looking for?" he called after her as she yanked open the trunk, leaned in, and began rummaging around.

"My candy." Bits of back seat padding came flying out from inside the trunk.

When she came up for air, she was holding her backpack, and his, and grinned up at him as she held them up. "No damage," she called up to him. "You have your chipmunk food and water and that chain, and I have—" She pulled a cup of plasma from her pack. "Whatever this stuff is."

Ripping away the tinfoil lid, she raked a finger around the edge of the cup and rolled the dollop into her mouth, ravaging it as she rejoined him at the edge of the country highway. James felt his desire spike beyond the limits of sweet misery into physical aching as he watched her dip her forefinger into the goo again, then wrap her ruby lips around the tip of her finger, and pleasurably murmur, "Mmmm."

She twisted her hip a little, and her eyes glimmered precociously at him.

Daelyn used both barrels blazing in seduction. And not subtly.

She finished off the plasma with the tip of her little finger, tossed the cup to the grassy shoulder, and they walked away from the jeep still belching steam from the gulch.

"Go easy on the plasma," James said. "We might have to ration, the way we're going."

"Where are we going?"

"My adoptive father's farm."

"Is that where you were flying to?"

"No. This is a detour." He tossed her a light castigation. "I seem to be suddenly on my own time for a couple of days—since a well-mapped plan went south."

"You're not very forgiving," she accused.

"Actually, I'm very forgiving," he countered, "or I would have staked you with a piece of plane seat."

"Should we be walking on this road?" Daelyn asked, glinting into the distance. "Since the ghost seemed more than a little determined we shouldn't?"

She dropped to her knees in the middle of the road and drew her hand in an arc over the asphalt. "The dust blowing along the pavement doesn't feel right."

Her eyes moved to a utility pole at the side of the road. She flashed to the pole, and placing her hands on the wood, drew them across the grainy pulp.

"This tree held birds of song," she murmured, then closed her eyes. "Shavings on a saw mill floor." She inhaled. "Curing agents." She exhaled. "It's laying in a company yard among others amid spools of copper, service trucks, wire ..." She opened her eyes and turned to James. "Evil traveled this road today, the being leaned against this pole to rest." She took away her hand. "And it was human."

James felt a new appreciation for her talent, and was beginning to understand why the Realm coveted that gift and wanted to keep her hidden away.

If she had the ability to read a presence in the recent past in a utility pole, she would be able to read objects that could reveal the stealth of the Shadow envoys.

As well as objects that would betray any traitors to the Realm itself.

For several moments, James continued looking down the lonely highway, wishing he could penetrate its secrets. His slayer's senses felt the breath of the tomb on that two-lane. Shuddering slightly, he turned his gaze to the friendlier pastures and ranchland adjoining the highway. "We'll take the shortcut," he said.

His cell phone vibrated in his pocket. While Daelyn snapped apart a portion of barbed wire fence a little way from him, he read the text. The Shadows were in the game. He was to hide out at the farm until he heard from Andre, letting him know his guise had not been compromised.

"There," Daelyn said, turning to him brightly. "A barb-free gateway to—wherever."

James put away his phone and wished she wasn't looking at him with so much trust in her big blue eyes. Considering he planned to lead her into Hell once Andre released him.

"We'll be walking under a crescent moon tonight," she whispered happily as they began to trek across a field of newly planted winter wheat.

Guilt ate away at his insides like strong bleach.

Horses, in an adjoining pasture, grazed behind a white wood fence lined with birches. Quarter horses, Appaloosas, a couple of paints, a couple of colts.

And a chestnut with three white socks and a star with a blaze.

"Race horses," James murmured thoughtfully as he took a moment to stand in the shadows of one of the birches and admire them while he took a drink from his water bottle.

"The one with the blaze reminds me of the greatest of the greats, an American Thoroughbred named Secretariat," Daelyn said brightly.

"Kind of what I was thinking myself," James agreed as the chestnut trotted over to the fence for a pat.

"Hey, Chestnut," James said gently. "Sorry, no sugar or apple, fellow. But you could sure get me to where I'm going."

Truck lights. Appearing on a side road a little way inside the fence.

A pickup truck carrying a new saddle bobbled to a stop near them.

The old cowboy clambering out was chewing on a cigar stub under a well-worn hat.

A light, muffled laugh escaped Daelyn's lips. "He reminds me of the supporting actors who always get knocked off first in old westerns. Cowboy Lean As A Stick rides up, looks down at you from his saddle, and tells you you're trespassing, just as he gets shot in the back and falls off the horse at your feet ..."

"How ya'll doin'?" he said, his Texas drawl congenial. "Noticed you two making along the road in the dark there as I drove in. Cincinnati Red here seems to like you."

He leaned his elbows on the top bar of the fence.

"How many races has he won?" James asked, giving the white star a pat.

"He don' lose, son." He chewed around his cigar.

James unzipped his backpack, pulled out a roll of cash. "I'd be willing to pay you over and above what he's worth."

"Naw. Naw, I don't think so," he said eyeing the roll suspiciously. The rancher's eyes moved to Daelyn, drank in her form—and her shredded clothes. "What're you two doing way out here in the dark? With that much green in your pocket, you couldn't be homeless people."

"We ran off the highway and totaled our car," James quickly explained. "We need to get to the Arkansas border. My mother lives in toward the hills."

"You on the run?" the old man asked, eyeing them keenly now, with open skepticism.

Daelyn moved in front of him, smiled, and let her eyes fall into his. Deeply into his. "Yes. Yes, we are."

Knowing she was about to use her vampira wiles on him to get that horse, James made a move to stop her, but then, why? What the hell, he was bone-tired, and tired of hiking through fields of gnats, and chiggers and goat head stickers that jabbed and stabbed at his ankles through his socks.

Within twenty minutes, they had the horse and the saddle, and were galloping away across the pasture under a crescent moon, while the old cowboy stood beside his truck staring dumbstruck at the wad of cash in his hand.

James felt Daelyn release her wings to enjoy the flow of the night wind through them as they rode.

And he tried not to love her.

"Look at the smile of moon hanging over the hills!" she cried in delight as she wrapped her arms around him. "It's beautiful here!"

"It's Texas," he said softly.

"You're a strong rider, Prince James," she whispered as she relaxed against him. The soft, feathery edges of her wings brushed his arms as she drew them in. And her legs sensuously gripped his hard thighs.

Damn, he wanted to make love to her ...

Daelyn alerted him to the gurgle of a creek cloistered in a stand of distant trees, and he stopped to let the horse rest and get a drink. She slid from the saddle and smoothed her mussed blouse, and her smudged, ripped pants. Her cuts and bruises were almost healed, but her clothes were a mess.

"I shouldn't meet your mother like this," she said, shaking her head as she stared at her shreds.

She pulled her blouse out from under the waist of her pants and began undoing the buttons. "Maybe it would be better if I didn't wear anything at all rather than show up in these awful rags."

James quickly put his hand over hers to stop her from stripping to bare naked right here at the creek.

The curvature of her breasts met his fingertips.

His hand lingered. She would be so beautiful in the slip of starry night …

No. Not yet. He would surrender to her charms when he willed it. "I know you haven't been in the mortal world much, Blues, but riding up to the farm au natural is probably just not a good idea. On two counts."

She began returning the buttons to their holes and he turned his attention to the horse, stroking the chestnut's neck, to take his mind from her buttons and her breasts. A desire to turn around and undo the little pearlies all over again was sitting on his groin like a hot rock.

"What two counts?" she asked, finishing the closures.

"I doubt my mother has many naked vampyres come calling."

"Oh. Right. Okay. Wouldn't want to offend any delicate sensibilities." She tucked her frayed blouse back into her torn pants, and her wings into obscurity.

"She's not delicate," he said. "She's an ex-sheriff."

He leaned over to check the chestnut's legs and hooves before they rode on.

"You said two counts," Daelyn pressed.

"I'm not a saint."

He mounted the horse again, and extended his hand.

She took the grasp filled with prodigious strength and swung easily up behind him. "Do you enjoy me riding pillion, Prince James?" she asked as she wrapped her arms around his waist again and leaned into his broad back. The horse pounded across the meadows and James felt his heart pound. A blazing torch fueled by a wind of perfume and a voice like wind bells was flaring and sputtering within him, casting shadows on his rough hewn wall of mental discipline. His control.

With an occasional rest stop at a creek here and there to give the chestnut a drink, and give James a respite from the vampyre body that licked his with flame, they made their way across the countryside.

Only once did James feel Daelyn tense. "I thought I saw something," she said, staring into the night sky as he questioned her, then she shrugged. "I guess it was nothing. Just my jitters. Probably an owl."

But as they rode on, James remained watchful until a slender skein of pale purple horizon finally ushered in the dawn and eased his own "jitters."

Thunderheads towered not far into the west and caught an advancing sunrise in a splay of gold lacing.

"There's a road to the left," Daelyn said suddenly, excitedly, "with a small vegetable and fruit stand and souvenir shop off to the side. When I lived in Santa Monica, sometimes the souvenir shops also had lacy little tops and wraps and things for the beach. Maybe we could see if they have clothes?"

James squinted toward where her heightened vision had spotted signs of early morning life. Sure enough, out of the clumps of pampas grass, a white washed shop rose into view beside a bit of highway. A hand-painted sign hanging from the porch post advertised rose rocks, semi-precious stones, and souvenirs. The adjoining vegetable stand offered homegrown everything.

The owners were up early to get a head start on the day. Both the man and his wife were lean, tall and weathered with the rugged tans of farm life.

As James hitched the horse to a porch post, he related the Jeep wreck to the owner to explain their tatters, and they stepped into the shop. A wood burning stove was newly lit and taking the chill out of the early morning air. A variety of rose rocks, stones, Western movie hero memorabilia—and clothes—were crowded into the one room collection.

Cowboy hats, jackets, shirts, pants, boots and belts hung around the walls and stacked a couple of shelves. Daelyn began uncertainly fingering gingham blouses and jeans.

"No lacy cover ups for sand and sea. This is cow and creek country, ma'am," James grinned, pulling a pretty blue checkered blouse from a hanger.

She draped it shoulder to shoulder in front of a long mirror to see how it might look. "Not bad."

Playfully, he plopped a cowboy hat on her head.

She pulled the brim of the hat up city slicker style, and winking at James' clear reflection behind her own oblique silhouette, teased lightly in a Texas drawl, "Is that a stake in your belt, Sheriff, or are you jus' glad to see me?"

He pulled her carefully away from the mirror, forcing himself once again to remember she was, after all, a vampyre. "I don't think the owner will think his mirror just has a dirty streak if his eye catches your hazy reflection," he warned in a lowered voice.

"Easy, pardner," she tossed with an audacious wink. "Don't go getting' yourself all twisted in your stirrups." Pulling a man's hat from the shelf, she plunked the Stetson on his head and laughed lightly, her face close to his, lips slightly parted as she reached up and cocked the brim of the hat. He pulled hers low over one eye at an angle, unable to resist her precociousness.

But they were too close. The air sparked with heat as their eyes melted into a singular stream and electrified them both, sweeping him away as much as it did her. He stepped back, fighting her unpredictable, playfully dangerous power.

He placed the hat back on the shelf.

She put it back on his head. "Looks good on you, Prince James. How about a new belt to go with it? The one you're wearing looks—worn—in places." She eased her fingertips between the soft cotton of his shirt and his belt.

Slowly, with her thumb, she rubbed the dog-eared spot where his pack usually hung.

James knew as she kept her eyes on his that she was not only trying to excite him. Her hands were seeking to know him, and were beginning to feel his past in the leather. Felt the ones the weapons from the pack had slain.

"You are a Shadow warrior, a stealth hunter, and powerful," she murmured in a whispery voice.

The fingertips touching his past trembled.

James mentally blocked her touch a little. The deftness with which he held his weapons, sprayed his crossbow bolts, and slashed evil to shreds would instinctively terrify Daelyn in spite of her wonderment of him, her trust in him.

More recently, James had relinquished his protective pack for the quest that was consuming his heart like an inferno.

She would be able to read that.

He felt her pouring more heat from her fingertips into the leather, to read past the clouds he was forming to block her.

"You are a knight with a shield—but no sword," she said, looking up into his masked eyes, puzzled.

"Stop, Daelyn," he said, shaking away the rustling of the deadly soft, vacant breeze across his mind, and taking her hands from his belt. "Are you playing me, to delve into my past and read me, gypsy girl with bewitching blue eyes, to find a weakness?"

"No," she swore insistently. "It's something I often do without any reason, without thinking, just to 'read.' I've been doing it since I was a kid. While other kids were reading children's books, I was reading—them." A tiny wrinkle crossed her forehead. "Why did you relinquish your weapons, James?"

"After I clear the air with my father about some things, you and I will need to talk, and I'll answer that."

"Talk, or touch?" she teased softly, her eyes sliding into his one last time from under their long lashes before she sashayed away to a closet doubling for a fitting room.

I'm traveling with a friggin' stick of dynamite, James thought.

Momentarily, she walked out in the blue gingham shirt, bandana to match, the hat, and a pair of jeans that looked like she had been sewn into them.

Make that dynamite a mule pack full of nitro. "You gonna' be able to ride in those?" James questioned, his eyebrows arched.

Smiling deeply at him, she turned her hip in a half-twist, and gave the side of her thigh a light smack. "Spandex. Greatest invention of the twenty-first century. Moves with you as you move."

The double-entendre was not lost on him.

"You're determined to make me crazy, aren't you?" he said, shaking his head lightly.

"Yes." She pressed into him, enfolding her body into his, and he exhaled hard.

Taking her waist in his hands, he drew her closer, harder, letting his body want her, letting the electricity flow.

Her hands smoothed across the shirt covering his hard-muscled chest, and the waters in her eyes became waves, washing over him. "You want to be with me," she whispered softly, seductively, "but you are—a slayer, of course."

9.

As they headed for the counter to pay for the clothes and hats, Daelyn glanced wistfully toward a jewelry counter at the earrings on display. She had loved earrings, when she was—mortal.

"Which would you like?" James asked, following her glance.

"You—want to buy me something?" she asked in surprise.

He lifted a pair of Black Hills gold earrings with turquoise insets from a counter display. "They would look nice on you. Kinda match the gold flecks in your irises."

Her eyes cut deeply into his. "I have gold flecks?"

He looked at her oddly. "Some."

Hesitantly, fearing the answer, she asked, "They're not—red, fire?"

"Oh, they're fire all right. But not red. Not yet. And never will be—if I have anything to do with it."

"And how do you plan to rescue me from Hell, Prince James?" she laughed drily. "Ride in on your gallant chestnut steed in shining armor and crash the Dreadful gate, then sweep me up behind you, and outrun the devil?"

"Nope," he said. "I plan to stake him."

She glanced at his ring. "Your ancestral uncle would have that ring, and your head, impaled on a pole before you could even entertain the thought."

"Then let's not entertain it," he grinned. He bought the earrings, and a thick bracelet of gemstones—turquoise, citrine, aquamarine, garnet, and smoky topaz.

Taking her hand gently in his, he slid the diamond bracelet covering the tattoo, down and over her hand, and replaced it with the less ostentatious, but beautiful band of stones.

The touch of his palm against the sensitive part of her wrist as he clasped the stone band in place sent ribbons of excitement through Daelyn—almost human pleasure.

But the sensation of his pulse throbbing against her wrist heated her without mercy, shocking her as her veins throbbed with the curse of the undead.

Control. Keep your desire for him in control. Find a freakin' cow if you have to ...

"Have to keep you incognito," he said, his smile a sexy twist. "That diamond bracelet would draw too much attention to that lovely wrist. Diamonds catch the eye by their very nature and beauty. Like you."

Oh, damn. He is so sinking me. Love me. Love me, James, so I can know what it would have been like before it's too late.

They left the shop, and as James unhitched the horse, she glanced at the heavens cast in gray above them. The thunderheads had taken the sky, demolishing the morning sun behind a wall of rain-laden cloud. He would not need to find a place to hide her from its rays.

"Do you need to daysleep?" he asked her, also appraising the incoming storm.

"No. But I don't think I want my wings slushed from a deluge. Those clouds look pretty sauced."

The shop keeper came out on the porch to check out the dark, gray-blue clouds. "Looks like we're in for a little cloudburst," he informed them. "If all you got is a horse, you won't make it home before that cloud hits, even if you live close. You're welcome to stay in the warehouse shed until it passes over, if you like. Wouldn't want to see that good looking stallion catch his death in a downpour."

"I'll take you up on that offer," James said, as a large raindrop made a circle on the porch steps.

"The shed roof is well shingled and will keep you dry."

James led the chestnut into the shed.

Daelyn followed them, gazing around in curiosity as she stepped into dim light, sawdust and apples. Working her way between empty crates and buckets, she moved toward the back of the shed and crunched into a corner where the sacks would cushion her.

And hide her.

Enwrapped in the corner, she was no more than a slip of movement. She opened her pack and searched for one of the large cups and a straw.

She stared at the straw, then at the tinfoil seal on the cup. Within her, from some dark, horrible place that crushed her spirit into desolation, from a chasm of emptiness, a wrenching rose upward and constricted her very heart, cutting a slice out of her humanity, and replacing it with an inhuman, fierce thirst. She felt the sharp tips of her fangs touch her tongue.

Though his back was to her as he leaned against the shed entrance and gazed out into the horizon of gathering rain, the slayer sensed the darkening. "Better you strike that cup than me," he warned quietly.

The squeezing sensation rose up through Daelyn like a geyser. She struck the cup and drank deeply, replenishing her existence with the processed product though she would have preferred the slayer.

Could he not become—her mate?

Daelyn felt a delicious warmth travel through her at the memory of what it felt like to be held by him.

The chestnut sauntered up behind James and nuzzled him. He pulled an apple from a bag on the floor and gave it to the stallion, then stood at the side of the shed door, quietly but steadily watching the trees and terrain across the road.

A flash of lightning briefly outlined his lean, strong-shouldered silhouette in the entrance.

And the black silhouettes of the vampyres in the trees on the other side of the road.

"Janus Vanguards!" Daelyn breathed in a whispery cry.

"Three of them," James said quietly.

He turned, walked to the back of the shed, and knelt on his haunches in front of her. "Janus are soldiers of the First Order. You're not exactly just an escapee, are you?"

"I rose very quickly in the ranks. He—told me … things," she admitted.

"He. You mean Dracula." James' brow furrowed deeply. He stood up, took his cell phone from his backpack, and texted rapidly.

Daelyn craned her neck and leaned forward to try to read the text, but it was in a language she did not understand. French, maybe? Spanish?

As replies flashed back in, his face was grave.

He helped her to her feet, and handed her the reins to the chestnut. "Go out the back door. And ride hell for leather. Don't look back. A horse and rider will join you, coming out of the orchard just beyond the shed. Don't slow down. The pace will be punishing but she'll match it. Exchange saddles with her. She'll break pace and head in another direction, back into the orchard. You'll be led into woods by the black horse, woods so thick only night could dwell there. Trust the Black. He will take you where he will. He knows where to go. He belongs to a friend of mine."

She refused to go. Her eyes cascaded with tears. "You have no weapons, James!"

"I'll be all right," he assured her with a smile. "We're just going to misdirect them."

Indecision held the remnants of Daelyn's human heart strings suspended, and her foot hesitated in the chestnut's stirrup. She wanted to flee the heavy-handed vanguards. She was terrified to try, and she was terrified to leave the slayer prince to them. She wanted to ride away, but she also wanted to stay with him ...

He helped her make up her mind. Before she could protest, he lifted her bodily into the saddle and gave the horse's butt a light slap. "Get going!"

She grabbed the reins and was out the back door and flying through the orchard before she could blink. Trees and trees and trees sailed by on either side.

"Trade places!" a woman's voice said suddenly beside her. A black horse was hoof to hoof with the chestnut, kicking up clumps of rain smacked dirt and breathing hard.

The two riders leaped, saddle to saddle, wings extended to balance the jump.

What in the name of sanity am I doing? Daelyn thought wildly with a silent sob as she grabbed the horn of the Black, fell into the saddle, and took the reins.

A walk on the beach. I was just taking a walk on the beach.

She wrapped the reins and a twist of the Black's mane into her hand and held on tight. He turned, and took to the left at full gallop. The other rider moved on and off to the right.

Daelyn dared a glance backward in spite of the slayer's warning. Three black shadows were rising from the trees.

To follow the wrong rider.

The wrong rider!

If she hadn't been so terrified, she would have laughed out loud. Laughed hysterically.

The clouds suddenly tore open and slapped the countryside with wind and rain. Her hair became drenched and the wind whipped the wet tresses across her cheeks, stinging her face. The horse ran on. Her clothes became soaked in the cold autumn rain. A full gallop. Mud and water flew out from under the Black's hooves as they pounded at the flooding ground. On and on. A wild flight through wet and wind and an eternity of trees.

Then Daelyn understood why they were called cloudbursts.

As quickly as the clouds had unleashed their wet fury, they were gone. A few scattered sprinkles and the storm was over. High overhead a light layer of clouds lingered to create a dim curtain over the countryside. But by that time, she was deep within the woods where only night could dwell, the slayer prince had said.

And he was right. Not even a bird's song. A woods filled with an unnatural silence. Suddenly, she felt vastly alone and vastly desolate. All she had wanted was to rest hidden in a pile of apple bags, watch the thunderstorm from the shelter of a shed, and be with the most mysterious, intriguing, hard-assed, gentle, exciting man she had ever met.

The Black galloped furiously, making his way with nimble footing in the dark past snags and twigs and over broken limbs. The trees thickened, closing in on them. Daelyn warily watched the branches above her for signs of movement, for vanguards.

But there were none.

After what seemed an endless journey through lightlessness, the tunnel of leaves finally widened, opening up to a stretch of flat, grassy ranch land. The Black slowed briefly to get his second wind. An L-shaped wood and stone, two-story ranch mansion with a pillared porch rose from between two creeks.

The horse went into another full gallop in that direction. Daelyn could see a swirl-shaped swimming pool with a waterfall at the far end tumbling over a shady fern and canna wrapped terrace. Stables lined a well-tended lawn and riding path, and a couple of oil wells pumped away in a distant field.

The horse must be lost! Daelyn thought frantically, trying to rein him in. They were supposed to meet James at a farmhouse, not a dynasty.

Daelyn couldn't turn the Black. He was whipping through the last of the morning with the strength of ten horses.

She spread her wings to leap from the saddle and leave the crazy horse behind …

A drive gateway appeared with the name of the spread in silver colored letters.

Just Another Texas Farm.

She folded her wings, stayed in the stirrups.

The Black took an easy leap over a chain link fence, then raced through the lead way of a stable to an empty stall, where he stopped abruptly. Daelyn dismounted, and the raffish horse began munching contentedly at the loose hay stalks in the stall like he had never been on a mad romp through a Texas cloudburst and wicked woods.

Daelyn filled a bucket with water from a stable faucet and gave him a drink. "There you go, fellow, not a picnic in the park day for you either, was it?"

After the horse had his fill, Daelyn crawled into a corner of the stall and tucked sweet smelling hay around her and under her for a cushiony seat. And to hide her.

Where are you, James? she thought, her blue eyes darting around. She sniffed the air and tried to find his scent. No one was about, and she didn't know what she would do if she was discovered. There were some ceiling beams above her. Maybe she should just shapeshift into a mouse and hide there until he came.

The other horses in the stables shuffled nervously, sensing an unfamiliar presence. Sensing the undead. A murmur of uneasy neighs passed through the stalls.

Daelyn looked up at the Black. "How about you tell them to settle down and stop gossiping about me, so we don't get found out?"

Too late. Another shuffling at the front of the stables. Daelyn sniffed the air. A human presence. Bacon and biscuits.

A woman, probably in her mid to late fifties with a tough, weathered exterior, dark brown hair and lively, intelligent eyes appeared at the stall entrance with a short-barrel shotgun. Her gaze traveled over Daelyn from head to foot—to wing. "James said I'd probably find you out here. Well, come on in the house and let's get you liquored up."

Daelyn was too dumbfounded to speak. She blankly rose and followed the woman out of the stables. But as the matron Daelyn assumed must be the "sheriff" pushed open a corral gate and started across a wide, manicured lawn, she urged Daelyn to hurry on ahead. "That sun's threatening to break those high clouds into bits."

A long, lone prism of light skimmed through a cloud and struck a patch of marigolds in front of her. Daelyn leaped around it and raced to the porch, her wings smoking. The woman leisurely continued on to the porch, observing her, the shotgun trained on her heart.

"You must be James' mother?" Daelyn gently prompted when she finally found her voice.

"That would be me. And you would be the vampyre."

She opened the front door, motioning with the end of the shotgun barrel for Daelyn to go in first.

So she could not be ambushed.

"James is running late," his mother said as they entered the foyer of a "farmhouse" that was an architectural confection. Oak, granite, stone tile floors, rich colors and airy windows—but now with their elegant drapes drawn to block the sun.

"I'm generally known as Belinda," James' mother said as she led Daelyn into an entertainment room and opened a liquor cabinet. She pulled out a cabernet. "James said you fancy a full-bodied red." She poured a full goblet, set it on the bar counter, and motioned with the shotgun for Daelyn to take it and go sit on the couch nearest the bar. Then she swung a swivel bar chair around to face her, and eased onto the seat with the shotgun steady in her grasp and trained on the vampyre.

"The bullets in this .12-gauge are mahogany and silver," she said. "One hundred percent pure. And will scatter buckshot into your chest that will feel like cannonballs of fire when they hit. Are we clear on that?"

Daelyn didn't have to ask which side of his adopted family James took after. She nodded, and forced herself to drink slowly, politely from the glass.

"Did I mention I was a sharpshooter?" Belinda added.

Daelyn averted her eyes, and her gaze fell on a glass case resting against an adjoining wall. The shelves held baseball trophies, game balls and pictures of James in baseball uniforms from boyhood through college varsity.

"And James is a switch hitter," Belinda said, following her eyes. "He can swing a baseball bat, or aim a crossbow, or throw a stake, right or left-handed."

She handed her the whole bottle of wine.

"I'm Daelyn," she said, refilling her glass. Then she had another, and another until the bottle was empty. She looked around sleepily, uncertainly, not sure where to daysleep.

"James said you're used to sleeping here, there and everywhere," Belinda said, a brief flicker of pity in her eyes. "The couch would probably be more comfortable than the cellar or the basement. But truthfully, the floor carpet in here isn't bad, either. I've fallen out a few times there myself. The pile's thick as a lamb's coat, and warm."

"Will James be here soon?" Daelyn asked, choosing to curl up on the couch under a soft, sweet smelling throw in forest green. If vanguards came calling, she decided it would be best to be near Shotgun Annie there. They might be able to slip into the cellar, or through a dark hole in the basement and nab her while she dayslept, but she had a feeling they wouldn't get past that sharpshooter if they crashed this room.

"James should be here by the time you wake up," Belinda assured her. "Are you drunk yet?"

"Just—tired," Daelyn said, and closed her eyes.

10.

The sprawling Lauren home was lying lazily in the warm afternoon sun, its oil wells pumping tranquilly, as James pulled a leased Mustang into the drive.

He found Daelyn dead to the world on the couch in the game room, and his mother on a bar stool quietly sipping a mineral water behind the barrel of a shotgun. Dropping his car keys on the bar, he pulled a bottle of beer from a small fridge behind the counter.

"Where did you pick her up?" Belinda asked, studying him as he slid into the bar stool next to her.

"She sort of fell into my arms." He grinned, slightly sheepish.

"Umm hmm. You in the habit of picking up vampyres now? How about bringing home a nice human girl? Who is she?" She set the gun on the counter next to her.

"Dracula's consort," he said, taking a long swig of beer.

His mother's startled eyes swept over the vampyre on the couch. "What are you doing with her?"

"She's a renegade," he said. "And she's going to go to work for us. She just doesn't know it yet."

"Us, as in, the Shadows?"

James nodded and took another draught of beer, though it did little to boost his courage to tell his mother why he was here.

He slipped his arms around her shoulders and gave her an affectionate, longer-than-usual hug. "Thanks for handling things here."

"Something's on your mind," she said.

"You always knew, didn't you, when things were on my mind?"

His eyes moved from her to a patio doorway, then traveled out across the back lawn to a fenced, grassy area under a towering Texas elm.

"I need to talk to him, Mom. I need to tell him—that it's all right. Doesn't matter that he can't hear it. I need to say it."

"Tell him what's all right?" she asked, her voice suddenly a little jagged.

"Did you know about it, Mom? That Dad set the fire?"

Her eyes welled with sorrow. "Not until the day before he had his stroke. Just couldn't live with it anymore, I guess." She drew in a deep breath. "He was always curious about the ring. He started searching into your past, first at the adoption agency, then he took off one morning—and flew to Europe. Whatever it was, whatever happened over there, it—shook him up."

She took James' beer from his hand, and swallowed about half the remainder. "He came back a changed man. He was silent, sullen, withdrawn. He wouldn't talk about what went on there, just kept saying he couldn't let 'them' take you ... he started drinking. Heavy."

"And there's no way to know what happened because he can't tell me now," James said bitterly.

"He told me there wasn't a minute gone by after that night in the lab that he hadn't been riddled with guilt," she said, her voice breaking. "He said he didn't know your fianceé, Corinne, was there, and he never forgave himself. Over the years, the horror of what he had done ate him up alive. And the regret and remorse he buried in the bottle caused his failing health ... He was going to go see the sheriff and confess."

James clenched his hand into a fist of frustration. After the fire, and in the years that followed, he had struggled with the bewilderment of trying to understand the change in his father. The drinking bouts, the nights he would sit on the porch with his shotgun, watching the woods and the skies as though waiting for invaders from Mars, nailing the windows shut, never letting any strangers past the front door.

His mother had blamed the liquor, and faced the bouts of depression with courage and dogged determination, but the daily struggle drained her vitality and finally took the shine from her eyes.

"In his confused mind he was trying to save you from something, James. He loved you. I believe that with all my heart. He could never just—do something like that." Her gaze became distant. "I didn't know what he was planning, or that he was planning anything. Why didn't I see the signs, something, anything?" She dabbed at her eyes with a tissue from a box on the corner of the counter. "I didn't even know what he had done until the day before the stroke. All those years ..."

James exhaled in a deep sigh and glanced out the window. All those years.

He took the hand of the woman who had been mother to him, and eventually, had to become father as well. "It's all right, Mom."

He glanced toward the elm again. It was time to walk the walk, reconcile his life. He might not be coming back this way. He might not be coming back at all. He set the empty beer bottle on the counter, and slid from the stool.

Daelyn was sitting at the corner of the couch, leaning on the arm rest, her cheek resting in her hand, studying him.

How much had she heard of his life's story? he wondered. All of it, apparently, from the way she was looking at him. Her eyes were flashing with intense hunger after daysleep, but her lashes fell against her cheeks with sadness for him.

He opened the small refrigerator, pulled out a bottle with red liquid and tossed it to her. "You're doing better." He smiled at her.

"Your pistol packing mama there makes a good case for staying in control," she said with a glance at the deadly shotgun as she caught the bottle.

He laughed. "That's the sheriff in her."

Lugging the bottle with her, Daelyn followed him to the patio door.

"Don't want to stay in the house with the long arm of the law?" he grinned.

"With the silver shotgun sheriff? No," she said flatly.

He headed out across the lawn, past the swimming pool and pool house.

"This doesn't look much like a farm and farmhouse," Daelyn said. "I thought you said your father was a farmer."

"He was," James returned. "When he was young, he was an alfalfa farmer. Until his plow hit a patch of bubbling crude one spring. Then he was a young, rich alfalfa farmer. He began raising a few horses, and making a few investments that turned a nice profit."

James walked Daelyn in the direction of the elm tree. A small gate in the square of fence surrounding the trunk opened up to grass and shade, a large boulder—and a single tombstone.

"Dan might have survived the massive stroke, the doctor said, if his body hadn't been so maimed by alcohol," James explained. "And he had no will to live, though at the time, we couldn't figure out why."

James knelt down before Dan Lauren's grave, closed his eyes, and clasped his hands together. For several moments, his lips moved in inaudible words to forgive the only father he had ever known and repair the past with prayer. Then he moved his hand to his forehead, touched it with his fingertips, moved his fingers to the center of his chest, crossed over to the left shoulder, then the right.

He heard Daelyn suddenly constrict like she couldn't breathe, like the breath was being squeezed out of her. He turned, knowing what had happened.

She was shrinking in horror against the boulder, her fingernails digging into the rocky surface. Terror had swallowed her eyes, and she hissed in agony. "What was that?" she cried, slumping, clinging to the rock in open anguish. "Why did you do that?"

"I'm Catholic."

He held out his hand to her. "Come on, Daelyn. Let's take a walk."

She shook her head violently, clinging to the boulder.

"It's all right," he said gently. She was like a wounded wild thing that needed to know he would not harm her.

Slowly, she let go of the rock. Trusting him. But breathing like her lungs would burst.

She gave him her hand and he led her from the family plot to a stream winding past an alligator tree. A tall cottonwood eclipsed the alligator tree overlooking the contented currents, and James lifted her onto a low, large limb. He grabbed a handful of stones from the creek shore, and hopped up beside her.

He tossed a rock from the pile in his palm absently into the stream and tried to find his voice. How was he going to tell her he was contemplating taking her back into the desolation she'd just escaped?

He averted his gaze to the pasture lands rolling past the stream and an old gabled house in thick, overgrown green foliage. The original farmhouse. Friendly, quiet. A hummingbird darted, a mockingbird somewhere in the alligator tree imitated a host of other flyers. But behind the tranquil stream and placid pasture, a growing dark against the evening sky, a long curve of horizon broke the peace.

James took off his ring and turned it slowly in his hand, studying it. "I was told this was found in my car seat with me. I guess I'll never know why. Was it only because my mother wanted to give me something to remember her by, or because she wanted me to acknowledge a dark legacy?"

Easing her cool hand over his warm one, Daelyn asked, "Maybe it was neither. Would you like me to read it?"

His thoughts clouded a little under the heat of her cool touch traveling through him, and her voice seemed like it was traveling through a mist. But—

Damned if he cared. Those blue wells were calling him.

She smiled, then turned her palm outward. "Read it?"

For several moments he gazed at the dark sapphire gleaming at him, shining through the shade. What would she find in those facets? Slowly, he dropped the ring into her palm.

She rubbed the golden band between her thumb and forefinger, searching. "She's squeezing the ring into her fist. She's terrified. Her heart is beating rapidly ... Time to go. There isn't much time. She has to go. She wraps you in a blanket ..." She ran her fingertip across the sapphire, and her brow furrowed as though puzzled. "There is great fear within this ring. She was afraid for you. She's running toward—a window, I think. She can see her reflection in the clear glass. She's lovely, James. She has great fear. She's afraid of the window ... Someone runs beside her, but I can see only as she saw ... His shoes as she looks down ..."

She gasped. "A—slayer!"

Her eyes melted into a blue glow, reeling from the impact of melding with the ring's past. For several moments, she was silent, then her eyes glazed over again. "The wind is cool, the trees full of green leaves. The ring is swinging on a chain ... She's nervous. Her hand comes up. She clutches the ring, looks back over her shoulder ... She catches you smiling up at her from your stroller and she's happy—evening, then night. Night frightens her. Locking the window latches. A bat flaps its wings, almost angrily, against the panes. Dawn. Running breathlessly, haphazardly, holding you to her breast. What to do, what to do? She can't run very fast. A supermarket parking lot. She's pulling your car seat from the car, puts you in a stray grocery cart, presses a kiss filled with tears to your cheek. Presses the ring into the folds of the blanket." Daelyn paused and looked up at James. "There was no malice in the giving of this ring, James. She loved you. She needed to give you something, something for a remembrance. It was all she had, all she knew to do, then begins your own journey." She handed the ring back. "Should I continue? I did not feel that you would wish that."

James drew his hand gently down her cheek. "No, I would not wish that. I'm a slayer."

"This ring has Dracula's touch everywhere in its history. But I cannot read past the curse to find how it found its way to your mother's hand."

"You gave me enough," he said. "You had to get past a lot of pain, and the inherent evil in that gold to enter the ring and find my answers for me. I—appreciate that."

He slid the ring back on his finger. His mother had loved him. He hadn't been left in a grocery cart because he was unloved, or unwanted. She was afraid for him. She just didn't know what else to do.

He could live with that.

"Since my plane contact met with a rather early departure, I need your help, Daelyn," James said.

"Don't tell me. Let me guess," she said knowingly, unhappily. "You want me to go back." She stared gloomily down at the ground below her feet as they dangled from the branch. "I knew it. I knew it when you wouldn't slay. You want in, to pretend to be a bad boy. The Count's new wiseguy. Let me guess, all that angst inside you has one channeled target. You want Dracula. And I'm your ticket in."

"That's part of it. But not all ..."

Her eyes shot holes through his. "I should mesmerize you, right here and right now and suck you dry, and we can both die. Right here on the ground. You can bleed out and I can sling myself across your chest, and moan for love lost till I die from your poisoned blood. The two lovers who never were. A touching finish. Your mother the Sheriff can give you a shotgun funeral. And I can be the dirt around your tombstone."

"Stop it!" he said, taking her roughly by the shoulders. "I didn't want to lead you on or lie to you, Daelyn. And I couldn't lie with you in a bed of lies. No false pretenses. So I'm laying it all out for you. Yes, I need you to go back, to back up my ruse as a defector, and find out where's he's hiding the Roses." He paused and released her. "You can stay or you can go, Daelyn, but if you go, you have to realize you can't hide forever, not from the Realm and not from yourself. And not from—me."

"Let me be!" she cried, jumping to the ground and running from him, tears stinging her eyes as she skirted the creek.

"Damn it," he muttered to himself, running after her.

"I have a friend," he called to her. "I have a friend who can salvage you. You would be able to walk in the light, as long as you remained on the side of absolute Truth. You would become a Vampyre of Light, Daelyn, a Valkyrie."

She stopped running, and stood silently for several minutes, her back to him. Thinking it over, James supposed.

"Is that what the other one was, the rider with the pearl white wings? A Valkyrie?" she finally asked.

He slowed his steps and stopped a little ways behind her. "Yeah."

"What—happened to her? Where did she go?"

"She rode the horse into the orchard and lost the vanguards in the chase. She's hell on wheels—and in the saddle."

She turned to him, and extended a wing. Stroking the inky feathers, she asked, "Will my wings be white?"

Haloed in the light of the sinking sun, Daelyn was beautiful, encased in a golden aura that tinted her shimmering brown hair and flecked her eyes with sunrays. But a tinge of melancholy lay on her smile.

James studied her, this vision of mischief and mayhem and sweetness and loveliness all wrapped up in feathers and fangs.

"Probably not. You've got an unpredictable hot spot."

She laughed, the melancholy faded. "How do you do that?" she asked.

"Do what?" he countered, puzzled.

"Make me—happy," she said, almost inaudibly.

James waited patiently for her to give him an answer to his "proposal." The thought of having to stake her was not something he wanted to contemplate. He didn't want to slay her. Lingering humanity meant she would feel lingering, excruciating pain before she died. Deep pain. She would suffer. The life would drain from her slowly, and she would gasp for every last breath in continual, open agony.

It would be hard to kill this one, he thought.

James looked away from her, down into the dark currents of the stream.

A cool hand touched his shoulder, drawing him from the water. "James?"

He turned, loving the little wind bells in her voice when she spoke his name—

"I guess if I have to go back into that hellhole with you on whatever this insane journey is that you're planning, at least you're a man I don't mind traveling with and sharing the risk—because I know you will be courageous." She paused and smiled. "And just so we have it straight—maybe a courageous lover?"

He definitely didn't want to have to slay her …

He pulled her to him and kissed her, long and slow, to let her feel human warmth, human desire. He wanted to let her know there could be more to a kiss than "that damned, drunken castle." She melted into him, and her passion for him suddenly spilled over into her kiss in fiery splashes. Her lips parted, inviting him in.

He smoothed his tongue across her lips, carefully, forcing himself to be patient. Far be it from him to deny this beautiful creature her offer, but he wanted to be sure she absolutely, resolutely, wanted this *baiser avec la langue* with him. The tip of her tongue lightly brushed his, teased a little. She wanted it. He slid his tongue into her mouth, and groaned with pleasure as the silken tongue he had wanted to feel for so long welcomed him. Her breasts rose and dipped into his chest in excitement.

His tongue tantalized. She curved into him, and caressed and explored his body with hers. For several long moments they enjoyed the hot exchange, then James realized—too much too soon. She had not slept with a human male. His hard body, his kisses, were like an inferno sweeping across kindling.

She moaned. He felt a fang tip.

Reluctantly, he eased back, ending the fire.

"Wow," she murmured through her breath. Her eyes were wet, shining. Azure seas.

Oddly, James felt sparks of strange embers within him that refused to cool.

Damn. He had surrendered to her charms more deeply than he had intended. And she had subtly stolen him a little. Though damned if he knew how.

He was captive.

But not a prisoner.

"So when do I become a vampyre of light?" she asked with her wind bell voice.

"When you let me go," he said.

She released him.

Damn, I picked a dangerous one to invite into the Shadows, he thought.

11.

Daelyn cast a glittery gaze toward the bright, black water trickling over a bed of small stones. "I haven't waded in water since … since I can't remember when. I want to feel the cool rush tickling my Valkyrie toes! Do we have time, James? I mean, we don't know if we'll ever be near a stream again …" Her eyes fell into his in a plea.

"Don't know why not." He shrugged.

His hands lingered on her bare legs as she sat on the ground. He pushed up her jeans and tugged at her boots.

"You are so wanting me!" she laughed, arching back on her elbows. Under the gingham blouse, her breasts rose delightfully into his eyes, into two exquisite points.

As riveting as an untamed sea in moonlight, Daelyn excited James into uncontrollable, fervent heat. She was becoming his body's desire, and the delight of his heart.

She jumped up, and rolling up her jeans legs, splashed into the water. "This is sooo heavenly scrumdelicious!" she cried. In irrepressible abandon, she sloshed across the stream bed stones and through the thin strands of rippling water toward a boulder in the middle of the stream that created a perfect, natural seat.

Wading to the boulder, James sat down beside her while she sunk her "Valkyrie toes" into a tiny waterfall cascading from a bit of sedimentary shelf.

"Can't we just stay here, James?" she asked, looking up at him pleadingly. "It's beautiful. It's secluded. No one would find us here. Your ritzy little farm would hide us."

"The world has a slight problem right now, Daelyn. For some reason, the Realm's vamps don't seem too overly concerned when they're spotted above ground, so to speak. Like the ones that thought nothing of hijacking that plane and deplaning the passengers in the middle of nowhere. When an informant told us what was going down, I went on board covert. I was supposed to be drugged by her, and hauled in to the Count. Presenting me for purposes of Royal insemination would elevate her and she could infiltrate on a deeper level. She was supposed to help us locate the Black Roses. But, of course, that didn't happen. Do you know anything about those little here and there incidents, like airbus hijackings, disappearing planes and people, Daelyn?"

"I'm not sure," she said as she drew her feet back and forth in the water. She cast her eyes imploringly at him again. "Please, James. We could splash in your pool and let the world go up for auction. It's a rotten place anyway."

"It may be rotten, but it's all we've got," he said. "I know life hurt you, Daelyn, but there is hope for you. And we can't let the only world we have die in a pool of blood, without any hope."

"They're not planning a pool of blood," she said.

"I thought you said you weren't sure what they were up to?" His eyes narrowed toward hers, probing.

"I was usually drunk, sodden, but I know it's not that. Not outright killing. I remember them yakking about how they wanted to domesticate humans, create a minion world, farm camps, feeding pens—maybe that's what it's about. With the Royals birthed from the Roses rising to rule this torn world?"

She shrugged again and leaned over to pluck a leaf floating down the creek, caressing its golden veins, innocent, an accidental vampyre.

And their encounter, an accidental desire.

"Daelyn, look, I know it's not going to be easy to go back, but ..."

She raised up suddenly, her eyes, and her demeanor bright, tight, changed.

She was bristling.

"Daelyn, I don't want to fight you."

Her eyes flitted like butterfly wings in the direction of the house. She sniffed the air. "The evil one. From the road!"

James yanked her from the water. "My mother!"

They ran toward the house.

At the gated entrance to the pool, James scooted Daelyn behind him, and they slipped past the waterfall to the patio. Hiding behind a built-in barbecue, they had a clear view to the game room windows.

His mother was strapped to a thumb back chair with twists of rope, a piece of duct tape slapped over her mouth. A young man who looked to be about in his twenties was bent over pulling a beer from the fridge, his back to them.

But James recognized the profile. Rage flooded his heart. How could he have been so careless? In his business, suspicion out of necessity always took precedence over trust. He crept around the brick barbecue as quickly and stealthily as his footsteps would allow, to take the quarterback from the train by surprise.

Daelyn flashed past him, almost knocking him down, and was through the patio door and at the refrigerator before Muscle Kid could straighten his back. She threw the trespasser over the game room bar counter and he went sailing head first to the floor. "You don't hurt Mama Pistola!" The beer bottle went flying and busted against a far wall. Beer poured down the wallpaper, streaking through a swirl of green and gold leaves to the baseboard.

James leaped in through the patio door to stop his rookie Valkyrie before she misdirected her sense of justice again and there was a repeat of the train thing.

She went into stance and picked the kid up by his throat.

She didn't attack.

Dropping the quarterback at James' feet, she began untying his mom with lightning fast fingers.

The kid curled into the womb position and didn't move, assisted in his decision to remain perfectly still by James' persuasive boot resting on his ribs ready to crush them if he even flinched.

"Did he hurt you, Mama Pistola?" Daelyn asked Belinda gently.

"Something about you is different," Belinda said quizzically as she gingerly rubbed her mouth, chapped from the tape, and studied the vampyre.

"You all right, mom?" James asked, looking back over his shoulder at her. His heart was torn, but the ex-sheriff had always been tough, was tough now.

"I'm fine."

Belinda Lauren had never been one to lick her wounds. Or anyone else's. "He used a high kick to knock the front door off the hinges, and rushed me. When I wouldn't tell the little upstart where you were, he tied me to the chair, and said he was going to wait for you no matter how long."

James pulled the train kid from the floor and urged him, not graciously, to the couch, then forced his voice to remain even—while he helped the kid understand the error of his ways. James smashed his fist into his face. The kid fell backward and burrowed into the couch pillows. "A man has the right to defend his life, his property, and his family, those he loves," James reminded him through clenched teeth. "Now talk before I continue exercising my right on your face."

The kid shriveled deeper into the couch and rubbed his jaw. But he said nothing.

Daelyn touched James lightly on the shoulder, and stepped in front of the quarterback. "Now, you're going to tell this man everything he wants to know."

"Like hell." He tossed her a stark, defiant gaze. Right into her eyes.

He's up the creek now, James thought. *He has no idea what those Kryptonite eyes can do.*

"No, you won't like the hell I'm about to put you through," Daelyn said softly.

He started to shake, all two hundred pounds of him.

She took a step forward, to mesmerize him—her eyes flew to the hallway stairs. "He's not alone!"

The other youth from the train, leaner but just as mean-eyed, was skulking down the staircase, knife in hand. He took aim, the blade was in the air.

Daelyn rushed forward—

"No, Daelyn!" James cried.

But she was already flashing toward the stairs to leap between him and the blade with death in its sheen.

She gasped, and toppled backward.

The knife that had been slicing the air toward him protruded at an angle from her chest.

James snared her in his arms. "It was a silver and wood alloy, Blues, honey," he moaned forlornly. "There's no way you could have caught it. You're too new to the game."

"Silver and wood," she uttered. "I couldn't—see it."

The assailant raced down the stairs to finish the job. An arrow rocketed through the open patio doorway. He stumbled forward, and rolled down the steps, then crumpled to a stop as his hand and arm caught in the spaces between the banister posts and twisted through them like a lattice crust on a pie.

A broken arrow protruded through his ribs and back.

An Indian, tall, muscular, with an eagle feather braided into his long, inky hair, stepped through the door, his bow now trained on the kid on the couch. "Your stupid, insignificant other there would've lived if he had better balance," he said. "I only disabled him. The fall turned the arrow and drove it in. How's your balance?" The kid didn't test him.

"Seems you're always center fielding my falls," Daelyn said in a weak whisper as James lowered her to the floor.

"And you're always saving me," he smiled tenderly.

Tears seeped from the corners of her eyes as she lay in his arms, and she gasped in deep pain.

"She dying, James?" Belinda asked as she roped the pseudo college student on the couch like a cow. She taped his mouth shut, then hurried to the staircase to check on the wounded vampyre.

"She has a chance. It hit just under her breast bone," James said. "But it's close, in at an angle."

"We need to get her upstairs," his mother ordered expeditiously. "Take her to your room, James. It's the closest."

"We'll have to move her carefully, or the knife could move," the Indian added, coming to his side.

James gave the Apache slayer a quick warm smile. "Glad you showed up when you did, Jon T." Daelyn moaned and James turned back to her. "She's hurting."

"She's also bleeding like hell," the Apache said. "And she's in a lot of pain." His forehead knotted in puzzlement. "A damned lot of pain—how old is she?"

"A little over a year."

"Damn." He shook his head remorsefully.

James lifted Daelyn gingerly into his arms, and carried her up the stairs. Once in his room, his mother pulled back the bed covers, spread towels over the sheets, and he placed her on the bed. The towels were soon soaked to blistering red.

"We have to get that dagger out," the Indian said somberly.

"Call Christa, mom," James said. "She's going to need blood. Because her humanity is still with her and not in shadow yet, it will take her a few days to heal. And she'll be weak."

He smoothed the vampyre's hair back away from her forehead while the Apache carefully tore her shirt away. She started shaking. James unsnapped her bra and lifted the left cup. "This is going to hurt, Daelyn. I'm sorry."

"Could I—have some wine first?" she begged in a whispery, pain-ridden voice.

Belinda pulled a flask of whiskey from her front pants pocket. "You don't need social creek water right now, honey. You need some southern comfort."

Daelyn took several deep, breath grabbing swallows—and so did everyone else in the room.

James took the flask and handed it back to his mother. "We might need a refill on that," he grinned slightly.

"Why is he here?" Daelyn asked suddenly, her eyes wide, staring starkly at the opposite wall.

"Who, Blues?" James asked, perplexed.

"The man. From the road."

He followed her eyes. The ghost was leaning against a dresser, his arms crossed, his gaze grave—and riveted on Daelyn.

"You can't have her," James said firmly, desperately. "Get the hell out."

"Don't look at him, Daelyn," the Apache said. "Just look at Jim Boy there."

Daelyn looked up at James imploringly. "Hold my hand?" She slipped her palm under his.

James entwined his fingers in hers, then leaned toward her. "Just don't break my fingers," he grinned.

She managed a small return smile. "You have nice hands, Prince James."

"You can use that other hand to keep the towel in place, your highness," the Apache smirked as he wrapped a towel around the protruding portion of the blade then wrapped his hand around the handle of the knife.

"Another friggin' slayer," Daelyn groaned, her body trembling suddenly, violently.

"Easy, Daelyn. You need to lie still," James said, knowing she could feel the Indian's profession and his heritage deep in his strength and in his touch. Instinctive fear was walloping her insides.

She clutched his hand. Belinda put a blanket warm from the dryer around her legs and waist, and the trembling subsided. "Don't I get a bullet to bite, pardner?" Daelyn joked weakly toward James.

Then the Apache was slowly pulling the long knife from her rib cage, and she was crying and squeezing James' hand and screaming and passing out.

"Straight out, steady, easy does it, so it won't knick her heart," James instructed worriedly. The ghost had not gone.

Jon T. tossed him a slightly disdaining glance. "I've been at this a long time, Jim Boy. Relax."

Finally, after what seemed like an eternity, the knife point was clear of the wound. James tossed the knife into the trash, and they worked quickly to apply towels and pressure to stop the bleeding. In a few mere minutes, the bleeding became seepage as her body began to seal the wound.

The ghost dissipated.

"Friend of yours?" the Apache asked amiably.

"Hell, no." He stroked Daelyn's hair away from her forehead as she lay unmoving, unconscious.

"So how's that cousin of yours, Jon T.?"

"In love," he grinned. "So who's the spirit of Christmas past?"

"Long story. Seems he has nowhere to be so he's everywhere."

They left his mother to watch over the vampyre, now succumbing to the deep sleep vampyres fall into to heal when heavily wounded, and went downstairs.

The stairs were clean, the body gone. Shadow Sweepers had worked swiftly and silently to restore the home.

Andre DuPre was sitting on the couch, his arm across the back rest. The "student" was gone, taken away for interrogation.

"You should be more careful who you pass out business cards to," Andre directed pointedly at James, and not gently. He had the look of a schoolmaster about to rap his student's knuckles with a cane.

James dropped to the couch, and pushing his hands through his hair, stared at the floor. "I wasn't thinking too clearly after I got planked with a railroad tie. Concussion had me cloudy. I know. I should have gotten his name, checked him out."

I was cloudy on a lot more than just the college kid, he thought, glancing up the stairs.

"He was human backup for the guards on the train," Andre informed him. "When he called the number on the card and gave his train story, he was given your last name. Realizing who you were, he and his sidekick decided to strike out on their own for personal gain. Certain New Royals, it seems, will secretly pay quite handsomely to see the fabled slayer prince dead rather than kidnapped. They do not want the Count's bloodline, in a blend of vampyre and slayer power, sitting next to them some day in Council."

James leaned back and closed his eyes. Pain etched his face. "And Daelyn took the blade meant for me."

"Fortunately for you, they kept their get-rich-quick scheme, and the location of this farm to themselves. They planned to claim the bounty after the deed."

"So we're cleared to continue to Paris, then?" he asked in an exhalation of relief.

"Unless you've still got a concussion and have been wandering the streets aimlessly handing out business cards like we're a damned lawn mowing service."

12.

After two days of daysleep, Daelyn finally stirred. Slipping a cup of plasma into his pocket, James went upstairs.

She opened her eyes and smiled dreamily at him. "Seems a shame to be taking your whole bed. I'll share."

He grinned. She was, apparently, recovering nicely. "I've got a stern, wise old mother who can also be a wise-ass and wouldn't go in for me sharing my bed in her house, vampyre or otherwise, unless an exchange of rings and a champagne wedding were involved," he said.

She pressed her hand lightly against her rib cage. "How am I doing?" she asked.

"It's almost completely healed."

"Completely healed? In a few hours?"

"You've been out for a couple of days, Blues," James said tenderly.

She looked startled. "Oh."

He didn't tell her that sometimes she had cried out, and moaned as though trying to break free of chains. He took the little cup of plasma from his pocket and handed it to her. "Thought you might want some 'candy' when you woke up. You've had a pretty rough time."

She flashed him a deep smile, and the cup was empty almost as soon as it hit her tongue.

By midday, Daelyn was walking down the hallway, a little unsteady but determined, with James at her side.

He was in swimming trunks, and she was in an aqua blue, two piece swimsuit with a sash tied at the side of the bikini bottom—a skinny little bit of two piece nothing that barely covered her curves.

James had bought her the little bit of nothing to go swimming with him. So she could have a taste of Texas sunlight and water instead of a damned drunken castle for a change, he had said.

But as he reached the patio door and she looked outside, he felt resistance in her hand. "Thought you wanted to splash in my pool," he smiled invitingly.

"The afternoon sun is in full force," she said uncertainly, dropping his hand and pulling away. "Even autumn does not diminish its force."

She shrank back into the shadows of the drapes. "Maybe we can swim later," she said. "When the sun is lower."

James pulled a drape to the side until a pencil of sunray stole into the room and fell to the floor next to her. "Tell you what. Let's give it a trial run. We can ease your arm close. If it starts to burn, it won't be more than a smudge of heat, but we'll know you can't tolerate the sun yet."

He held out his hand. "Trust me, Daelyn."

Slowly, she eased from the drape, trembling, abhorring the tiny line of light. "I'll touch that horrid sun, but I won't like it," she said, her blue eyes scorching his. "Will it scar?"

"It isn't even going to burn, Daelyn. Unless you're heart's running in dark alleys again. Is it?"

"My heart's running amok," she said, wind bells returning to her voice. "Because a slayer who runs in dark alleys has filled it with fire."

He kissed her. "And the vampyre who mesmerizes me when we touch fills me with her fire."

She gave him her hand, he held out her arm, and held his breath. Watching for any curl of smoke and pain, he let the rim of the sunray sweep an edge of skin.

Her arm was unscathed. "A Valkyrie yes, you may yet become, young Jedi," he said with a pleased grin.

She looked into his eyes as though he had just given her a handful of diamonds. She turned her arm to the inside, let the sunray splash across her wrist, and laughed lightly, elatedly. Then her eyes glistened into his like bright blue water. "It's—beautiful!"

James exhaled with relief. There were times he had his doubts with this one.

Daelyn Bakerville was his responsibility. She was also his beautiful bane.

She walked gaily out onto the patio. Tossing her towel on a chaise lounge, she twirled in the sunlight in pure elation, and the sun haloed the brunette tresses cascading around her bare shoulders and down her back. She tilted her head upward, relaxed her wings, and stretched her arms outward to catch the warm, rich sun on her body, a sun she no longer had to run from, or be a victim of its golden terror. James gazed appreciatively at the lithe body twirling in wind bell laughter—the oval face and strong, soft shoulders, the firm lift of her breasts, her slender waist, the hips curving delectably as the sash swirled against them.

"Lordy, James, she's beautiful," Belinda exclaimed as she brought out a tray of lemonade, sandwiches and a bottle of blood. "Delicate, yet—"

"Wild?" James finished, arching an eyebrow knowingly.

His mother gave him a light glance that stated clearly he still needed to watch his heart, and his steps, with this one. Then she set the tray on a table next to him. "I'm headed over to the Knights of Columbus hall for Bingo," she said. "Dinner's at six sharp. The cook is somewhat of a pain about that."

"She won't spit in the sweet tea if we're late, will she?" James laughed.

"Might," she said, and left.

James draped his towel on the back of a chair, then dove into the pool and waited for Daelyn to follow.

She didn't join him. She sat on the edge of the pool's tiled border, hesitant, and only reluctantly eased a foot into the water, then the other, moving them slowly through the aqua liquid shimmering with sunlight.

"What? You want to sit in the sun all day?" James teased from the middle of the pool.

She didn't answer him, just stared downcast into the tiny ripples around her ankles.

He swam over to her and rested his arms on the pool ledge. "You know how to swim, don't you? Or do you just splash in creeks?"

She laughed. "I'm from a beach city. Of course I know how to swim, silly!" She paused and became solemn again. "It's just that— sometimes if it's deep, water—hurts."

Water. Water could weaken a vampyre's earthly-supernatural

powers, as well as present a real threat and a serious risk. And Dae-lyn was, of course, still a vampyre, very much a vampyre, though James was finding it harder and harder to keep reminding himself of that small, rather significant fact. She wanted him to surrender to her. He knew that. He sensed her desire for him in every nerve in his body. He just didn't know yet how it would play out.

James cupped his hand and swept it through the water, catching a palmful, then he smoothed the water gently across her bare waist. "Does that hurt?" he asked gently.

"No."

He poured several more across her waist and thighs, smooth-ing the watery streams down her legs in slow, easy strokes. More across her neckline, tributaries that trickled downward, soaking her bikini top and glistening in the curvature of her breasts. Her eyes became riveted on him. As the streams flowed down her body, she held onto the edge of the pool tightly, but she didn't fight him. Pouring more water across her shoulders, James smoothed the cool rivulets onto her arms.

She was soon drenched, wonderfully wet, and liquid in his hands.

And she wasn't hurting.

He took her by the waist and pulled her from the pool ledge slowly, carefully, into the water. She threw her arms around his neck, breathing hard.

Her wings disappeared beneath gossamer blue liquid. He eased her deeper. Her body tightened against his. "Don't let go," she whis-pered. "Don't let go of me, James."

"I won't," he promised. He drew her under the water with him, let her test the blue depths surrounding her, let her gaze at him under liquid spells of aqua.

Then he brought her up for air. "No power outages?" he smiled.

"None that I can tell," she said as he pressed her close, and she snuggled him. Every inch of him.

Then she laughed, and in a burst of new found freedom, she dove away, diving to the bottom of the pool. For a moment he couldn't see her, then her slender form pushed to the surface in ec-stasy, a dolphin freed from the net. She kissed him, a quick splash that made his heart pound with desire, then she was flash-diving away from him, and all he saw were ripples parting the water.

She surfaced next to the waterfall. Reclining on the top step under a shallow shelf of water shaded by ornamental trees, she dangled her bikini bottom provocatively from her fingertips. She was wreathed by red and gold leaves of the low hanging branches, and colorful autumn flowers.

Is she dove, or raven? James thought.

"So the rules of the house are you can't share your bed. What are the pool rules?" she cooed.

Raven. Stealing his heart like a dove.

James felt the unbearable tension demanding he go to her.

Logic told him she could fail when she was surrounded by vampyres and blood again—and lose the light within her; he needed to wait, wait to be with her. Wait until she had proven herself. He had to be patient.

But James didn't feel patience, in that moment, was much of a virtue.

She turned to sit sideways on the shelf, arching back under the waterfall to let the cascades splash over and down her body in thousands of cool drops and streams as she reveled in her newfound joy of water.

"This feels so wonderful, James!" she cried pleasurably.

James wanted heavily to share in that pleasure with her. He dove under the water, to swim to her—

"Jim Boy?"

A voice, calling down to him through the water.

He swam back to the surface.

Jon Tyree Quintero was on the patio with two airline tickets.

Daelyn flashed from the shelf into the water to hide, making barely a ripple as she dove.

James climbed out and toweled off. Wrapping his towel around his shoulders, he poured a glass of lemonade for the Apache.

"Have a seat, Chief," James invited, and dropped into a metal back chair at the patio table.

"Hard Mike?" Jon T. asked, holding up the glass.

"Hard water."

Jon T. set the glass down and handed James the tickets.

"Ethiopia?" James asked inquisitively in surprise as he glanced inside the folders. "I thought my destination was Paris, then Scotland."

"Pighead sent word the Realm is riddled with unrest. We've alerted Tani and the African night fighters to keep you under wraps for a day or so. He needs time to nose around, and time to make sure he's not being watched before he will agree to guide you through the Empire of the Dead." He paused. "If Pighead even thinks anything's amiss, he'll disappear, and we may never get this close again."

James turned toward the pool. "Daelyn," he called toward the pale shadow of a woman's form drifting just below the surface of the water. "You may as well come on out. I know you can hear all this."

She hoisted herself out of the pool, and eased toward the Indian cautiously.

His eyes flickered briefly with an appreciative glance at the body glistening with beads of water.

"What is the 'T' for?" she asked as she tied her towel around her waist.

"Tyree."

"Tyree. What does that mean?"

"Chief, I'm told."

"You're a full-blood?"

"So I'm told."

She slid into a chair at the table. "How did you become a Shadow?"

"I'm a mountain vampyre hunter, in your words, 'another friggin' slayer,' and you're a curious piece of nonlife. Why so many questions?"

She shrugged. "You helped save me. Thank you."

"Don't make me regret it," he said.

His voice was as dry as the bottom of a wooden ship coated with pitch.

Once more, she was reminded she was in the presence of heavy-hitting slayers.

13.

The sprawling, Addis open air market was dense with buyers hedging their way through bustling avenues of shops and stalls and commodities. And the streets were dense with homeless faces peering close, ragged beggars' hands reaching out, and the city's weak sleeping near on patches of grass, the deformed forgotten.

"I saw some pictures of this market, and a lot of others from all over the world during a cultural exchange week in one of my college classes," Daelyn said as her hand melted into his and they cut deeper into the crowd of shoppers. "The class even shared traditional foods and ceremonies from other countries." She laughed suddenly. "Speaking of the ceremonies, I think I might be married—to more than one guy. Or at least engaged."

"You might be engaged to the Apache. That was his horse you took and rode into my ranch—and watered," James grinned. "If a young maiden accepts a suitor's horse left at her doorstep within four days, and feeds and waters it, it's a done deal."

"Not funny." She shuddered a little. The Apache was cold and mysterious, a secret heart. His feather had told her little about him as it brushed against her while he leaned over her to help save her life.

"The feather belonged to a shaman. Is he a shaman?" she asked.

"No, but his cousin is," James said. "His cousin gave him that feather."

Daelyn's blue eyes drank in the stalls filled with colorful things to purchase. "I still don't understand why you won't let me carry any money," she said, slightly irritated. "I won't break the bank!"

"That's not the point. Too many layba, thieves," he said.

A wine merchant called out to them to peruse his wares.

Relenting, James pulled a small, leather pouch from under his belt, from underneath his zippered fly, and gave her some money. Then he put it back in under his belt.

"I can't believe that's where you keep your money," she said with a light laugh.

"In Addis Ababa, Ethiopia, I do," he said.

"So, next time, can I just—help myself to a zipper full?" Her eyes glittered softly.

She bought fresh figs and a rich wine.

Another seller motioned her toward brightly dyed scarves. She bought two as she relished the bottle of wine and James enjoyed the figs.

They walked on. The shoppers became thick as bees, shoulder to shoulder, buying spices and teff grain, pots and pans, needful things if they were to survive this country.

"Are we leaving soon, James?" Daelyn asked, starting to become uncomfortable in the sea of mortals, starting to feel closed in, feeling—hungry. People, people everywhere, and not a one to drink.

It was becoming unbearable.

And James was watching her closely. "Our ride should be here soon," he said.

I'll never make it, she thought. *This Valkyrie is for getting her ass out of here and away from this street salad or I'll never make it. Besides, the scent of all these vats of spices are about to make me retch.*

Someone bumped her. One of her scarves slid from her shoulder. She tried to reach for it. People were suddenly close, crazy close, a group of about five, crowding her. They chattered into her face, asking for coin. Her handbag disappeared from her shoulder into the press. James grasped her arm and yanked her through the circle of faces concaving toward her—the necks, the throats, the pulses, throbbing in her ears ... She could nip and nibble and no one would even notice.

She left the scarf on the ground as he dragged her into a café, noisy but quiet compared to the merkato.

"You all right?" he asked.

"Hell, no. I lost my pretty scarf, and I lost my handbag—in fact, I think someone stole it. I liked it, even though there was, of course, nothing in it to steal, basically. Thanks to your zipper."

"That's not what I'm asking," he said. "And yes, they did steal it. It's what they do. They're pickpockets. Now, how are you?"

"Oh. You mean that. Yeah, yeah, I guess I'm okay. A vision of those beady little eyes of your boss, Momma Pistola's shotgun, and Dracula's waiting, clammy hands, ran successful interference with my—wanderlust."

"If you can control your 'wanderlust' in a horde of humans, whether it's an open air market, or the streets of New York, you'll be able to retain your walk in the sunlight," James said tenderly. "We're also scheduled to have supper with a few of the most aggressive vampyre fighters on the planet. We'll see how you do with them. And as for Dracula, I plan to vocally exercise my princely privileges to claim you so he'll have no choice but to keep his mitts off you. Aren't those the rules and regs of the game in the underground?"

Her eyes filled with elation. "I—will be—yours?"

"Business. This is just business, Daelyn."

"And you will be—mine," she murmured in deep pleasure, barely aware of the rest of what he had said.

A woman was suddenly beside her. A young Ethiopian woman. She had weaved through the restaurant tables toward them without making a sound.

How ...? Daelyn thought, then reeled as every fiber in her body screamed, *Slayer!*

Daelyn instinctively backed her steps to fight her. The African slayer emanated a strange, frightening power.

James quickly stepped between them. "She's a friend, Daelyn," he said. "And you don't have many, so I wouldn't piss her off if I were you."

"Hurry," the hunter said. "I have a cab waiting."

James swept Daelyn out the door, and they piled into the back of the taxi. Once in the cab, Daelyn dared a careful glance toward the Ethiopian slayer. With exquisite facial bone structure, high cheekbones and a noble jaw line, she was the epitome of her people's exquisite ancestry. Large gold bangle earrings dangled against an elegant long neck, her skin a soft, caramel brown. If Daelyn could have pictured what the Queen of Sheba might have looked like, she would be it.

The cabbie began tackling the crowded streets of the city.

"So you are the One of Light," the Ethiopian Shadow smiled. "I'm Taniesha Telahun. Known by most as Tani."

"This is Daelyn, a Bakerville," James grinned with a sly wink at Daelyn. "Mistaken for a Baskerville."

Daelyn desperately held onto James' arm and moved closer to him, away from the Aftrican hunter whose steady brown gaze was unnerving her.

"Hmm," Tani murmured, tapping her chin with a mauve fingernail. "Thomas Baskerville. Related to the Dukes of Normandy, who had helped William the Conqueror in 1066. The Baskervilles lived relatively tranquilly in the 19th century, I'm told, until that strange business with the hound. According to Kathyrn, the bizarre affair was a challenge for Mr. Holmes, but he was marvelous in his solving of the mystery. Were you also there, in his history, Daelyn? I would loved to have known him."

"Holmes?" Daelyn cast a look of puzzlement at James.

"Sherlock Holmes. Of Baker Street," Taniesha explained. "In London. A renowned detective of his time, famous for his analytical solving of complex crimes. Kathryn even met him once in her— pre-Shadow days. His carriage started to wobble and the driver stopped to check the axle and wheels. Holmes took advantage of the short stop to stretch his legs and smoke his pipe. He walked a little way from the carriage, and she appeared out of the fog like an opiate dream. He offered her a ride into the city, then completely captivated her with his quick mind as they rode together. She found it impossible to attack. They exchanged pleasantries and he dropped her off at her apartment building. She said he remained in the carriage, but peering out at her from the edge of the window, thoughtfully drawing from his pipe as he watched her ascend the stairs. They never met again, but she was certain he knew he had encountered a vampyre."

"And we're kind of damned glad she's on our side now," James grinned.

Taniesha drew her hand through the air so close to Daelyn's cheek, Daelyn felt the wind in her fingertips.

"You are young!" she murmured in surprise. Then those searching brown eyes, two exquisite almonds, turned to James. "The young one has the gift."

"Tani's also a precog," James explained to Daelyn as her breath, and her fear, and her defenses, intensified. "She also has a quick wrist."

The last statement was a warning. A warning which Daelyn decided was well worth taking seriously as she looked into the dark, mysteriously masked eyes of the Ethiopian.

The precog's eyes fell on Daelyn's left arm. Holding it up to the light in a soft grip, she drew her hand down the inside in a slow stroke. "You were tempted in the market," she said knowingly as she gazed at her skin.

Daelyn looked at her arm, at the splotches of pink.

Sunburn.

She hadn't noticed the burn marks until now.

"Be wary of your thoughts," the precog exhorted her. "Our desires can become our own tools of destruction, and we the fools that wield them." Those orbs of mystery cast a quick glance into James eyes, and Daelyn was pretty sure the words of precog wisdom weren't meant for her alone.

The cabbie dropped them off in front of a tukel just outside the city.

As Daelyn entered the dim coolness of the thatch roofed, stone house, she stood still as a brick, her defenses flaring. A power was flowing into the room from somewhere within the further recesses. A power reeking with danger to her. Shrinking from the unseen force, she grabbed James' arm. Her instinct to survive was telling her to flee, hide, smother herself in a deep, dark, safe place. An empty monastery cellar, a cave, a tunnel …

Four African men entered the room.

Slayers.

Their presence enveloped the whole house.

Their bodies, the muscles rippling under white shirts and pants, were seething with power, and Daelyn felt like she was going to faint. In this small, tight room with slayers' practically oozing out of the walls, her quaking insides were screaming.

Flash and fly, idiot! Get out of here! Now!

Her whole body was constricted, telling her to spread her wings and flee this tukel, this continent. Swimming pools and sunlight be hanged. Black gold and saving humanity, and hoping for love with a prince—it just wasn't worth it. She wanted to go home. The devil got the world into this mess—let God fix it.

She just wanted to go home, but she could never go home. A sob rose up in her throat.

"Daelyn," Taniesha's voice said softly as though reading the pain within her, "we will not hurt you. We are at James' command tonight. Come, join us." She led them to a larger room and invited Daelyn and James to sit together on a low, comfortable divan.

As Tani left the room, Daelyn pushed as close to James as possible without becoming his Siamese twin. He was the only protection she had in the middle of this room swilling over with vampyre killers.

"You can breathe now," he whispered.

"I don't think so," she whispered back, shaking her head, still staring fearfully, defensively at the dark giants in white.

Tani returned shortly carrying a handmade table. Wicker, with an hourglass-shape and a domed cover. She set it down in front of them.

"A mesab!" Daelyn cried delightedly, her fear diminishing somewhat as James squeezed her hand reassuringly. Not much, but a little.

The other "guests" sat down on stools eight inches high covered with monkey fur.

"There are underground human spelunkers in the Parisian vamp tunnels," one of the men informed James in a business-like tone. "They sneaked in yesterday and set up housekeeping. They could be a problem. We're trying to figure a way to run them out, without causing undue attention."

Daelyn cast a careful, quick, corner-of-the-eye glance toward him. He was put together like a body builder. And his face was handsome with strong, sensitive eyes and a square jawline. There was nowhere this African could go and flex a pec, and not cause undue attention.

The fighter next to him with dark, intelligent eyes, carried a strength in his voice that said when he wasn't playing with barbells, he was used to commanding. He was taller, older.

"Pighead is now realizing he is openly aiding and abetting and he's starting to get antsy," he said. "He is not sure he wants to continue with us."

"His hatred of the Realm is not as deep as his desire to keep his head out of range of a Realm executioner's ax blade," Daelyn piped up, before she thought.

The room was suddenly silent.

"You know him, Daelyn?" James asked.

"He—helped me escape once."

"Can you talk to him? Convince him to stay tough?" the older hunter asked, suddenly avidly interested in her.

"I could try," she said, shrinking under the intense, steady stares all now funneled in her direction.

"Tani could probably use some help," she said quickly, rising, and forcing herself to keep her back straight as she felt their gazes on her while she walked calmly from the room with Tani. But she wanted to run like hell.

14.

Holding a long-spouted, copper pitcher for washing in her right hand, and a copper basin in her left, Daelyn moved next to James. Tani draped a soft beige towel over her left arm.

"Tani tells me you pretty well know the dinner ritual, and that you're rather fond of the local cuisine," Daelyn smiled. She poured warm water over the fingers of James' right hand, holding the basin to catch the excess.

James wiped his hands on the towel on her arm, taking longer than necessary, just to be close to her, she was sure. His eyes smiled at her, returning the desirous looks she cast at him, with warm affection. They were in the beginnings of transcendent union. It bewildered her, but she liked the way it felt when their eyes would lock. Pleasurable and powerful.

James fought it a little. But only a little.

He wanted her. She was certain of it.

And she wondered if she was beginning to—love him.

Strange. After she was bitten, she had felt only a sting in her heart, a wistfulness, and even that began to vanish with each fading heartbeat.

Should she even entertain the idea a mortal might want her, perhaps even love her? She had barely a heart throb left to return that love. Her heart had died in a Realm cavern. In more ways than one. But now—

Tani took the mesab away, and when she returned, she removed the dome.

The table was covered with what at first appeared to be a gray tablecloth, but this "tablecloth" was Injera, the sourdough pancake-like bread of Ethiopia.

Daelyn helped Tani bring out an assortment of wat in enamel bowls and dip individual portions of the stews onto the table cloth. "Doro Wat, a chicken stew and the lamb are usually the most peppery," Daelyn said as she ladled delectables onto James' area of the Injera and let her breast rub against his arm. "Seasoned with Berberi and Awaze spices." Her eyes glittered slightly at him. "To heat you up."

His eyes said he was already pretty hot.

A milder version, alecha stew, also graced the elegantly laid table.

Tibs was next, a hot dish with vegetables mixed in, a dish to show special respect to a guest.

They were honoring James tonight.

Like giving a condemned man his last meal, Daelyn thought.

When the entire Injera was colorful with different stews, Daelyn tore off a piece of about a two to three inch square of the "tablecloth." "Spicy, or a wussy wat?" she challenged the prince behind her smile.

"Doro Wat," he laughed.

"Ah, the adventurous type." She rolled the dab of Injera and spicy stew like she was rolling an old west cigarette. Then swoop, scoop, she moved close to him and popped the little roll into his mouth.

Which he accepted enjoyably.

As she gave him another one, his enjoyment deepened, into sweet heat, his eyes as spicy as the evening's fare, his desire for her becoming straight Awaze. She laughed lightly, loving the heat, then spoke to him softly, her voice like silver bells that unbalanced even the four fighters a little. "It takes a bit of doing, but once mastered, you cannot help but enjoy it, yes?"

"Yes," he smiled, his eyes filled with the knowledge he knew she wasn't referring to Injera wrapped stew.

Dessert followed the stews: Iab, cottage cheese and yogurt with herbs for an acidic, lemon flavor; Kitfo, ground raw beef marinated in mitmita, a spicy chili powder; and niter kibbeh, seasoned clarified butter.

Tani took a long-necked bottle from a table close by. "Would you like to try the Tej, Daelyn?"

Daelyn studied the amber-colored honey wine with misgivings.

"If it doesn't agree with you, I have a nice red," Tani offered.

"She doesn't mean a red wine," James added.

Tella—homemade beer, and weakly carbonated water, along with the plasma cups and cups of the red liquid she carried to sustain her were also on the side table.

"I'll try the Tej," Daelyn decided, hoping she wouldn't retch.

The night fighters drank coffee from tiny Japanese cups, black with sugar. More hand washing, then incense burned while they indulged in the coffee and Daelyn dared a cautious sip of the Tej.

"It's delectable!" she said.

"Before our Texas pact you wouldn't have been able to stomach that," James informed her.

Before James, she thought with a smile, *I couldn't stomach this godawful earth.*

After coffee, the lights were lowered for the night and Tani led Daelyn and James to a room at the back of the house.

The only object in the room other than a small table was a cottony, thick-piled, brightly colored pallet in the center of the floor.

Only one.

A lighter blanket, also brightly colored, in diagonal patterns, lay folded next to the pallet.

In case the night became cool.

A round terra cotta bowl of sweet smelling, warm oil was sitting next to the blanket.

In case the night became hot—

Tani left, closing the door softly behind her, and leaving them staring at one another.

"Well, I guess you can take the bed and I'll take the couch," Daelyn spoke first, gathering the coverlet into her arms. She found a darkened corner and curled into a ball, becoming an almost imperceptible shadow.

James picked up the bowl of oil and began dragging the quilt over to the dark corner.

"The presence of Team Olympic in there doesn't exactly add ambiance to a romantic night out," her voice said from the darkness.

"They won't disturb us," he said, his voice husky.

Her blue eyes peered out of the darkness, into his. Questioning. This slayer wanted to make love to her. He wanted to lie in webs of surrender with her.

"Are we going to hurt one another, Daelyn?" he asked, his voice low, and rich. "Or ...?" He held up the bowl of oil.

His eyes were seductively wet.

She moved onto the quilt with him, trembling. Excitement at the thought of being touched and touching, sensuously, intimately, with a human was suddenly raging out of control inside her. "Is this—just business?"

"Business has been postponed for the night."

Forcing the wildness pelting her in throbs to behave was like the addicted gambler trying not to flip the one unturned card. The delicious depths inside her were saying slap dash him to the floor, straddle him, and take him, unbridled—

But—he was human. She unbuttoned her blouse slowly, controlling the urge to simply rip it off. She eased her arms out of the sleeves, unbearably slowly, then lowered her bra straps to let him gaze at her, though he had basically already seen quite a bit of her when she was wounded.

She had seen most of him in the pool, and now ... He showed her the rest.

And the rest was worth waiting to see.

Oh, yeah.

As she pushed her jeans from her waist, Daelyn could hear his heart begin to beat harder. Through the whole room. And she could acutely feel and sense the crush of desire pressing through his body.

Being able to sense so completely such mortal need, delighted her, sent hot thrills through her.

But this mortal was—more than need. There were drops of love intermingling with his desire.

Love.

Were there a few drops forming for him in her heart as well?

Do I love you, James Lauren? Or am I just your ticket to Dracula's hole, and you my ticket out?

He looked away from her briefly as though needing to say something, but not sure how to say it. "When you chased my attacker at the train, Daelyn, was it because he was trying to kill me, or simply because he was trying to kill your way out, your escape?" he finally asked.

He was revealing his heart, drop by drop.

"I won't lie to you, James. I saw you as my escape. But then—well, I guess it was a fifty-fifty split. You were my escape, but I—liked you," she said truthfully. "And now ..."

"And now?"

"I—want you. I want to be your obsession, James Lauren."

"Obsession." He pulled her to him, let her feel the full breadth of his desire. "Obsess with me, Daelyn."

"Are you—claiming me, James?" she asked, almost shyly, in soft, low tones.

She gasped as he drew his lips to hers and she felt the warm, human body encasing hers, sinew more exciting than she had expected. His kiss seemed to melt the walls, urgent, needing, pleading, and he pressed her back against the quilt. Tipping the bowl, he poured the light, fragrant oil in a small stream over her, and she gasped again under the surprise of the potion's delectable warmth and fragrance. She felt as though she was being bathed in velvety softness, as velvety as rose petals under a warm sun. He smoothed the stream across and down her body with both hands, interspersed with kisses virtually everywhere, and her enjoyment exploded into regions deep within her, places she never knew could exist with a mortal male.

More oil. The smoothing became deep caresses. He was massaging the smooth liquid into her skin so she would be warm under him. She felt her body go crazy. Crazy for more of the warm oil and James' warm hands.

More.

More.

More.

Heat traveled through her arms, her legs, her body ... Would the slayer prince drive her into love spasms she had come to believe could never be hers? Ever? Except in her wistful thoughts, her sad dreams? Lonely wishes in the sand ...

But wishes can come true.

She moaned and arched, penetrated with need, while he kissed her and kissed her and kissed her. Then his hands moved to her thighs, massaging in slow, smooth upward strokes between her legs, deep into tissue and muscle. Wonderful, warm hands, making her sizzle.

She was making love—for the first time.

She encircled her arms around his waist. Desire was becoming a command and she called to him through the night with her eyes. He trembled, but yielded, and the veils flowed between them, pulling him into the melting vortex she herself barely understood, but could control however she willed.

"You're wild, Daelyn," he said as he raised back to accept the pleasure in the kisses she was planting passionately across his chest.

"You're wonderful," she responded, letting her own voice flow like liquid silver. "I won't say I never thought it could be like this. I always thought it could be like this. I thought about it every day, all day, knowing it could be like this. I just needed—you."

Neither of them could control the tension any longer. He consumed her with his passion, and she cried out, the warmth he filled her with strange, but exciting, a wild thrusting warmth that she had never felt, and that she never wanted to stop.

This was not cold fire. This was living flame.

She held him in throbs of heat with her silken sea, drove him forward, and taught him what it could be like with her as they became one in mind and body.

A final rush of pleasure, and he groaned, his body tightened, then relaxed. But he lingered, as though not wanting to let go of the passion, the sweet, wild Tej that they had both drunk so deeply from, and that still encompassed them.

Honey wine.

He tasted it more than once during the night.

And the night's heat left a lot of smoke behind.

"You're gorgeous," he murmured drowsily, waking as a meddlesome sun poked its nose through the window. They caressed, touching places lightly they had explored during the night, with renewed interest.

A knock at the door let them know the rest of the house was also up.

Fresh clothes had been left outside the door. Warm, hooded jackets in black, two sets of black jeans and black long-sleeved shirts for him, a black jogging suit and black silk blouses and black jeans for her. Wherever they were going when they left Ethiopia, they apparently needed to blend in with the night. They bathed quickly, conserving water, then dressed and met the African Shadows for breakfast.

The breakfast table offered a simple but palatable fare of fatera, fried pancakes of flour with a layer of egg, and accompanied by honey with bowls of fresh pineapple and melon, cups of plasma, and a bottle of Tani's "red."

Daelyn decided it would be best not to ask her where she got the blood. Or whether it was even human. She was afraid she would tell her it was monkey blood, or wombat, or pole cat …

Ugh.

She held her breath and drank it.

Within the hour, she was on a charter plane with James on her way to France.

"The Count may not have officially claimed you as his own, Daelyn, but I felt his union with you in your vortex of thought," James said. "He will know. He will sense even from a continent away that you made love to someone else last night."

"Like I give a damn," she said. And kissed him.

15.

The Eiffel Tower's sparkling ladders of lights cast their spell of romance across the Parisian sky. But James in a construction helmet with a headlamp, and Daelyn in her black hoodie and matching sweat pants, were not out for a romantic stroll beneath the starry lights. They were in a taxi, skirting a shop-lined avenue wrapped in a cocoon of rainy sleep. The smell of baking bread and the sound of street musicians and car horns would not return until morning. The cab driver dipped onto a deserted back street between two sleeping buildings. And the two "spelunkers" were left standing at the curb in the dead of night.

"So what's the plan, Prince James?" Daelyn asked. "Since we seem to be a little alone here?"

"One you probably won't like too much, but it's all we've got," James said, then he turned to her and stroked her hair affectionately, his pain in his eyes. "I'm not going to let him have you, Daelyn. The word is out that I have you, so he'll let me come calling, thinking I'm bringing you home, but there's no way I'm going to give you to him."

"You may not have a choice, Prince James. But it's okay. Realm walls won't hold me," she responded. She had flown the coop before. She could do it again.

"Once I face off with him," James said, "I'll be working to convince him I want to create a bloodline with the Roses and take my princely place at his side. When I find out where they're holed up, you and I are going to free them."`

"What? You make this sound like it's just a drive-through coffee run!" she cried. "Are you crazy? We're dead where we stand!"

"We also need to try to find out how many Rose-born, high

powered vamps are forming ranks to overtake the envoys, and take them out."

"Just you and me. Alone against the world. Right." She smirked sarcastically.

"Not—exactly," he said. "We'll have a little help."

A head emerged from a hole in the sidewalk.

The face was a crossover of Peter Lory and Edward G. Robinson. A flat, wide nose, sunken eyes, and cheeky pockets wrinkled into a toothy grin above the ribbed collar of a black turtleneck.

"This way," Pighead urged them in a lowered voice, waving them over.

James hurried Daelyn toward the manhole, and thick gushes of pungent, warm air rose from the hole to meet them.

Pighead disappeared back down into the manhole, his voice ascending behind him. "Hurry! Before we are seen! I do not want to spend the night explaining to the French police why I am covered in mud and mess!" He scrambled down a ladder of iron steps into a deep, vertical well.

"Mud and mess," Daelyn grimaced with a glance tossed toward James that said, plainly, *Thanks a lot, Pardner,* as she dropped into the hole.

James adjusted the headlamp on his construction helmet, then shimmied down the iron rungs behind her.

The night sky became a pin point above them then disappeared as the manhole ended and they were in a dark sloping tunnel. Bracing their boots at an angle, they half-slid, half-hiked down an angled trench to an abandoned underground railway track. The light on his hardhat glinted off the rails.

Trudging down the middle of the track to avoid the rats, they hurried until a quick turn to the left took them from the rails and into tunnels that soon became narrower, the wet limestone ceilings lower. Another turn at Pighead's leading. They found themselves almost in a crouch in front of a small opening no more than double shoulder wide and about the same height.

"I may be obsessed with you, Prince James, and like the way you warm me to Fahrenheit Crazy, but I'm not crawling into that hole," Daelyn said, stopping abruptly.

"Don't tell me you're claustrophobic," James said with a grin.

"Didn't you ever see 'The Great Escape?'" she said, and shuddered. "The thought of dirt falling all over me in a cave-in just doesn't wow me somehow."

"We do not have to crawl very far," Pighead assured her.

"Key word, crawl," she muttered. Her eyes narrowed, stating plainly she did not feel very assured, and was definitely not enjoying spelunking in the carrières, the old limestone quarries of Paris—and she was definitely not going into that hole." You didn't tell me this job meant I had to crawl around on my ass through ant holes."

"Can you shapeshift?" James asked.

"Some," she said, gazing at him with a puzzled expression. "I'm not very—accomplished. Why?"

"Shapeshift. Preferably into something I can carry," he said. "I'll take you with me. We can move through together. Fast and smooth."

"So we can drown in dirt together," she said, rolling her eyes. Her lips turned down in a pout. "Not a very romantic ending to our partnership, Prince James."

He kissed away the pout. "We'll be all right, Blues," he coaxed.

"Humph." She shadowed and shapeshifted.

Into a chicken.

"You expect me to carry a friggin' chicken?" James exclaimed in shock, exasperated, but almost laughing at the ludicrousness of it. She shadowed and returned to herself. "Well, what then?" she said, irritated.

"How long you two going to quibble?" Pighead said, his tone edgy. His eyes darted around the tunnel walls in every direction. "We need to be moving. You might have all night and all day. I don't. And your contact won't hang around long, either."

"Well, I'm not doing a rat," Daelyn said, stiffening a little.

"Okay, okay. How about—a kitten?" James suggested. "I'll put you in my pocket."

She smiled suddenly—wickedly beautiful.

He gathered the calico kitten into his hand, dropped her into his shirt pocket, and began working his way through the small space.

"Ouch!" he exclaimed as he felt tiny claws suddenly pierce the material of his shirt pocket and stick him in the bare chest. She might have been enticed by the idea of being a kitten in his pocket, but now she was clinging to him, hanging on for dear life as he turned and twisted under and around raw stone in overhangs just inches above his head, or scraped his arms and legs in the tight tunnel. "You could purr or something," he said.

She hissed and spat.

God, he loved her! She was full of vinegar—a sexy, dynamite spirit charged with sensual electricity.

In the space of a few moments more, they were kicking out through a narrow opening into a corridor of cave. The ceiling was shored up with pillars of rock and rubble. James carefully set the little ball of fluff on the ground and Daelyn shadowed and became herself.

But she gasped, her blue eyes wide, startled, as she looked around. "What is this place?" Her voice shook.

Empty eye sockets stared at her, dead black holes from rows of skulls, no matter which way she whirled and turned. Eye sockets, and walls and walls of bones.

"Catacombs," James said. "Once upon a time in history when no one knew what to do with the dead overrunning the city, they dumped them here, in the abandoned quarries. Millions of them."

Daelyn did not touch the bones, or sculls, or femurs, or even the stones. She did not want to brush against the history of this place. Ever.

"It's said Marie Antoinette is around here someplace," James added, glancing around. The remains of kings dwelled here, and the remains of men and murder and rebellion and revolution. These were the remains of lives lived, whether for better or for worse.

Etched into the stone of an arch above them glistening with water droplets, was a simple warning. *Arête! C'est ici l'Empire de la Mort*—Stop! This is the Kingdom of the Dead."

This subterranean chamber was the Empire of the Dead.

"So while the rest of the world is taking a romantic stroll above us under canopies of chestnut trees and laughing and enjoying late night open air cafes, we're in this hole, hanging out with the haunts, with dead people." Daelyn moaned.

James ditched the hard hat. Pighead led them on.

Voices began to drift toward them through the stone hollows.

The living also haunted these limestone corridors.

They passed a few spelunkers, a few lovers, a few painters of stone walls, a few who just came to see, see what lies beneath.

Laughter. And music. An old wine cellar had been converted into a secret club where the surface dwellers could escape the above ground monotony of being the masses.

Further, deeper—

The tunnels changed, felt odd.

Daelyn sniffed the frothy air. "Something is different."

She touched a stone wall, and dared a brief touch to a pillar of blocks bracing the ceiling, a pillar with sculpted rock. "These tunnels were not made by mortal hands," she murmured. She stepped away quickly, astonished.

"Vampyres roam these quarries!"

Pighead grinned. "There's a great club. Under here, with the dead, we are all the same. No one calls me ugly. We are all hiding from the light. Some wine and blood, and we are all the same, all having a good time."

"So good you want to help slayers?" she scoffed.

"The New Realm will eventually add us to the list, missy. All of us. They want to dump us in heaps and leave us to rot like the dead back there. Anyone who is a misfit, or is deemed to have outlived their usefulness, or who they just don't like." He paused and appraised her from her halo of hair to her hiking boots laced to strong ankles. "You, they will keep."

A draft moaned through the labyrinth of caves. The darkness ahead murmured.

A vampyre, a long, thin profile, appeared from out of a small opening between two walls. Blood trickled from his mouth onto his bare chest.

A small, weak moan drifted out from the dark alcove.

James felt his blood boil, and his hand began to curl into a fist. Pighead was immediately at his ear, his lips moving urgently. "You cannot help. It is too late already. And you have a bigger fish to fry, yes?"

The vampyre's savage, unearthly eyes traveled from Pighead to Daelyn, to the human. They flared with interest, an interest like the mosquito zeroing in on the scent of a blood host.

The vampyre moved toward them slightly.

"He is ours," Pighead threatened with a hiss, stepping in front of James. "You have your own, party boy."

Daelyn was silent, but her stance warned the intruder she would kill to keep her "catch."

He retreated back into his secret place. They moved on.

Side tunnels became deeper, darker. James swallowed hard. The rock flooring took on a weaving sensation, the seepage from the walls dripping down the stone like droplets of blood.

These tunnels were haunted. The three travelers were getting close to their destination. He stopped and took Daelyn by the shoulders. "Daelyn," he said softly. "You will need to hide the fact you can walk in the light."

"I can hide," she smiled coyly.

She was smart. And James was really, really glad about that. She had the wiles to stay alive.

A different blend of music moaned through the stone from out of this darkness, different from the mosh pit frenzy of the spelunker club. Guitar strings meandered through the caves as though winding through a graveyard, drumbeats echoed behind them in a funeral procession of heavy percussion.

An eerie, glowing green light emanated from beyond the hollow of a bend, then the limestone doorway to the "club" appeared, outlined in neon. Beads of moisture from the sweating rock glimmered in watery green.

James and Daelyn stepped inside.

The place was packed. A mass of shapes of moving bodies alive but without life, death at an impasse.

As James and Daelyn made their way with Pighead through the crowded cave club, James felt a slight, sharp sensation on the back of his shoulder, quick, like two needles. He pressed his hand to his shoulder, felt tiny spots of warm wet through his shirt. Someone had pricked him.

He kept moving, toward a table recessed into one of several small overhangs, following Pighead and keeping Daelyn close.

James could feel the cold desire for his blood circulating through the club—but more than that, a sense of general fear that had nothing to do with him, an uneasiness, a watchfulness.

"There were beheadings last night," Pighead explained in a lowered voice. "Someone was mouthing off about occupying the Council. The New Realm dissolved the uprising before anyone could rise from daysleep. Many of those you see about you are afraid. They're afraid they will be accused."

James slid into a chair behind a black tablecloth that fell flush to the floor, making the small, square table and the three figures in the darkened alcove almost imperceptible.

Pighead left them and meandered into the crowd to get a drink at the bar.

From between two dancers, a hoodie above a pair of Wrangler jeans made swift headway toward them.

As he slid into a chair with his back to the crowd, two red slits peered out at James and rested on the two red dots on James's shoulder. "He wanted to boast he had bitten a slayer and lived to tell about it," the hood informed him. "We had the remains taken discreetly out through the back. Hopefully, there will be no other incidents. The thirst for vengeance is strong here tonight, an anger that could find a voice against anything and anyone if disturbed. Everyone is edgy. It would not take much to cause a swarm. Watch out for the female and keep her in line." He paused and the amber stones swept Daelyn. "Speaking of the female—"

His words were cut short as a flying head, fangs extended, crash-landed smack dab in the middle of the table, bobbled off onto the floor, and rolled away into the darkness.

A sudden din of screams and shouts, panicked voices, rose above the music, from the front of the club.

Then a whirring beheading whip, and a shirring of wings and swords in response.

The sounds of battle.

The beginnings of war.

Vampyres fled in all directions to escape the impending pogrom.

The lights, what few there were, went out.

"Quickly!" Pighead said, his head popping up above the table edge. "Under the table! They are here to kill those who speak betrayal!"

The hood moved like lightning, disappeared under the black tablecloth.

James grabbed Daelyn's hand, and they followed suit.

Pighead was holding a manhole cover open, and urging them into a circular hole.

"Not again," Daelyn moaned.

They dropped into the well of inky black, with no choice but to choose the unknown in preference to the known that was devouring the cave club in a blood bath. An echo of death cries and slaughter followed them down the shaft.

James could hear Pighead behind him closing the cover hard and locking it as they descended into God knows what, into a darkness that promised only darkness.

16.

Running in a black vacuum, James kept Daelyn at his side, her hand wrapped in his. She clung to him and they chased behind Pighead and the Hood until the close, grainy halls came to a sudden dead end—at an elevator shaft.

The elevator doors were rusty, old, but the Hood forced the doors apart easily with his bare hands.

The wobbly, dark cube was filled with cobwebs. Slinging her arms passionately around James' neck, Daelyn melded her body with his. "Just in case we don't get a chance for another obsession in Addis," she said, and kissed him hard, kissing him with the fervor of every hot heartbeat left in her heart.

James wrapped his arms tightly around her and pressed kisses filled with love against her lips.

"Come on. Run like hell now. Sex later," Pighead said impatiently. He pushed James and Daelyn into the hanging cobwebs of the elevator.

"We rarely use the elevator itself," the Hood informed them. "We use the shaft. It's a convenient corridor straight up to the surface, or to dive bomb to the bottom, wings folded close like a peregrine falcon." He glanced out from the hood slightly at James. "Have you ever seen one descend on their prey? They can dive at over two hundred twenty miles per hour. Wonderful predators." Then he said, simply, "Hang on."

"Hang on?" James and Daelyn exclaimed in startled unison.

The four cave runners sank against the rusty metal walls, the doors closed, the elevator spun upward like a rocket.

An experimental rocket.

The square box rocked and creaked and rumbled and tossed

them against the elevator walls like a salad spinner as it hurtled. James had shed a single drop of sweat now and then in a vampyre sweep or raid, but in here, in this little box of horrors, he was sweating buckets.

When the metal cage finally slowed, clunked, dropped a few feet, then thankfully stopped, even the Hood stepped out quickly.

Relief washed across Pighead's stale features. "We are on the first floor of a brewery gone dry. And I for one wish it hadn't."

James and Daelyn breathed the musty but welcome air, and wanted to kiss the even more welcome solid ground.

"There is a limousine waiting outside," the Hood said. "I threaded a friend for help in view of the—circumstances."

"Pretty nifty, huh?" Pighead remarked, with a broad grin. "We don't need cell phones, just good, clear telepathic thread. Drunkenness clouds it, but otherwise ..."

"Yeah, got it," James said, his tone narrow.

"Climb into the car quickly. Don't speak, and for God's sake, don't throw up on the leather seats!" the Hood warned, then he and Pighead were flashing away between the kegs.

"Batman and Robin of the Underground," James smirked.

"What did he mean, 'throw up?'" Daelyn asked as James whisked her from the building and toward a black limo.

"It probably means we'll be traveling rather fast again," James answered.

The limo began brushing the night traffic like a blur of black ribbon almost before Daelyn had her seatbelt buckled. "Rather fast?" she cried.

The limo was as haunted as the vamp built tunnels. James could feel the loss of equilibrium, the night seeping in to assault him, the darkness of powers beyond the force of nature weaving into his slayer's senses. He collapsed back against his seat, devoured by the forces propelling the car forward, toward its dark destination.

He wanted to throw up. All over the black leather seats.

Daelyn shoved a piece of mint gum into his hand. "Chew it," she said. "Quick. It will settle your stomach."

He chewed like his life depended on it. *Don't vomit. Don't vomit. Whatever in hell were we thinking, Andre?*

"You are being taken to the River Mosell," the driver said, turning around to grin at them, his voice filling the interior of the limo as though he was talking through a chasm in his throat. His bluish skin was so thin, his skull and skeleton seemed to show through. Or rather, glow through. "You will travel the river into Germany. The Count has relocated."

"In other words, he's in hiding," Daelyn said.

"How do we find him?" James asked.

"We will get you there. What you tell him to explain how you got there is up to you. I would suggest a lot of lies." His smile was ashy, then his face seemed to fade behind the smile and the skull shimmered through.

His sunken gray-blue eyeballs rolled to James full on.

"At the river's edge, you will board a wine barge."

Daelyn's eyes regained a few flecks of sparkle. "A party boat!" she whispered to James. "I guess they're giving us the last great bon voyage—" The sparkle faded a little. "Since we're probably gonna die in this venture."

The "wine" barge was not the party barge French wine and dinner tour she was expecting. She stared at the lightless, flat bottomed boat filled with crates, lightless as a night in new moon. She would not be lounging on a tiled deck and sipping a locally produced wine. James would not be sitting alongside her waiting to be served a delicious meal.

At the river's edge, they were stuffed on the wine barge, literally, to float down the river with a silent man robed like the Reaper at the helm.

James settled down and propped his back against a couple of crates, and she—pouted.

"We are floating on a scow, and we have a river spectre for a boat pilot," she sulked. She finally spent her time checking out the variety of smaller crates. She pulled one forward, sat on her knees and loosened the lid to search through the straw packing.

"Wines of the Upper Mosel!" she smiled as she pulled out a long, green hock-style wine bottle. "The region's finest! Sonnenfeuer, Sternengold, Kuhlen Modlichtschein. The fire of the Sun, the gold of the stars, and cool moonlight!"

After looking at the labels of a few more crates, she discovered boxed wine glasses, and gift packs of cheese and dried meats.

"Well, looks like we at least get a complimentary breakfast on this Best Western Boat," she said, turning and stretching out with two stemmed glasses and the wine. She poured a goblet for each of them, and settled comfortably next to James. "Party, Prince James?" she coaxed as she handed him a glass. "You've been staring at the river like it's the river to eternity. And not a very pleasant eternity."

He managed a smile, and sliced a hunk of cheese and dried meat.

Washing down the complimentary breakfast with wine, James gazed into the bit of dawn touching the river water, a river clean and clear after a dedicated people had spent years salvaging the river from industrial waste. He sighed. "Someday I'd like to come back here as a tourist."

"Someday, I'd like to come back with the tourist," Daelyn smiled. She clinked her glass against his. "To us. And the romantic River Mosel."

They kissed, another long, "I may never see you again" kiss. Then another—longer, harder. Fire enveloped his belly, and James wished he could have had a last night with her. A night to measure eternity by.

"We'll come back to the romantic Mosel on a champagne and party barge, not a friggin' boxed cheese and crate barge," he promised, kissing her.

"To us."

"I'm in love with you, Daelyn," he whispered into her ear.

"Are you saying that because you think we really might die?" she asked. "If so, then don't say it. Say, 'We are now, or forever.'"

"We are forever. I'm in love with you, Daelyn. I want to say it, in case I lose my humanity and can no longer feel it."

"No," she said, tears suddenly stinging her eyes. "I just got you, damn it. I'm not going to lose you. I'm not doing this Valkyrie thing alone." She wiped at her eyes with her sleeve.

Taking her right hand gently in his, he slipped his ring on her middle finger. "When we're separated, let the ring remember for you."

A coldness, like a brush of cold river wind, traveled across the barge. Daelyn took her sable tresses in her hand and watched them being tussled. "We are being visited," she said in a lowered voice, then she looked up, at the higher stacks of boxes in the center of the barge.

The transparent outline of a man materialized, sitting on the top of the stack, one foot propped on the crate supporting him, the other braced on the crate below him. The ghost, his cane resting on his lap, nodded from under his top hat in greeting.

"In case you hadn't noticed," James said in return, "I don't happen to like you very much. Haven't liked you since the night you said the road would be long for me. You gonna say that again?"

"The river will be long for you tonight," the ghost said, and vanished.

"Hide!" the voice at the helm said urgently. "Under the tarps. Quickly."

He guided the barge swiftly in under a secluded overhang of tree branches at the shore line.

James pulled a tarp over himself and Daelyn, his heart beating like a wind gone wild as they listened to the shirring of wings pass over, close. Vampyres flying in low over the river.

The whipping sound filled their ears and peaked into a roar like an incoming train, then just as quickly diminished.

James lifted a corner of the tarp.

"New Realm warriors," their helmsman said. "Returning from a hunt."

"I did not catch the scent of blood on them," Daelyn said, puzzled.

"A vampyre hunt."

"Why do I feel like I'm traveling with the last star fighter?" Daelyn sighed and polished off the bottle of wine.

When she was deep in much needed daysleep, James crawled over the crates and ventured toward the tall, muscular being manning the helm.

"Did Andre send you, Henri?"

Henri De LaCroix pulled back the dark robes cloistering his shape and form. His blue eyes shone and his black hair caught the wind.

"I cannot be close enough for the Count to sense me," Henri said, "but I will come if you need me." He paused and his eyes searched the distance. "This morning is rising on the back of a bad moon."

"Why didn't Daelyn recognize your voice?" James asked. "She said she knew you once, rather well, in fact."

"She does not know me as I am. Her memory searches for the

one who was." He paused. "And I will be gone before she awakens."

The master Royal glanced at her lying quietly with her head resting on a stack of cheese gift packs. "A shame, that one," he sighed.

His eyes caught the glimmer of the ring on her finger and flashed to James. "That's a move that could end in your destruction," he said.

"Is Drac the jealous type?" James tossed off lightly.

The master vampyre's eyes burned into his, looked knowingly into his soul, stripped back its sheath of secrets, and peeled back his heart. "Perhaps Dracula is not to be your greatest challenge. Perhaps it is yourself." He studied James intensely. "When did you allow her to place you momentarily in capture? Don't deny it. I can see it. I've been down that centuries-old road. No wonder that damned ghost is hanging around."

James averted his eyes to a castle rising high beyond the shoreline, its parapets rimmed bright gold in the rising sun.

"He won't be found in a mist-shrouded castle," Henri informed him, following his gaze. "He's hiding in plain sight, in a house, in one of the incorporated villages near Koblenz."

The barge moved crosswise across the currents toward a small pier jutting out from an overhang of pine branches and red maple. The hull of the barge bumped the wood pylons, and the vampyre—was gone. Daelyn opened her eyes and helped James anchor the barge then gathered the last of the food and wine, their backpacks and their courage. Stepping out onto the pier, they began what they believed to be the last leg of their journey, the hike to Koblenz through the Black Forest.

17.

The Black Forest. Mysterious. Beautiful. Slightly sinister. Almost impenetrable, fog-wrapped slender tree trunks surrounded James in dark gray colonnades. A pine and birch canopy doused the light and he moved through feathers of mist with quick steps to keep Daelyn in sight.

The vampyre slipped in and out among the trees as easily as a forest spirit, as though birthed from the hidden, magical depths that had given birth to tales of werewolves, fairies and elves.

A touch of wing slipped around and behind a tree trunk, then re-appeared beyond another. Then a glimpse of mist-drenched sable hair appeared as she turned and whipped a smile past a branch. She gestured toward James to follow, that the way was safe. He hurried to follow his enchanting dark spirit of light, his fledging Valkyrie guide.

Would she be able to resist Count Dracula, her now former master? he wondered. Would she be able to lock away her identity and hold her guise with him? *God be with her. He will destroy her on the spot if he discovers she is a Valkyrie.*

James became watchful, more than a little uncertain of this picture post card forest Dracula had chosen as his latest conquest.

To claim as his imminent domain.

The enemy could be everywhere, and nowhere to be seen.

They walked on. The ruins of an ancient abbey nodded in sleep through the trees at the side of a foot path, its mossy corridor and aged gates pointing the way to a broken bell tower.

"Lunchtime," James said.

Daelyn took the hand he offered her, her eyes sparkling as they passed through the gate and climbed the stone steps to the remains of a church porch. "I have never seen such a beautiful forest," she whispered. "Touches of ancient secrets and history in every leaf—"

"And I hope the Erdmännlein, and any other forest dwarves, are as friendly and helpful to humans as the fireside stories claim," James said. "Since we're damned deep in trees and don't know where the hell we are at the moment."

"The path has to lead out eventually, to the village. All paths have a destination," she said. Not an inkling of worry brushed her words.

"Hansel and Gretel thought so, too," he laughed. Relaxing on a stone bench, he pulled his backpack from his shoulders. "This looks like as good a place as any to have lunch."

"Lunch for you and a cup of Joe for me, or whoever it was that volunteered in the blood drive to keep me happy," Daelyn added, letting her own pack slide to the ground. She took a cup from the zippered compartment. "I'll have a tall please, easy on the sugar, two pumps of pumpkin spice to celebrate fall."

After a lunch of cheese and crackers and dried sausage, and a bottled water, James scrutinized the blue-eyed vampyre with luscious legs. She was enjoyably sipping her cup of "Joe," and basking in the forest breeze that played among the fallen leaves on the porch. "Daelyn, you're accompanying me into a world that will be unforgiving if they discover your treachery."

"We'll always have Addis." She smiled.

"We could turn around," James said.

She put down the cup. "Excellent idea. That's exactly what I was thinking." She tossed him a coy smile, then turned around to lie down on the stone on her back and gaze up at him. "I was thinking I could turn around and lay like this, and you could turn around and lay over me—like this." She pulled him off the bench and across her in one quick easy little movement and folded her legs comfortably around his. "I was thinking we could make love—since it may be a while before I can escape m' quarters, Cap'n, and sneak in to see you in your princely quarters."

She smiled into his eyes, and he drowned in wanting her.

Under the adroit quickness of her hands, she had unbuttoned his shirt and pulled it from his shoulders before he could find a logical reason why she shouldn't. She briefly caressed his chest, then he was pantless, shirtless and shoeless, and she was beautifully clothesless except for the ring.

A small clap of thunder rumbled through the trees and a light, forest rain began to dot the forest floor, soon creating a watery, silver veil around them and the porch.

"Keep rhythm with the rain, Daelyn," he said, pressing his hands into her shoulder blades. "Let me feel the thunder in you." She led him, slow danced her thighs against his …

"You're throwing a little lightning in there, Blues," he groaned. He pulled her up and swept his arms around her, holding her and caressing her and loving her, memorizing the liquid flow of her silken skin as though this might be their last day together. She made love to him as though there would be many, many more days like this. Little rainy breezes flowed over them, a misty leaf floated down now and then around them, to settle on the stone porch flooring.

When the rain dissipated, a warm, late afternoon sun scattered a few needles of soft rays through the trees and across their bodies entwined together in a last, forever moment. He drew the back of his hand slowly down the side of her back, her thighs, her legs—lightly, committing her to memory.

"If we don't pass this way again, I will at least have the thunder and your rain to remember," Daelyn said softly with deep pleasure still lingering within her.

But will I remember it? James thought as they dressed and left the stone ruins. The memory of Jane's fangs in his neck stabbed at him. The possibility of her re-entering his life—and his neck—was still all too real, still vivid.

Jane was a nightmare reality show. And her fangs could take Daelyn's memory from him with one lost heartbeat.

Evening closed in on the forest, swallowing the last points of light that had managed to linger in the skeins of the canopy. They hiked across moss-covered snags and broken limbs of older growth forest. Pinpoints of light from a gibbous moon fell across the forest floor.

"The New and the Old both have reason to assassinate you, James," Daelyn broached anxiously as the trees began to thin out and they knew they were drawing close to their destination. "They could both come for you and kill you in your sleep or something because they don't want you taking the seat of power next to your uncle and fathering the ultimate heirs—Dracula's own bloodline."

"Maybe," he shrugged. He was more concerned with Jane coming to him in his sleep. Don't think I'll be sleeping much, he thought, and made a mental note to pick up some Red Bulls, five-hour energy drinks and coffee.

"So do we fight them with our bare fists, or run? And where do we run to?" she asked despondently.

He twirled her to him and kissed her. Lingeringly. "You have more power in your fists than they have in their whole bodies, Daelyn. New or Old."

"Are you serious?" she laughed, looking at her hands.

"Try it," he said.

She smacked a small boulder.

Her curled hand pulverized the center of it, leaving a fist-sized hole behind.

"I'm strong, but not that—"

"You're a Valkyrie." He paused. "At least, semi."

"So do I also stop speeding bullets?" she asked with a cocked eyebrow, somewhat astonished by the hole in the rock.

"Not if they're silver. Use discretion."

"Gotcha," she said, her hand moving to her ribs where she still ached a little.

The village where Dracula had chosen to "mainstream," finally appeared as the trees opened up and the path intersected with a road, deeply rutted. The lanes had seen more than a few decades of carriage wheels and probably a few horseless carriage wheels as well.

Filled with quiet side streets lined with quaint, picturesque half-timbered houses, the fairytale town was serene, the inhabitants bustling about in the daily business of buying bread and beer and potatoes—and utterly uninterested in the visitors rising out of the forest. James and Daelyn crossed the street near the four-story house at the end of the street, the house with every single curtain drawn tight.

As he gazed toward the windows, the hairs on the back of James' neck began to stand on end and Daelyn's senses fired to alert her to the presence of one of her own.

"Looks like the proprietor of the house is at home."

"Something in this town isn't quite right," James said as he studied the picturesque German houses lining the street.

"Yeah. Dracula lives here."

"Something else," James said, searching his slayer's senses.

Then he knew.

"They have garlic hanging outside their doors."

Dracula had struck.

But the townspeople had no idea the half-timber at the end of the row was sheltering the very evil they were trying to defend against, that it was not just the resurgence of a blutsauger. It was the rising of *the* blutsauger, the Count from Transylvania.

James took Daelyn's hand as he crossed the street, entwining his fingers tightly in hers. "Are you okay?"

"Hell, no. Are you?" Her eyelashes feathered heavily upward into dark crescents above her blue eyes.

"Hell, no."

Daelyn brushed her hand slowly, deeply, across the door frame as James lifted the hare's head wood knocker.

"This is definitely his house," she said as he let the knocker drop, and the clapper smacked, wood on wood, a deafening explosion to nerves drawn taut. "But no Roses passed through this door."

The door opened a slit, slowly. Ever so slowly. So slowly James felt the sun could have risen and set a dozen times as they stood on the doorstep.

"Cut the theatrics and—open the damned door!" James ordered sharply as a plump little lady in a housekeeper's crisp uniform peeped through the slit. "I'm here to see my ancestral uncle."

She continued staring at them, neither smiling nor frowning. Her round face was expressionless.

More endless moments.

Daelyn took a step forward, her eyes flashing her displeasure.

The housekeeper scowled and stood back, holding the door to allow them admittance. "You're expected."

Expected.

So, what did that mean? Expected for dinner? Expected to be murdered? Expected to become a vampyre?

James fought to control his thoughts and the sweat that threatened to break out on his forehead at any moment.

Expected.

Expected to father a race.

Expected to destroy Dracula.

Expected to restore the world's axis so vampyres could not destroy men. They were doing a good enough job of that on their own.

James and Daelyn stepped across the threshold into the picturesque foyer—and the housekeeper led them to a darkened, not quite so picturesque library.

There were few books on the sculpted shelves, and the flameless fireplace with ashy remnants of logs was not friendly.

The housekeeper disappeared into the recesses of the house.

Dracula appeared.

He was hidden in shadows as though a deep, desolate black chasm of shadows rose up around him to protect him.

From the chasm, the eyes that had torn maidens from their souls for centuries erupted through the dark, traveled to Daelyn, and flared as they landed on the ring on her finger.

Then the snake gaze moved to James and his voice traveled into James' soul. "You son-of-a—"

Well, that made that easy, James thought. "Yes. I am. And she was worth the claim."

The room itself seemed to tremble as the eyes widened.

He stepped out of the dark.

Odd, James thought. *There's a touch of gray at his temples.*

Other than that, and the usual pallor of one who avoids the sun, he was unobtrusive in appearance. Nothing to alert a stranger to the difference within him.

Because of course, he was Dracula. He emanated his power subtly, easily, a graveyard of power he could use in the blink of an eye as he walked past an innocent or brushed their shoulders.

Innocent shoulders. The shoulders of his victims.

"And you?" Dracula said coolly, his voice a sepulcher. "Are you worth—claiming?"

James gave him his story without pause, without an iota of the terror, hatred and anger, he could feel at the bottom of his stomach. Squelching the desire to grab a hot log and whack the blutsauger, he calmly told him the story of betrayal he had rehearsed over and over until he had ironed out every wrinkle of emotion from every word that could alert the Count to his deception.

"I was betrayed by my adoptive father because of my bloodline, because my uncle was a welder of vampirism. The human didn't want me, and tried to destroy me because I am your descendant. I bear the scar of his hatred. And now, I'm being rejected at every turn because of that fateful revelation, a tainted bloodline. Now I receive uncertain stares from those who had once called me friend. No one is sure they can trust me. I'm becoming an outcast—" He took a step toward the being he believed to be his ancestral uncle. "Am I an outcast here? Do you also want to destroy me? I'm here to embrace the bloodline that brought about my shunning. Here, I would have a place, a position where I will not be looked on with disgrace, be the subject of whispers, spoken to as though I should be killed, or turned away, or turned out, because my power is now feared. They do not know the meaning of fear. But they will. They do not know the fear I can instill. The prodigal prince has returned. I will return to power and create a dynasty to destroy those who contemplated my destruction." He paused. "There is dissension in the Realm. So I simply used those who believed I would kill Dracula for them, to find my way to this village, this house."

Dracula didn't move, and when he spoke his voice was level, controlled. "And who betrayed this house to you?"

"My guides were nameless, shadowy wisps who rarely spoke. And I could have cared less who they were. My purpose was to reach you, and return the wench, and take my rightful place at your side—but she's a spitfire and I liked her. I figured you wouldn't mind, she's just another pair of wings in the crowd—"

He pulled Daelyn to him, hooked his arm around her waist. In a discreet declaration of possession.

But in reality, his stance was in case they had to fight their way out. He could not see acceptance of him in the Count's eyes or still-as-death demeanor. And he knew he might have to fight to protect her.

"I will have my housekeeper prepare a meal for you, and show you to the rooms you may use for the night," the Count finally said slowly, his voice superficially amiable. "We will find the truth in your words by tomorrow, I would think." He turned to the dead fire and his eyes glowed into the hearth. "Your loyalty, or your fate, James Lauren, will be sealed here. No one leaves the House of Dracula once entered."

He did not join them for dinner. They sat alone at a hard wood table in fruit wood chairs carved with leaves and acorns, in a small kitchen nook. The housekeeper flopped German potato salad, pink cabbage and apples, and a variety of sausages and breads onto the table with a begrudging sneer. The beer was dark, strong, and James drank very little of it. Being even a little drunk in this house would be an act of complete stupidity.

The housekeeper stood by through the whole meal holding a pitcher of water, and watching them closely.

No doubt she would break that Tole-painted pitcher over his head if he even sneezed wrong.

Daelyn sat across from him, her eyes saying the thousands of things her voice could not say in this amber painted room of sausage and pitchers and horrors. The Count would hear even a murmur in the halls of this house.

"I wish you could thread," she finally said with a sigh.

He took her hand, squeezed it and moved his lips close to her ear. "Let's find the suites where Uncle Dearest said we could bunk."

He turned to the housekeeper who hadn't moved a centimeter in her stern, little boots with steel toes. "Wanna show us where I can get some shut-eye other than in the attic roped to a chair, or the cellar in shackles and chains, sweetums?"

"Fool." She scowled, and showed them to their rooms—on the third floor.

When the German left, James sat with Daelyn on the bed. "At least our charming host didn't order her to give us separate rooms and lock us in," he said tenderly.

"Probably because he knows locks don't hold me very well," she responded with a small shrug of her shapely shoulders.

The mist at the corners of her eyes told him she missed Texas. He pulled her to him and held her. Letting his hands hold her cheeks, he moved his lips over hers and let his heart tell her what his voice could not in this house.

18.

The miasma that encompassed the house seemed to lift a little. Was the Count crawling out to skulk around the town and the woods?

Sequestering himself at the side of the bedroom window, James had a clear view of a tiny courtyard and alley below. He pulled the corner of the curtains back slightly and risked a glance outside.

The Count was sweeping along the ground, away from the house … another figure was hurrying to meet him.

Jane Weston.

She embraced him, and the two slipped away in the direction of the forest.

The appearance of the infamous vampira complicated things. James had not expected to have to deal with her so soon. "Apparently, she found her path to power in the Count after Nicholai met his final end," he murmured to himself.

He turned quickly to Daelyn. "He's gone for a while at least. We need to search the house. I need you to read the rooms, the walls, anything you can to see if any Roses have been here. They may not have used the front door, but they might have come or gone another way."

He kept her protectively behind him while he peered out into the hallway to see if the housekeeper was anywhere in sight.

The hall was empty—frighteningly empty. Not a sound of settling in the house or creak in the hard wood floor as they crept out into the corridor past the single ceiling light. Melting their bodies against the walls, they inched their way to the stairwell banister to check the fourth floor first.

Several rooms later, Daelyn had come up as empty as the hallway. The only room left was behind a set of double doors at the end of the hall.

James opened the doors carefully, half-expecting to find the Count's own room behind those imposing doors.

The room was comfortably sized, but somewhat smaller than one would have expected behind two large boudoir doors. Two paned windows with a view to the street let in a bit of lamp light.

A full-sized, but simple bed with a patchwork quilt filled the opposite wall, a vanity with a hand painted music box scrunched beside a round-edge headboard on another.

The furniture was plain, unadorned—except for a cheval mirror that stood out a little way from a corner. An outlay of carvings traveled the entire length of the oval cherry wood frame.

James lightly traced the elaborate engravings with his fingertips. "This mirror doesn't fit with the rest of the room," he said. "These hand carved, raised characters in the wood are runes."

He turned to Daelyn. She was standing in the center of the room, silent but for a slight rustling of her wings as she gazed at the mirror oddly. "Runes," she said in a curious voice.

Her beautiful smooth brow was drawn taut, the lips he loved to kiss pressed into a puzzled line. "What's wrong, Daelyn?"

She stared past him, at his reflection in the mirror.

"Turn and face the mirror for a moment, Prince James," she said softly.

Wondering at her strange behavior and the dry somberness in her normally glistening, vivid blue eyes, he nevertheless did as she asked.

"Raise your right hand," she continued, studying his reflection in the mirror.

He raised his right hand.

"Your reflection is not a mirror image," she said. "It's a mirror opposite."

"That's me. Can't even get a good image of me," he laughed, but he was getting a chilly flow in his veins. She wouldn't be this serious without good reason.

"You raised your right hand, and your image's right hand raised in the mirror. A normal mirror image would have given the appearance of being the left."

James gazed at the hand in the glass. It was as though another man stood on the other side of the mirror face, raising his right hand. James had been so intent on the runes, he hadn't noticed the mirror itself, that the reflection was not inverted.

"The Law of Mirrors states that one can only see what is in them, regardless if it is what is actually present in reality or not," Daelyn said, looking back behind her, then at the mirror again.

"The music box is on the wrong side in the mirror. Everything in the room being reflected in the glass is on the wrong side," she frowned. "Nothing is inverted. Nothing is a mirror image."

"It's like another me is staring back at me from a parallel room rather than being a reflection of me," James said, then grinned, and ran his hand through his hair. "A rather handsome me. Could that be?"

"The hair's a little on the wild side," Daelyn answered with a snicker.

James studied the runes, brushed his hand across them all the way around the frame. "One symbol keeps repeating. If you picture the mirror as an oval clock, an arrowlike symbol pointing up is in the ten o'clock, two o'clock, three, six, and nine positions."

"But not in the twelve o'clock position," Daelyn said. "That symbol looks like the less-than symbol in a math equation." She ran a fingertip across the small, carved bars of wood.

She jumped back. "It turned under my touch!"

"Be careful," James admonished her quickly. "We don't know what we're dealing with yet."

"Following the six o'clock arrow to the left," Daelyn said, tilting her head to the side to study them, "the two vertical bars enclosing an X running corner to corner don't make sense if you try to form a word from the normal reading position of left to right."

She raised her hand toward the highly polished frame to trace and read all the symbols traveling the wood. James caught her fingers gently in mid-air, folding them into his. "Sure you want to do that, Blues? This attic find isn't exactly trunk junk."

She looked into his brown eyes, caring and burning anxiously under their feathers of dark lashes. He didn't want anything in that mirror to hurt her. "I'll be careful."

She knew the secrets in those runes could explode in her precog senses like grenades. "The Count has this mirror for a reason," she said. "Vampyres do not, as a rule, keep mirrors—anywhere in their dwellings."

She moved her hands slowly around the dark wood oval, pausing at each symbol to study the rune with her touch.

Then she circled the wood again. And again.

"What'd you find, Blues?" James asked, disconcerted as a thousand emotions were sloshing in her eyes when she finally looked up, and he couldn't read even one of them.

"This is an enchanted doorway," she said, almost inaudibly.

"As in fairytale?" he almost laughed.

"As in vampirical," she said, unsmiling.

"Enchanting." James smirked sarcastically. "The images reflected in the mirror are not reflections at all. And there are symbols but no words. And I'm chasing the White Rabbit in *Alice in Wonderland*."

"This is the sequel," Daelyn said pensively. "Alice, in Through The Looking Glass, went through the mirror." She paused, and her countenance became downcast. "Went through the looking glass ..."

Excitedly, James immediately began searching the wood for a secret lock, a secret hinge, an opening. "We don't have a lot of time, Daelyn. Did the Roses travel through this mirror? Is it hiding a door? To the outside of this house? Or another room? Is that why the rune at the top turned?"

"That's not what I meant. Let go of that practical mind of yours for a moment, James, and stop looking for concrete answers. It's— a gateway. Allowing changes in time and spacial direction. Time running backward. Or forward, depending on how you set the runes."

"Damn. You're telling me this is a time gate? Is that possible?"

He put out his hand, and pressed it to the glass.

His fingers disappeared into the glass as though into a layer of clear plasma. And something, from the other side, tugged at his hand. A strange pulling sensation ...

Daelyn grabbed his hand, yanked it out.

"Did the Roses go into this glass?" he asked, then murmured to himself, "That such a device even exists—a dangerous device. Yet fascinating."

"I—felt no Roses," Daelyn said. "But I did feel the past through the wood. And one small traveler ..."

One small traveler. James laid down on the bed, on top of the quilt with his back against the headboard and studied her. Her wings were a tad on the droopy side, and he was not sure he wanted to hear what she was about to say next.

"I have a confession, James," she said reluctantly.

"I thought you might," he responded quietly.

She sat down on the bed beside him. At least his voice held no fury. Only that narrow intelligence dissecting her like she was a potion, shaken and stirred with a drop of vampyre. "When I told you your mother gave you the ring in love, it was the truth. But I—I've discovered I made a mistake."

She lifted her face to his, and the sadness startled him. "What mistake, Daelyn?"

"You looked so unhappy," she blurted. "I just wanted to make you happy! I wanted so hard for you to be happy, I missed it!"

"Missed what?" His voice was a narrow ravine.

"She gave you the ring in love, but not as a gift. She gave it as a warning." She exhaled sorrowfully. "I saw her fear for you, and her love. I should have seen the deeper terror. But I didn't. Not until I touched the mirror. James, I am so sorry!"

James sat up straight, and leaned toward her. His face was dead level with hers, his eyes holding hers inescapably, loving her, but demanding truth. "What warning was in the mirror, Daelyn?"

She threw her arms around him and clung to him, her eyes pleading. "I love you, James. I love you! Please, let's go. I will be your Valkyrie. I will be your slave, if you want. Just let's go!"

He pulled Daelyn close to his chest, desperate to comfort her, her tone was so forlorn. "My heart is already your slave, Daelyn. What did you touch in the runes that's made you so distressed?"

"Dracula's handmark is all over the runes. And a sense of vengeance permeates them. He wants you dead, not undead."

"Why? I thought I was the chosen one," he said in surprise.

Her lips parted, but her whisper was lost in a dying echo. James heard only the wolves howling in the forest.

He looked over her shoulder at the room, the room that was changing. The walls grayed, the air became thick. The room became permeated with strange essence. The evil in the house was about to engulf them.

He felt her heart spasm. She was losing her light, recanting her vow to him. "Daelyn," he whispered, holding her tighter. "Stay with me. This house, this room, the evil in the mirror, is calling you back. Fight with me. What did you see? Let go of it. I'm sorry. I'm sorry you had to read things you didn't want to know, glass and wood that held too much evil, too much of my evil uncle, but you have to tell me what you saw within those runes."

"He is not your uncle." Her words were like a hollow hole from the depths of a dwarf star.

She looked up at him. The gold flecks in her blue eyes were pitted with red. She stroked his chest, his arms, his thighs. "I haven't had fresh blood in so long. Your body is so warm ..." She touched his throat, moved her fingers of vampyre magic to the side of his neck, stroked his jugular in a heavy, deep massage. The little Hibachi briquettes in her eyes became a wham bam double burner grill full of hot coals. He was pulsing hard, and she liked it.

He grasped her hand, fighting the urges within him, the desire to let her take him. He was dizzy, suffocating. The room was sucking the very oxygen from his lungs, taking his breath. He tried to rise. But he felt only her soft body, her knees pressing against the sides of his thighs as she sat across and over him, her free hand caressing his chest. Magic fingertips. Could he ask for more?

"You'll die, Daelyn," he managed as her gaze swept through his, deepening his urges into a hard yearning.

She kissed him. Long and slow. "I don't care." She slid his ring from her finger, let it fall to the floor. He reached down and put it on his finger.

The ring burned. He felt a helplessness driving away his logic, his will, as the ring imprisoned him while her fingers moved caressingly back and forth over the sapphire and his hand. For the first time since picking up a crossbow, he was being derailed by a lithe, beautiful body holding him in ecstasy and trance. Words slipped away in mid-thought.

Her lips moved to his neck, her fragrant hair fell softly across his throat, her fangs traveled the nape of his neck, tracing, testing, tasting.

"I need you, James. Come to me, my love."

"I love you, Daelyn. Don't do this," he said weakly, aching for her. "The darkness that rules this house is calling us into a unity of death—"

"Die with me. We will live forever," she whispered.

James looked into the Tej in her eyes. Honey wine. Filled with fire. She was forgetting, forgetting as she became lost in the need stabbing at her that his blood would destroy her. He exhaled deeply. He was also forgetting. "Daelyn, I—can't want you this way." He took her waist in his hands, to hold her away. "The house is evil, seducing us."

She gazed at him, then at his neck, wanting, struggling, needing, battling. She was in a war against a dark fairytale town and a storybook room with a magic, evil mirror.

"You sought to escape, Daelyn. Don't embrace again what you sought so hard to escape," he implored her.

James forced his mind to obey him, brought forth all his strength to fight her fire in his brain, pushed her from him to save her life.

She whipped away and sat on the edge of the bed, and stared at the floor, breathing hard, her hands clenched into fists. "I'll die if I'm not fed!"

Wings extended, she flew to the wall and back again, pushed the heavy vanity like it was a feather and knocked it over, then smashed the music box that survived the jolt into tiny pieces.

James lurched toward her. She whirled, ripped up the pillows, yanked the quilt from the bed. He caught her, slammed her to the floor and straddled her, pinning her arms against the wood planks. "You're in the house of Dracula! Fight it!"

She writhed. "He's calling me, James! I can feel it! He isn't willing to give me up. He felt the ring leave me. He's calling me to the woods. Let me go!"

"Where did you put your backpack?" James demanded desperately.

"The bedroom, under the bed, or maybe the closet, I dunno, I can't think ..."

He could see her shimmering. In moments, she would be swirling specks of light, whirling out the window and into the woods. To Dracula. He pulled her from the floor and ran with her to the bedroom.

The backpack was gone.

"The housekeeper! Can you feel her, Daelyn? Do you know where she is in the house?"

"No," she said, then her nostrils flared. "But I can smell my pack."

She flashed away so suddenly, he could not see what direction she went.

She was back within ten minutes. Her mouth was dripping red onto her chin.

"Did you ...?"

"Naw. When she saw me coming, she jerked open the refrigerator and started throwing bottles at me. I fouled off a couple to left field against the wall, then I realized what was in them and switched from batter to short stop." She smiled and wiped her mouth with the back of her hand. "Pretty good catch."

"Where ...?"

"She's locked herself in the pantry, scared to death. She'll probably stay there the rest of the night. At any rate, I guarantee she won't touch my pack again."

She'll probably get the hell out and never touch this house again, James thought.

19.

James heard the front door open, then slam shut. Hurrying to the window, he drew the curtains apart just a crack. Below him, the housekeeper, pulling a suitcase behind her, was running into the street, hailing a taxi and taking off for parts unknown.

He turned to the vampira who had almost cost him his life, and almost lost her own in the taking. "This house isn't exactly a five-diamond bed and breakfast, is it?"

"Dawn is breaking," Daelyn said in a nervous voice, looking out the opposite window. "He will return soon."

He and possibly Jane Weston with him, James thought with a shudder. "We need to talk about the mirror, Daelyn," he insisted, moving to her side.

Sighing, she plopped on the bed. "The runes travel in a clockwise direction, and because of that the symbols run backward as they move around the frame. 'Time turns but is not a door. Enter through the gate at the turn of the lock.' If you move the runes to the right places, the gate will open."

"Who was the small traveler, Daelyn?"

She looked up at him, her eyes saddened again. "In a manner of speaking, it could be said you're not exactly a twenty-first century man, Prince James. More like nineteenth."

James stared at her in shock.

"Sometime in the nineteenth century, a rumor was deliberately spread that you died as a baby," she said. "There is a force of fear traveling through the runes, fear that vampyre vengeance against the slayer might include his son. At your 'death,' your mother feigned insanity. I felt iron bars. You were hidden with her in a locked, gated asylum. Then suddenly, for reasons unclear, she was moved in the dead of day … to a mirror like this one. She fled through to this century. The gate was to be destroyed behind her."

"Why was she taken away if she was so well hidden?" he asked, puzzled.

"Glimpses of what appeared to be tall, dark figures near the sanatorium." She paused. "Within Dracula's touch on the runes, I read the rest. He certainly has a high opinion of himself. He was so elusive and clever, according to himself, it was not known at that time if he was fable or fact. It was he, the elusive Dracula, who discovered her hideaway and informed them. Spying on the professor suspected of being a secret slayer, he had followed a doctor after a park bench meeting with said slayer in which he slipped him a letter. The day she fled, Dracula heard a cry carried on the wind and knew the babe lived. He burned with hatred toward your father and desired to kill you. He searched through the decades until he found the mirror that was your mother's entrance to this side of time. He studies it insanely every night, searching its secrets. He wants to go back, reverse time, kill your father." She turned to James, and set her eyes solidly on him. "I don't know who you are, James Lauren, but I do know you are not the Count's descendant." James stood at the window and twisted the ring back and forth on his finger. Then his gaze narrowed toward the forest, hardened, and became fiery.

"I know who I am," he said.

He turned and surveyed the demolished room. "We need to leave this room quickly, Daelyn. The Count does not yet know what we discovered here or that I was even in here. He needs to continue to think I believe I am his descendent, but how do we explain this mess, and the blood all over the wall in the kitchen?"

Daelyn shrugged and smiled. "That's easy. I'll just mess up a couple more rooms, tell him I got hungry and chased the housekeeper all over the house and into the kitchen. She threw bottles of blood at me to ward me off, then ran out screaming."

"And he'll believe that?"

"Yeah," she said, avoiding his gaze. "He'll believe it."

•

He believed it. "Did you get rid of another one of my housekeepers, Daelyn?" he addressed her mildly as he entered the house and found the kitchen a wreck.

She shrugged sheepishly.

He turned to James. "And this is the creature you want? Filled with wildness and her own designs?"

The Count seemed tired. As though the night had been long. He did not seem refreshed or bloated with blood as he should have appeared if he had been on a successful hunt. His eyes were drained, empty, his pupils large. James sat down in an overstuffed chair and draped his legs sideways across the armrest while he studied him.

"You look like you were on a bad date," he ventured boldly. "I saw her with you in the courtyard."

The Count turned to leave the room without responding. "I will see you this evening. I suggest in the meantime you also find a place of peace. Away from her." He turned back briefly to Daelyn and his gaze became menacing. "He is destined for the Roses. Chase the butlers and the maids as you will, but leave this one unpricked or you will suffer by my hand."

Daelyn trembled under the iciness in the heated threat and the cold power that rippled through each word, wrought with cruel flame. Her shoulders drew in to show subjection. "I will not touch him."

"See that you do not."

The elite vampyre's command carried a venom and viciousness unlike any James had ever imagined, the voice unbelievably calm as it carried threats worse than death for her.

He breathed a little easier once the mogul was in daysleep.

Daelyn collapsed into the corner of the couch in the library. "I suggest we run like hell from this place," she said.

James sat down beside her and drew his arm around her shoulders. "I was thinking that myself. But we also need to help the Roses run like hell."

"We don't even know where they are," she sighed.

"Yes, we do. They're somewhere in that forest. He knows where. And before he grinds me into hamburger for his wolves, he wants a Rose to conceive by me."

"Why?" she asked wonderingly. "He knows you are not his descendent."

"Blood vengeance. The deepest, most vicious, but most victorious form of revenge. He wants to create a powerful vampyre from the seed of a slayer he hated, a vampyre hunter who secretly pursued the undead, and later in life, him." He glanced at the ring and turned it slightly. "My father should have scattered his ashes in the sun ..." His voice trailed off.

"I don't understand any of this, James," Daelyn said, draping her slender legs across his lap. "This is going to be one of those 'if we live' things, isn't it? So I guess we might not be spending Thanksgiving at the farm?"

"We'll live," James said, taking her chin in his hand. "I'm not going to let that don of the ditch dwellers put his hands on you."

It was a beautiful promise. But one Daelyn could not feel he could keep. She was a subject of the Realm, a vampyre, after all.

She reached up and ran her fingers through his thick, soft, dark hair. Then her eyes began to shine as she studied his face. "Intellect. And power." She traced the line of his broad shoulders.

"You're the descendent of the Dutch slayer!"

"I must have my mother's eyes. His were blue."

"You do," she smiled, "if the window, the mirror, gave a true reflection of her." But Daelyn's smile faded as her eyebrows almost came together with hard thought. "When I was still a Rose, there was a Dutch Rose named Katrien. She was nice to me, felt sorry for me." Her eyes flashed into his. "But that's not possible, is it? That you have a sister?"

"Of course it's possible," a feminine voice like liquid silver flowed into the room from behind them.

Jane Weston stood in the doorway.

James tensed, breathing hard as he turned to face her.

She was wearing a mint green Grecian gown, and her curls were pushed up from the nape of her neck, held in place with pale green, crystal chaining. A slender belt of gold chain was tied at her waist and fell downward in shimmering links.

She was, as always, beautiful.

She floated full into the room and gazed with open desire at James as she smoothed her hand across the folds of the green gown. "I love the ancients. So much intellect and freedom." She smiled winsomely.

Daelyn eased her legs from James' lap and swung them to the floor. Stiffening, she hissed at Jane in warning.

Jane ignored the younger vampyre. "I will tell you where the Roses are enjoying their chains, James. And I ask nothing in return."

"Except what?" he responded coldly, knowing her coquettishness well.

"You." Her eyes began to glitter excitedly, violet beams, with horrific, glittery stars in the pupils. "I want the son of—"

"Hell, Jane. You would want him if he was the son of a friggin' troll," Daelyn interjected, easing from the couch. She stood up, her wings extended, her voice cold as January ice.

Jane hissed hotly in return, the stars in her pupils turning red in violet eyes now blazing. Her hands extended in warning. "Release him to me, you insolent sobriquet!"

They circled, "fairie dust" shimmering all over them and the floor.

Damn. They're going to fight over me, James thought.

But he knew the power behind Jane's claws. He moved quickly to protect Daelyn.

Jane smiled coyly at James, and playfully tossed her head full of black curls. "She will kill you, James. In the end, she will kill you. Her insatiable thirst will destroy you."

"When the Count hears his house getting trashed again, and all his antique German furniture and Black Forest valuables being smashed to bits, he's going to be trashing you both," James said.

Daelyn secretly, briefly, entwined her fingers into his and squeezed lightly. "That's quite a belt you're wearing, m'lady. I wonder how it would look wrapped around your neck?"

James understood. He stepped forward, to divert Jane's attention and let his rookie Valkyrie take her. "So what kind of baubles does the Count buy you? He gave his castle firebrand here white diamonds. A whole damned mine full."

It was enough to unbalance her. Her eyes flashed in a frown with the blow to her ego he had effectively launched. She swept toward him to knock him against the wall.

In one leap Daelyn had grabbed the chain and whipped it around and around the vampira's neck, tightening with each twining wind, and pulling her backward.

Jane tried to put her fingers between her neck and the chain that could slice through her neck and behead her if she resisted Daelyn's grasp.

Daelyn yanked hard. Droplets of blood trickled from between

the links of gold.

"Now, walk with me backward up the stairs," Daelyn instructed her firmly.

"I would help you, Jane," James said with a shrug, "But well, you know how it is. I have a—passion—for Daelyn."

The room practically smoked with her anger, and her hatred, and her terror.

They took her to the room with the mirror, and James tied her, standing, across the width, lashing her to the posts with his links of silver. Sinking her partially into the plasma-like surface, but leaving her face clear, Daelyn set the runes and said, softly, sweetly, "Now you know what this will do to you if you try to move, m'lady. You'll be sucked into God knows what, and only Hell knows where. Feel the tugging, Jane? The mirror wants you. Bad."

"If you call out for the Count," James said, "You'll be calling into the mirror. He won't hear you."

"But the mirror will hear you," Daelyn added precociously.

"Where are the Roses?" James demanded.

"He didn't tell me," she spat in spite of the danger facing her. "He doesn't tell me anything. I don't know and I don't care where he keeps his females."

They could hear and sense the Count stirring. He could feel Jane's peril even in his daysleep.

They hurried down the stairs, leaving her nose to nose with herself from a mirror that gave her back a reflection of her terrified face.

"Think she'll believe that load of bull about the mirror calling her?" James asked as they raced from the room.

"It isn't bull," Daelyn answered.

James didn't ask her anything else about the mirror. He wanted to break it to bits, crush the shards, and burn the runes.

But he knew he couldn't. There could be innocents stranded in the crystal streams, caught somewhere between the past and an unknown future.

"Guess you should have staked her," Daelyn said, "but I thought maybe she could tell you more of the New Realm's takeover plans if, you know, we got back from checking all the rooms before he woke up. Should have known she had her talons in him even in sleep."

They rushed out into the light where the Count could not follow.

"What did her belt tell you, Daelyn?" James asked as they skirted the courtyard toward a foot path beyond the alley. He knew the precog would not have left the gold chain untouched.

"Katie is your sister," Daelyn said. "And she lied of course. This trail leads to a dripstone cave with a natural illusion, a wall that isn't there. The wall becomes a walkway through the mountain. The Roses are within the mountain. A medieval royal hid there with his people when he was overrun in a surprise attack by a rival lord and his lands and castle became his enemy's spoils, and—"

"A sister," James repeated, a faraway look in his eyes. "I have a sister."

"You okay?"

"Yeah. Yeah, I'm okay. We just need to get there."

Daelyn could see his quest burning in his eyes. This was no longer about thwarting a Realm power play or killing the Count. It was personal.

"The dethroned royal and his entourage made rooms out of the caves," Daelyn continued, "and lived in the mountain. Tales grew up in the forest by people who caught glimpses of them here and there that dwarves lived in the mountain. He and those who were loyal to him would slip out at night and slit the throats of the enemy's outer castle guards and anyone else who ventured out. They communicated the positions of their victims by imitating wolf growls and howls."

"Werewolves. The Black Forest werewolf folklore," James murmured. Then he shook himself back into reality. "Hurry. As soon as Drac figures out how to release Jane from that goo and glop, we're in goo and deep doo doo."

20.

A sinister air saturated the forest, permeating its dark mysteries and ancient past. An odd, ominous feeling. James could sense the bitter flavor in every leaf, every pine needle.

"Getting colder," he said, pulling his jacket collar closer to his neck. "Autumn can bring snow in these here parts, pardner, if it clouds up. So I'm told."

Daelyn didn't respond. She had slowed her steps and stopped, and was tilting her head to the side, listening. James moved warily past the trees rising on either side of the road like Ents. She had heard something he couldn't hear or see yet. Something that didn't bode well, if her look was any indication.

"What's coming at us, Daelyn?" he asked, half expecting her to say her keen ears had picked up the reverberation of hoof beats. A spectacle of dark, powerful beings mounted on stallions, their capes turned into the wind as they bounded toward them through the forest, searching for them at Dracula's command, filled his thoughts.

"Are they on horseback?" he asked.

She tossed him a slightly disdaining smirk. "Not hardly. This isn't Medieval Times. They're in off-roaders. And traveling much too fast to be looking for anyone on foot. They would be winging, and traveling much slower, low through the trees." Her eyes began to glisten. "Quick! We need to get off the road and hide."

They punched their way down a low, descending slope and crouched in a stand of ferns.

As a roar of engines drew close, James raised up slightly to take a look. Almost twenty vampyres, bound by bloodlines, were shouting, laughing, cursing as they roared by.

The black SUVs with smoked windows following in the rear of the specter parade could stash a cache of Roses …

"We'll never beat them to the caves," he moaned despairingly.

"There's a shortcut on the other side of this creek," Daelyn said, casting her vision into the forest depths. "It's a long shot."

They cut through tangles of trees and brush until they spotted a waterfall cloistering a cave. The wide waterfall was thirty feet up to the crescent-shaped opening, then extended thirty more feet to a higher divide where the fall became two slender, silver lines

A rocky ascent did not promise the novice climber success in reaching even the entrance behind the lower cascades, but James and Daelyn were not novices and their legs were strong. They skirted the rocky, wet boulders, passed behind the cascades with agility, and were inside the cave in moments.

The rocky tunnel extending into the mountain was silent, empty, revealing nothing but darkness and stone. Daelyn read the stone walls, the granite halls.

The Roses were gone.

They turned, to return empty-handed and disheartened to the entrance.

Daelyn put out her arm and stepped beside James protectively. "A vampyre still lingers."

Pighead popped up from behind a boulder.

"He's not the one I feel," Daelyn said, frowning as she studied the darkness.

"I have your weapons for you," Pighead grinned enthusiastically at James. "I thought perhaps you might want them now, since things seemed to have taken a slight turn, yes? I have them hidden."

Smiling a crooked smile, he waved them toward him, to follow him.

He froze, his smile fled.

And so did he. He flashed into the recesses of the cave.

James turned to see what had frightened him away.

A tall, powerfully built vampyre stood in the tunnel walkway, caped in gold and white.

"The Vanguard Captain! He frightens the hell out of me," Daelyn whispered in a windless cry.

"Nicholas," James murmured. "I guess you're not deceased."

"In a manner of speaking," he responded coldly. "And it's Nicholai."

He was between them—and the cave entrance. The way out.

With a snarl behind his bared, white fangs, Nicholai unclasped his cape, let it drop to the ground, and launched himself through the air toward the slayer he hated. The impact sent both the mortal and the vampyre to the cave floor, reeling, locked in a death grip. Daelyn spread her wings to fly at the vanguard. This would be a fight to finish the slayer—unless Nicholai had second thoughts.

"I have spent hours contemplating the ways I would like to destroy your carcass!" Nicholai hissed toward James as they rolled and he smashed the slayer's head against the granite cave floor.

No second thoughts apparently.

Daelyn flew at him, grabbed him by the shoulders, pulled him off James, and decided to try the fist that had made a hole in granite.

Her curled knuckles sent the Vanguard against the far side of the cave. But she knew he would recover from the impact quickly.

Tightening her backpack so it wouldn't slide, she helped James from the cave floor, clutched his arm and hauled him toward the entrance of the cave. "Jump!" she cried as they ran to the edge of the heavy water veil falling thirty feet to a deep pool. "He won't follow us into the water!"

They jumped, plunging through a snowy cold water flow and icy autumn air. Sailing downward, they crashed feet first into the fathomless pool.

As soon as they came up for air, the pair swam through the pool to a stream that flowed away from the falls and into the trees.

Nicholai stood at the cave entrance watching them go, but oddly did not fly to follow them. He turned toward the inner chambers of the cave.

James and Daelyn swam furiously, fighting the dips and turns in the shallow, fast-flowing currents of the streambed and the deeper gradients of frothy waves when boulders would interrupt the flow and create mini rapids.

The water was arctic cold, and James soon found his arms tingling, then becoming leaden under the freezing currents. His backpack slid from his shoulders, was swept away.

The icy ripples began to numb his body, his arms grasped at the waves, pushed at the water, but he could feel his movements slowing. This river-stream kept trying to pull him down and toward its core. He felt his body being carried away by the fast flowing currents. "Daelyn ..." His call for help was weak, but in an instant she was beside him. She pulled him, and her backpack, through the rolling water toward a hidden eddy she had spotted. "Hang on, pardner, we're going to get you out of this range war."

Then the shore and dry, pebbly bank.

Wrapping her arm around his waist, Daelyn half-dragged, half-pushed him into a seclusion of trees into safety.

He collapsed beneath a giant birch, shivering and shaking, his lips blue. She began digging a lean to with lightning movements, then helped him in under its tiny roof of tree roots and dirt, and pulled off his wet clothes. "There, Prince James. That will at least block the wind and cold a little till I get a fire going." She rubbed his legs and arms to give him a little warmth while she looked desperately around. "Come on, Daelyn, you're a beach girl, you can do this. Make a pit just like at the beach only smaller. Find some rocks and stuff." She flashed out of the lean to and broke a stand of saplings into kindling and firewood. Then smashed large rocks into smaller stones.

A pile of sticks, dry tinder and small logs soon began to rise from a makeshift firepit through a moving, winged blur.

"Now let's see if I can get two rocks to spark the same way I punched that granite," she said determinedly, picking up two stones of about the same size each. Rubbing the two rocks together rapidly over the firepit wood, in a matter of seconds she had sparks erupting, and a fire was blazing in front of the lean-to.

"Come on, Prince James," she said, pulling him closer to the logs offering welcome flames. Stripping off her own soaked clothes, she spread their dripping garments over a boulder next to the fire.

"You promised me we wouldn't die, James Lauren," she sobbed, lying beside him and wrapping him in her wings to warm him. Rapidly, she stroked his arms and legs to create friction and warmth and get the circulation going.

"You rub any faster and I'm gonna' spark like those rocks did," he said through chattering teeth as he grinned at her weakly.

In an ecstasy of relief, she kissed him. He wasn't going to die an ice sculpture. She loved him so much she felt her heart would burst. He had given her the only chance she had at regaining a sem-

blance of life, and so much more. She would love him now and forever, she knew. Obsession had become possession—of her heart.

"I thought I was going to lose you," she said through another
ecstatic kiss. His lips regained their color.

She held him close to her, the muscles in his chest warming under her breasts, her own body enjoying its newfound bit of warmth
in shared body heat.

The fire began to wane. "We need more wood," she said and
rose to gather more kindling. She mounded sticks around the inner pit, and replenished the fire. "Not a bad pit for my first try," she
said with satisfaction, admiring the flow of flame. "Considering fire
scares me."

"You're beautiful, Daelyn," James said behind her. She was
standing before the firelight, a golden outline, and James could not
help but enjoy the effect the curvy, soft silhouette traced in gold
had on him. A bit of forest wind blew through her hair, tussling the
tresses.

She turned to him and her eyes fell on the desire expressed for
her between his thighs. "Well," she breathed luxuriously, "you've
recovered from your icy swim rather indecently."

"Can't help it. You're like the intro to a James Bond movie."

Her light laughter curled through the trees.

She lined a flat rock with the contents of her wet canvas backpack then laid it beside the fire to dry. First order of survival—
blood and a pack to carry it.

He turned on his side, leaned on his elbow. "You're kind of the
woodsy, camper-in-the-raw type, aren't you?" He grinned, his eyes
traveling over her like silk espresso.

Placing a well formed foot on his chest, she pushed him lightly
onto his back. "You've got a nice piece of hard wood there to build
a fire with. Think it will burn nicely in my little firepit?"

"It's already burning," he said, his eyes wet with want.

He leaned his back against one of the large tree roots forming the inner wall of the lean-to, and she lowered her body down
against his until she was sitting against him, straddling his thighs.
Scooting in against the hot, hard flesh, she wriggled, just a little.
Just enough. Enough to let him feel an edge of creamy silkiness, to
tease him.

The movement drove away his logic, made him moan. Made

him mad with desire.

"Let me in, Daelyn," he said, his hands moving to her waist, his voice throaty.

Her eyes drifted languorously into his. "Let me mystify you, James. Just a little. It will—enhance our enjoyment."

"If you bite, we die," he reminded her, but barely able to breathe under the heaviness of his desire.

"I might nibble your ear a little," she said in a light, whispery laugh.

He let her eyes take him, his thoughts floated away on her blue waves, and he became lost in her oceans of fire. Her hands were seductive, sensuous, as she placed them in under the backs of his upper thighs, sank them in, and pressed him upward.

He groaned and arched into her as soon as he felt the creamy sheath begin to envelope him.

"Tonight, you are mine," she said, her eyes shimmering with excitement as she claimed and accepted his willing surrender. They moved in rhythm, his lips pleasing her everywhere she wanted to be touched and kissed and stroked, taking her into physical love with him until she raked the woodsy night with her pleasure cries, and his own release matched hers. He barely remembered his own name, but he remembered the blue rapture in her eyes, and the voice like bells in the rain, and the body like a rapturous sea of forever.

Their clothes were dry. They dressed, and burrowed into the lean-to keep each other warm and wait out the night. She shielded her eyes from him under their veils of lashes and nestled against him.

A wolf howled, slow and low somewhere far away in the distant trees. Then a call answered. More followed. Wolves howled and called to each other all through the forest, all through the night.

"They're searching for us," he said.

"I know," she said, and pressed closer to him.

21.

At the first light of dawn, James answered nature's call, then returned to the campsite. A smoky, tantalizing smell of roasting meat filled the early morning air. In the short time he had been gone, Daelyn had caught a rabbit and built a makeshift spit over last night's firepit.

And she was turning it.

Breakfast would be roasted rabbit.

"You need your strength," she said in response to his astonished look.

He ate ravenously. She drank from her cups ravenously.

They would survive.

After breakfast, James doused the fire with dirt, stirred it, doused it again with river water, then began following the riverbank—back to the pool.

"We're going the wrong way," Daelyn cried in a panicky voice.

"I want my crossbow," James said. "If he didn't take it. The Roses are gone. No one will be expecting us to return to the cave. And maybe we can find some clue as to where they went."

"We can't help them," Daelyn said, walking backward in front of him to try to slow him down, stop him. "Your plan has been ripped apart. How do you think you can find them?"

But as she looked in his eyes, she knew what was spurring him on.

"She's my sister, Daelyn."

She moved to his side. "I understand," she said softly.

The cave was not deserted. As they entered to retrieve James' crossbow, bolts and belt pack, they were stunned to find one being still lingering.

The Captain of the Vanguards sat on a boulder, his short white cape ribbed in gold braiding draped around him as though he thought he was Julius Caesar.

His blond hair was in Greek curls. His white shirt was loose, toga-like over black tight pants tucked into stylish hip boots.

James' crossbow rested against the boulder next to his foot.

"Thought you might be coming back for this," he smiled ruefully.

James drew in a hard breath, tightening, bracing for a second battle. "So we're doing this again?" he said through clenched teeth.

"That punch your whore sent my way gave me pause to think," Nicholai said.

A fury of indignation rose up through every muscle in Daelyn's body at the word *whore*, and she curled her fist to send him to the wall again.

But she no longer had the element of surprise. He could kill her. She held her stance.

"You and I, slayer, at the moment, want the same thing," Nicholai continued.

"We want this mess cleaned up." He pushed away from the boulder and swept his cape to the side as though about to address Marc Antony. "I need you, though it sickens my stomach and makes me want to vomit maggots to admit it. And you, quite obviously, need me. Your little piglet has fled the trough."

"I need you for what?" James smirked. Nicholai wanted nothing less than to be a king, and had already proven in past dealings with the Shadows that he was the king of liars.

"I can play a trump hand and keep you alive," Nicholai said. "You, on the other hand, can no longer play your Ace card. You're a prisoner the moment you enter the Count's gates, and dead the moment you father a male child." He paused. "Or you might die sooner. You have no idea the power of those wannabe Royals. They're like a consuming oil spill. And they don't want a seed of the most hated slayer in history in their midst."

"I'm not a whore," Daelyn suddenly piped up. "I have claimed him. He is mine." She raised her chin with dignity. "And I decide his fate."

Nicholai laughed, raucously. And his eyes glittered at James. "You let her take you? Ha, you wanted a taste of those oceans! The righteous crossbow slayer has desires for darkness!"

"What do you want from us?" James demanded.

"I want them all dead. Every last one of them. Before I get snuffed like everyone else who makes the mistake of disagreeing with them. And I want the Count's head in the sun."

"Where are the Roses?"

"I don't know. But I have the wherewithal to find out where they have gone. They are not here, obviously. And probably not going to be found on this continent. And in case you're wondering why the New Royals never found you last night—I threw them off your scent. Spread a lot of bear manure around."

"The Devil may be the author of lies, but you wrote the book. Why should I believe you?" James said.

"James!" Daelyn said suddenly, grasping his arm and nodding in the direction of the illusionary wall.

A petite, shadowy form stepped out from behind the rocks at the site of the inner tunnel. "He speaks the truth, James."

As she stepped into the light, Daelyn caught sight of a mass of loose, blond curls and a pair of—"Violet eyes!" she exclaimed, her eyes widening in blue astonishment.

"Yes, she's a descendent of Jane Weston," James said, answering her unspoken question.

Another taller shadowy form in dark clothing rose behind her.

"Daelyn, this is our Shadow mystic, Angie Carter, and I believe you know Henri De LaCroix?" He was surprised as hell to see them, but damn glad in view of the circumstances.

"Henri?" Daelyn blurted as he moved into view. Her lips parted as Henri cocked an eyebrow and smiled at her, but she could not speak, only stare agape.

"Yeah, difficult to believe, I know," James said, "but he's one of us."

"Just one big happy family, we are," Nicholai mocked. "And if you want yours, we better get a move on. I'm assuming we are becoming bedfellows?"

"Drac's ladies are gone, and there's not even a scrap of cloth anywhere in the caves as evidence they were ever here," Henri said in a polished Parisian accent, a watchful eye on the Vanguard Captain.

"And you won't find any clues anywhere else, either," Nicholai said with a shrug. "You have only me. Take me or leave me. I'm all you've got. Admit it."

He was seething with power, wary, and James knew it would take all their strength and ability combined to behead him should the four of them make the decision to take him down.

The Vanguard's eyes read his taut facial muscles, and his own face transformed to red-hued hatred. "Someone would more than likely die if you try to take me, slayer. More than likely Daelyn. She's unstructured and undisciplined, zealous, but careless. You want to take that risk?"

"You're so full of yourself, Nicholai," Daelyn intercepted, undaunted.

"How will we reach you after you find her?" James asked, despising the thought of being in a conspiratorial bed with this monstrous blood sucker. But it was true, Nicholai was all they had now.

"I'll reach you," he said.

"How?"

"State of the art technology," he smiled wryly. He pulled a cell phone from under the cape, from an inner pocket of his shirt, and moved his fingertip lightly over the screen icons. "GPS, Internet, Camera, Texting, Facebook. But what the hell is Farmville?"

He looked up and his eyes did a stick and burn on James. "You do have a cell phone, don't you?"

"I have one," James answered quietly. "Waterlogged, but it should work."

Nicholai spread his wings, and took down James' number. "I'll call you. Wait for my text." He gazed at them all with a magnanimous intensity, disgust bordering on murderous, then he added, "You can spend the night in town if you like, in the Count's former abode. He took my mate and his damn mirror, and vacated the premises."

Nicholai had flown from the cave and into the forest before he could be discovered by any spy for the Realm that might be slithering through the dusk—or before the slayers could change their minds and kill him.

"Guess he didn't want to hang around too long," Daelyn said.

"How long would you stay staring into the barrels of four guns?" Henri quipped.

She tugged James' sleeve. "Nicholai knows what we did to Jane," she whispered.

"Yeah, I know. This treaty is probably going to crumble." He picked up his crossbow and Angie handed him a belt pack.

"Nicholai spoke the truth, but his words are as full of bad berries as bear manure," Angie said. "He has something else on his mind, a hidden agenda. But he's Nicholai, of course."

"Agenda or not, he was right. He's all we've got," James said. "He's all we have to lead us to Katie."

"Who's Katie, James?" Angie asked softly, studying him. "Your heart breaks at her name."

"One of the Roses was named Katie," Henri said, curious. "Singled out for joining with a descendent of the Count, Goran the Moron we called him, and she was isolated in secret quarters. What is she to you, Crossbow?"

"My sister."

Shock blew across both the Shadows' faces. "You have a sister?!"

"Apparently. I just don't know how the Realm discovered her."

"I have no knowledge of the particulars, either," Henri said, searching his memories. "The one called Katrien was trafficked in with two others, and placed in immediate seclusion ..." He halted abruptly as he saw James' jaw tighten. "So, Dracula had a more personal reason for her abduction ... Is there more to this story, Crossbow?"

"Nothing I care to share at the moment," James said, his throat tight. Fury raged within him like a tsunami.

"We need to go, Henri," Angie said, looking up at the ex-Realm Royal with strands of pure love in her voice. "It's not safe to linger here."

"You're a mystic. You have the ability to sense lies as well as truth, and read radials," Daelyn said, somewhat in awe of this petite mistress of mysteries. This mortal mystic has to be the reason Henri defected, Daelyn thought. It would be interesting to know her story. How else could an elite Royal as powerful as the mighty Henri De LaCroix, and the epitome of evil, have been swayed to betray his allegiance to the Realm?

"And you can see the past hidden within the present, I am told," the mystic smiled.

The foursome left the cave, descending between the rocks and pines to the forest floor below.

Once on the road back to town, Daelyn and Angie took the lead, and were soon talking non-stop in low voices, sharing secrets only women share, interjected with an occasional light laugh and a glance back at their two male escorts. Punctuated by more light laughter.

"What do you think they're talking about?" James asked Henri, curiosity burning his insides. Daelyn seemed delighted she had found a female friend.

"From the way they're giggling, I do not think they are sharing recipes for banana bread," Henri said drily.

22.

"You're wearing holes in that lovely carpet," Daelyn said as James paced the floor in the bed and breakfast inn lobby—again.

The half-timber turned B&B had been a much friendlier, inviting choice to wait out the day, than the creepy house in shadows at the end of the block, its rooms still tainted with the essence of Jane's malevolence and Dracula's cold death-smile.

"We will wait with the Shadows, James," Angie said. "If we stay, and Nicholai has decided to make a personal appearance at nightfall rather than text you, our continued presence here might frighten him away. He was jittery in the cave. Best we remain closeted."

"Either way, he will shortly be in daysleep and you won't hear from him until tonight," Henri added.

"A whole day lost," James muttered despondently to Daelyn after they left to find a place in the darker reaches of the forest for Henri to daysleep.

"We can wait for his call in the room," Daelyn coaxed, stroking his arm tenderly. "Truthfully, you could use—a bath." She paused and drew her fingertips across his three day shadow. "And a shave."

He laughed. "I guess I am a little ragged."

While he shaved, then turned the spigot to start a hot bath in a footed tub, Daelyn ran out to buy them some clean clothes.

Leaving his cowboy shirt and jeans on the floor nearby—just in case he had to jump and run, another habit he had acquired in his chosen profession—James sank into the tub. His clothes were soiled but wearable if he needed them. Leaning back, he closed his eyes and let the warm water work its magic on muscles that had been taxed to the limit in the past few days.

A drift of perfume, a sense of the Valkyrie essence in the room.

James' soft brown eyes opened a slit under the relaxed lids.

Daelyn was kneeling by the tub, smiling at him, holding a block of soap and a wash cloth. Every stitch of her own wrecked clothes lay on the floor next to his.

She drew the soap through the water, then rubbed it in her hands to work up a lather.

His neck and taut shoulder and back muscles were soon soapy and releasing the tension under her adroit hands. And his will power turned to soapy foam as she rubbed the block low onto his pelvis.

She moved the fresh scented bar around to the front to his hard chest, now rising and falling in breaths of arousal. Leisurely, she scrubbed in a warm circular motion.

"Nice," he murmured, feeling a luxury of fire growing in his groin.

"Nice," she murmured, easing her hand deep in under the water and lathering that growing fire into smoky, sweet-hard silk. "How long do you suppose the soap will last?"

"Long enough," he said, his voice husky under the spell of the eyes becoming as wet as the water.

She closed them away softly under their thick veils of lashes and kissed him, her lips on his while the soap encircled and massaged, harder and harder, until he felt he would die under that touch.

He pulled her into the tub on top of him. She laughed, a laugh like liquid silver, and slid against him.

"Guess I've worked up quite a lather, haven't I?" she whispered softly.

"One hell of a lather," he groaned as she settled her breasts into his chest and straddled him.

She placed her hands on each side of the back of the tub above his shoulders, and let her kisses massage his lips while she massaged his wet body with her own.

He felt her satin legs open deeply for him, sweetly, deliciously. An opening rosebud. His train dreams coming true …

The tub became a garden pool of delights.

She whispered again, a whisper no more than the rustle of a leaf in the forest, "Do what you will. Or shall I?"

"Oh, god," he moaned, sliding under the water with her.

"*Answer your phone.*"

James and Daelyn came up out of the sudsy water at the sound of the audio ringtone like an electric shock had hit them. Lurching from the tub, James hit the floor in a belly flop to grab his cell phone from his jeans pocket.

"Doesn't anyone ever daysleep anymore?" Daelyn said, miffed, as she climbed out of the tub and pulled two towels from a linen shelf.

"It's not Nicholai," James said, staring hard at the text message. "It's from Andre. Henri's been summoned to confer with the envoys to discuss the threat posed by the New Royals. I'm to let Andre know the location of the Roses as soon as I know so he can send back up."

"You really think an incoming fighter squadron will not be noticed by this new breed of throat suckers?" Daelyn scoffed.

"Right now I'm only concerned with the fact we haven't heard from the Vanguard carrying a double dose of deadly," he said.

He put on the new khaki Dockers and dark blue shirt she had bought for him, snapped and tied his belt pack to the new belt she had decided he needed, and went down to the B&B gardens to walk off a new wave of restlessness and uncertainty. Nicholai hadn't called, the Shadows were contemplating joining him in what could prove to be an inescapable arena of death, and he was emotionally entrenched in the middle of the mess. A mindless obsession to rescue his sister, and keep the wild vamp he loved from the Count's clutches and Jane's claws, could cloud his logic, leave him reacting rather than acting.

Then there was his legacy—and the subsequent questions overshadowing him.

Sitting on a stone garden bench, James absently turned and twisted the gold and sapphire ring on his finger.

He had to keep his wits about him—somehow.

The hairs on his arm began to prickle. And the air moving through the trees around him felt like a thousand demons had descended on the forest.

But it was only one demon. Nicholai.

A fog rolled across the ground, and Nicholai rose from its mists to face the human he considered his archenemy. He wore no weapons, or the white cape with the golden braid. Just a simple pair of casual black pants and a black shirt. James rose and stood away from the stone bench, his hand loose at his side near his pack.

Trust, of necessity, was discretionary when dealing with vampyres, but even more so with this one.

"I thought you were going to text us," James said, suspicious.

"Hackers," the Vanguard said roughly. "Not even the phones are free of New Royal handiwork."

He pulled a piece of tree bark from his pants pocket. "This is the address of a warehouse on the American coast, a sugar factory or something, abandoned after Hurricane Sandy's devastation. I will meet you there with the location of your—sister's—stateside residence as soon as I know exactly where she is. The mortal women are being herded to an undisclosed disembarkment point in the States."

He handed James the bit of bark. "Not much to write on when you usually just thread and text from the trees. And suddenly it's not safe to do so."

"So much for going paperless in the graveworld," James remarked with a smirk.

"Now," Nicholai continued arrogantly, knowing he had the crossbow slayer over a barrel, "if I even get a hint of a scent of a wood splinter from a Shadow stake following you into that warehouse, I'll fly through the rafters and disappear through the holes in the roof left by the hurricane and you'll never find your little Katie. I'll make certain of it."

"They won't come in," James said, his teeth clenched behind a tight breath. To have to yield to this detestable vampyre's demands caused hot indignation to flow through his veins, but he knew he had no choice.

"Have your vampira thread me when you arrive in the city," Nicholai said, then his lips twisted into a thin smile that played lustfully across his mouth. "She's quite a piece of fire. I don't suppose you'd consider—sharing her a little?"

Daelyn emerged from behind a tree, silent as a windless night, and both James and Nicholai turned in shock.

Neither had sensed her.

Her Valkyrie talents were emerging, and James knew the Vanguard was startled by her stealth.

She was becoming a Shadow.

"I think not, Nicholai," she said coolly, moving protectively near the slayer she was beginning to realize was in her charge. Forever. Valkyries. They descended after the battle to lead the valiant dead from the battlefield, to Valhalla.

She kept the Russian vampyre in her sights. "Go play Spin The Bottle with Drac and Jane."

Nicholai could not hide a slight frown at the mention of Jane and Dracula—together.

Then he shrugged in feigned unconcern. "You used to be such fun ..."

With a wary eye on Daelyn, he backed away from them, to become a part of the deep shadows lurking among the close columns of trees in the forest. But not without a closing statement.

"Remember—not a hint. Got that?"

"I got it," James said.

"I don't believe him," Daelyn said as James took her in his arms. "He's like a bad rain. Promising life—then it floods death."

"I don't believe him much either," James said with a sigh. "But he knows I'll come."

She placed her hand over his heart and smiled. "He knows how to play the strings that hold this intact. Your heart isn't pure, but it's damned near to bursting with tender honor."

He took her hands in his and she leaned her forehead against his, her eyes half-closed and neither of them spoke. They both knew Nicholai could break every bone in his body, and crush her beautiful wings with one hand.

Her tears traveled slowly down her cheeks and splashed in crystal drops onto the backs of his hands.

Two days later, their steps were moving with a marked sense of dread and uncertainty toward a warehouse chasm's heavy, metal truck bay doors. They were drawn down and locked up tight, but the single entrance door next to them was open.

"I love you, James," Daelyn whispered, squeezing his hand as they stepped through the door into utter darkness.

They moved toward the center of the room—

James sensed the presence of the New Royals just a hair of a second too late. Vampyres were sweeping from the beams, from behind the ducts, from every single corner in the building.

"Well, he was sure full of it," Daelyn said flatly.

The vampyres blocked every avenue of escape—every window,

every door, and every vent, then stood still as death, watching the Crossbow slayer and his Valkyrie, as though waiting for a command from within the depths of the building.

There was no sound in the depths other than a distant turbine, and the mighty captain of the vanguards did not make an appearance.

"Nicholai deceived us," Daelyn said. "His power even deceived your mighty little mystic."

"He would not have been able to lie to Angie," James insisted. "Something must have happened."

Daelyn spotted a devilish grin emerging out of the dark, in a face that vaguely resembled the Count, right down to the neon pits in his eyes.

"Randall," she spat dryly in acknowledgement. But she refused to lower her eyes to the Royal.

"Well. Daelyn the Desirable. The Lady Jane Weston is awaiting your presence," the vampyre said smugly.

Daelyn shuddered. Jane had probably made generous plans for her. If she didn't throw her in the mirror in a rage, or kill her outright, she would probably get out her whips and cat o' nine tails to torture her—before the beheading.

James gripped the crossbow tightly, and stretched his free arm out to the side to ease her back behind him.

"Drop the crossbow, son of Van Helsing," the vampyre said coolly as he approached.

Hearing his father's name for the first time jolted James momentarily.

The son of Van Helsing. It seemed—unreal.

"Drop it. Or we kill the lovely Daelyn right here, right now. All my hunters are trained on her."

"I think Randall just might be serious, James," Daelyn said with a sigh of resignation. "I mean nothing to them. And now, I am nothing to the Count. I have no promise of protection."

With reluctant compliance, James let the crossbow slide to the ground. They were surrounded by death waiting for an excuse to happen. The vamp motioned to his utility pack. He unstrapped it, tossed it to the ground.

The vampyre picked up the crossbow, and crushed it to bits. Then he wiped his hands in a back and forth motion as though to rid himself of feces-laden dirt. "Get in the SUV or your bones will be on the floor in bits like your crossbow."

Another taller muscle-bound New Royal grabbed Daelyn's arm and yanked her away as she moved out from behind James.

"Let her go," James said with clenched teeth, stepping forward.

The Count's protégé flashed between them. "I would let him kill you, slayer, but the Count doesn't want a hair on your head touched. At least not yet. However, he didn't say anything about your jaw."

In a lightning quick movement, James dodged the iron hand that came up to make contact with his left cheek. He also swerved and blocked a second try, but in a wind that crackled near his face, a fist came out of the dark from a vamp who had flashed forward and James was on the ground.

"Randall, you pig!" Daelyn screamed, and in one wrenching jerk, she was free of the arrogant hands holding her carelessly at bay.

The New Royal that had socked the human she loved, and Randall, were dead on the floor before any vamps could think to move in their behalf. Randall was bleeding from the slit across his throat that had knifed clean through and severed his head, but so quickly and sharply that his smile was still sitting on his neck as he fell.

"Looks like the Count has one less nephew," she said smartly.

"Dang, you're still a hellion!" The vampyre who had been holding her laughed. "And the Count will have your head for that one! What else can you do with those fingernails?"

"I'll show you," she said, turning and leaping through the air at him, her fangs now also extended.

It took five powerful Rose boys to take her down. And five more to subdue James as he pulled himself to his feet and came to her aid, his fists returning the favors he'd been receiving.

"Load the slayer in the car," a voice like lit kerosene said from a far wall.

"Damn you, Nicholai!" Daelyn cast at him in fury, straining against all the cold hands holding her like a clump of wet rags.

I've got problems of my own right now, he threaded as he moved into view. *Calm down, and let me take the lead, or you, and Crossbow here, are dead. I needed to get Randall's crew boxed in—you and Crossbow were the carrot to dangle in front of their noses.*

Keep your mouth shut and your fangs to yourself, he warned. *These are New Order and dangerous. They are like killer bees calmed only by the smoke pots. When the smoke clears, they kill. And there are more of them. This is just one swarm from the Count's hive. But one of the most dangerous. The Shadow envoys will be blamed for their unfortunate demise tonight, and you and lover boy will be free and clear to help me kill the Count.*

She forced herself to become still and stop resisting the ten clammy hands that seemed to be all over her, using the moment of bondage to touch her wherever they pleased. "Take your hands off me," she said in low, threatening tones. "Or a few decades down the road, I will deform every one of your fumbling fingers for you."

From out of the corner of her eye, she could see the unpredictable Royals dragging James to the back of an SUV and throwing him in.

A sob rose up in her throat, spilled out through her eyes.

"At least let me ride with him. He was mine," she feigned in a sulky, cheated tone, turning her blue, watering eyes on her kidnappers.

"No!" Nicholai said, stepping forward and stopping the vampyre who was about to release her. "You idiot. She would have him free before you could drive a quarter of a block, and you would never even know they had gotten out. Were you born in a barn like a brainless cow? Oh, I forgot. You were."

"A cave with sloths, with a bone for a brain, more than likely," Daelyn spat. "I've only seen that much stupidity in one other set of idiot eyes. Lem."

The insulted vampyre hissed, and his hand came up, smacked her face, sent her against the wall, and broke her jaw. As she sat on the floor, holding her dislodged cheek, Daelyn's eyes were filled with anger and hatred more than pain. Her eyes glared with flashes of red-gold through her hair as the strands fell across her face and spilled around her—promising him nothing less than death.

I warned you, Nicholai threaded into her thoughts.

As though appearing to want to help her, a New Royal near the wall held out his hand and pulled her from the dirty, debris strewn floor where she had been thrown. But his intention to be a dark knight in winged armor quickly died.

"You're warm!" he exclaimed as he took her hand, fascinated.

He began massaging the palm and fingers. "No wonder the Count put an ASAP APB out on you! Blood and play!"

He yanked her head back roughly by her hair, forcing her to turn her neck to the side.

She let him prick her, rather than become a punching bag again, or reveal the power she had sequestered deep within her. She had already revealed too much physical strength. To rise as a Valkyrie at this particular moment, in the presence of these graveworld vampyres of unknown "gifts," might not be judicious.

But as he began drinking ravenously from the holes in her jugular, wastefully sloshing gushes of warm red, liquid in his slovenly ravishing all over her blouse, a bevy of flaring nostrils and hungry eyes turned toward her from all over the warehouse.

She pushed at him, to push him away, try to escape the horrid, cavernous face sitting on her neck like a void in the night, and the faces moving closer, licking their lips …

She could see James kicking open the back hatch and fighting past the vamps left to guard the SUV to free her from the mouth enjoying the gluttonous gorging. He swept his pack from the floor as he ran, then wrenched her free of her blood captor. But the vampyre broke from James' grasp.

Nicholai threw the vampyre to the wall. "She is the Count's."

Two more New Royals stepped forward, their voices heavy, aroused by the smell of blood like rats to sugar. "Not tonight. Maybe later."

"Who says the Count should have it all?" her attacker directed angrily against Nicholai, wiping his mouth and licking the residue from the back of his hand. "The rest of us want a taste."

Vanguards moved to confront them. And protect their Captain. James placed Daelyn placed against the wall behind him. "Stay put." The atmosphere of the room began to change. More vampyres loyal to the Old Order moved beside and around Nicholai.

A silence clamped the warehouse, leaden, the moment of silence before the battle, when sword hilts glint in the gray, pale light of a dark dawn.

Then a distant low, slow, long scream from a far corner, hollow, terrifying, rolling across the warehouse, traveling across the floor to the walls.

As though a shadow from Hell was coming for its own soul.

A chorus of screeches erupted in answer, high-pitched howling, piercing, from a hundred vampyres as they arched their heads back. The predatory cries echoed through every floor of the warehouse, harbingers of the terror about to erupt.

This was a storm that had simply been waiting.

Someone parted a wing, slashed a vanguard. A sword responded …

Fangs and fists began flailing and flying and the whole place became a chasm of shouts and railing screams. Vampyres were flapping and flopping through the air, thrown and knocked and smacked, to somersault against brick walls, smash giant ducts scaling the ceiling, and tumble through dirt and blood-smeared, shattering windows.

Daelyn pushed away from the wall, ducked under Nicholai's arm, and she and James scrambled past the warring vamps. A war for dominance. They dodged dust, debris and flying streams of blood, to make their way out. They had been momentarily forgotten in the vampyres' enthusiasm to kill one another.

"Crossbow!"

James turned, leaped up and caught the car keys Nicholai flung at him.

Get him out of here, Nicholai threaded to Daelyn. *They'll drug him, and I don't want to find myself a few centuries from now fighting his Black Rose vampyre sons.*

Where are the Roses? She threaded back.

An abandoned plantation in North Carolina. By the coast. Dracula refurbished it. It used to have …

He stopped threading. A New Royal was trying to take his head with a machete.

James was yanking open the SUV's door. He jumped into the driver's seat, and Daelyn flashed to the warehouse bay door, opening it with a hard pull. Then she toppled in beside him.

But as the SUV roared through the doors out onto the street and vanguards were closing the bay doors behind them to seal in the New Royals, Daelyn caught a glimpse of the Vanguard Captain. He was deep in the skirmish, fighting with fervor. Fighting to save his position, fighting for his place in the only world he knew, and fighting furiously for his woman, to reclaim his place in her bed.

"On the lam again, I guess?" she said as James began driving like he was outrunning the border patrol.

He glanced at her purplish, lopsided face. "You look like you got run over by a bus."

"He isn't going to run over me again," she said flatly, pushing her jaw back in place again with her hand. Then she smiled at him, a crooked-but-beautiful curve of her lips. "We must be the scene from Beetlejuice that was left on the cutting floor."

He laughed behind swollen, sore lips, then muttered, "Ouch," and favored his jaw gingerly.

She drew her fingertips tenderly down his black and blue cheek. "You look like you got hit by the same bus."

"Bus full of vampyre fist," he said.

She tossed a short glance over her shoulder into the back seat. "You can come up for air now, Pighead."

The trembling little titmouse burrowed into the crease of the seat in a tiny, frightened ball happily shadowed and became himself.

"We should drop you off in the next sewage drain, you little coward," Daelyn said, infuriated.

"You don't know them," he said, pursing his wide, large lips. "They would have cut me up into little pieces." He paused. "And probably scattered me everywhere."

James flicked the blinker and the SUV sped onto the freeway.

"So, where are we going?" James asked, catching the Valkyrie's gaze intently surveying freeways signs. "Nicholai was threading, wasn't he? What did he say to you?"

She cast another, beautiful smile at him, straighter this time as her face began to mend.

"North Carolina." She paused and tossed him a teasing smile. "Oh, and he has a new name for you besides, Crossbow."

"I can imagine."

23.

"Looks like autumn is in full force on the East Coast," Daelyn said as oceans of gold appeared on the horizon.

The trees had turned.

"When I was behind the sealed walls in the castle, I sometimes wondered if I'd ever see another fall in the sunlight," she said, a brush of sadness in her voice. "Or any season."

"You'll see sunlight on the snow, if you can hang in with me, Blues," James said tenderly, giving her hand a light squeeze. He was determined she would not be lost to him, but he knew the worst was yet to come for her.

"I'm more of a warm fire and wine and amenities in bed type of girl when it's snowing," she teased enticingly.

"Fire and wine are good. Amenities are good," James returned as he pulled off the freeway and drove around to the back of a Denny's restaurant. "Don't think we want to be seen tucking Pighead into the trunk for daysleep before going inside," he said. After Pighead burrowed into the trunk, James slung his arm around Daelyn's waist protectively, warily watching the parking lot and they walked to the front of the restaurant. "Most vamps would be in daysleep by this time, but I'm not sure about New Royals."

"They sleep," Daelyn assured him.

The sleepy-eyed, middle-aged waitress who took his order for a Grand Slam breakfast stared at his jaw in curiosity. Stared at both their jaws. "You into your own version of the fifty shades thing?" she popped behind her gum.

A co-worker called her over, and began whispering excitedly to her as she turned in James' order, a hush-hush conversation interjected with glances in the direction of their table.

"You need some salt," Daelyn said suddenly, rising from the table.

"I do?" James asked, curious.

"The one flitting her beak like a nervous sparrow is saying 'all this' is none of their business."

The two waitresses became overly busy tallying receipts as they saw Daelyn approaching them. "Can I borrow the salt?" she asked amiably as she picked up a shaker.

But as her hand curled around the glass, she dropped it in shock. The impact of what she read in the glass traveled through her like a train.

"You okay, honey?" the waitress asked as she began scooping up the spilled granules with a rag.

"Yes, yes, thank you," Daelyn said quickly, and hurried to the booth with the shaker.

"James! Nicholai has been here," she whispered frantically. "His touch is all over this shaker."

James took the salt shaker and his lips drew together in a tight line. He walked to the counter, let out a slow breath. "Ladies, has anyone come through here, perhaps last night, perhaps a rather large body-builder type with sandy colored hair and very arresting brown eyes?"

"Arresting is an understatement," the sparrow twittered breathlessly.

Daelyn moved in close. In case the women should choose to lie, she would "suggest" they tell the truth.

The waitress who had served them leaned her elbow on the counter and lowered her voice. "Some big, really wicked looking dude came in right before sunup asking if we'd seen a couple of broken jaws." She glanced at Daelyn. "One of them on a brunette with blue eyes. And he didn't exactly look like the friendly type, honey."

"No, he's definitely not the friendly type. He's the reason we're banged up."

"I figured as much," she said. "Callie said we should just stay out it, but that fella looked like he might have a pretty nasty temper."

You don't know the half of it, James thought.

"Anything else?" Daelyn asked, as the waitress wrung out her cleaning cloth.

She reached under the counter, handed James a napkin covered in writing. "He said if I saw you, to give you this. Actually what he said was, if I saw anybody with a crapped up jaw—I left it under the counter by the cash register to remind me in case any customers came in who fit the description. Does it mean anything?"

"It means he ran out of bark," James snickered, then slipped her a twenty dollar bill in appreciation. He wolfed down his eggs and bacon, biscuits and coffee, paid the tab and they left the restaurant.

"So what does it mean?" Daelyn asked as he sped out of the parking lot.

"It will save us from having to visit every Chamber of Commerce and visitor's information center in every city along the coast," James said, entering an address into the SUV's GPS system.

He took the wheel, his focus of concentration on the road, but the Valkyrie's skirt was soon sliding up her thighs as she leaned back and closed her eyes. James found his gaze drifting more than occasionally to the silky skin that heated his thoughts with memories of bath water and lather. Those legs were a beautiful distraction on the long road up the coast.

Following the GPS directions on the dashboard screen, James turned onto a two lane highway leading tall grasses parallel to the distant shoreline, and by nightfall they were not too far from the address Nicholai had scribbled on the napkin.

Brake lights began to flash in front of them from the cars up ahead.

"What's going on?" Pighead asked, his head popping up above the back of the seat as James slowed his speed.

Cars were slowing, stopping.

"Looks like a highway patrol road block," James said, but the hairs were standing on the back of his neck. The air was steely.

Two units were parked sideways on the two lane highway, and two officers in uniform were halting cars and trucks.

Casting the beams of flashlights into the interiors, they were searching every face, then the trunks.

They detained every vehicle, but ushered only random occupants out and onto the shoulder to wait while other cars were allowed to move on.

Daelyn's eyes opened suddenly, she looked out the front windshield. "Those are not cops," she said. "They're doped on blood and looking for more."

"Are they looking for us?" Pighead asked in a panic.

"If they're looking, it's not for you," James said. "No one knows you were in the car."

"They're stocking the plantation," Daelyn said knowingly, watching them taking a sampling of humans into the woods. "They will mesmerize them, and—"

"They will recognize this car!" Pighead interrupted frantically. "They will recognize us!"

"Any suggestions?" James asked Daelyn. "We're getting close."

"There's a small road coming up on the right," Daelyn said. "Turn onto the road and pull over as soon as you are out of range." James took the turn and whipped up sand and dirt for about half of a mile, then whirled to a stop past a bend in the road that hid them from view.

"Now what?" Pighead implored nervously. "What do we do, Daelyn?"

"Shapeshift into a winged horse," Daelyn commanded the quaking vampyre.

He opened his mouth to sputter in protest, but her eyes flamed, and he fell silent.

"I've seen you do it. Shift. Now! This mortal is under my jurisdiction. He's mine, and I don't intend to lose him to some damned bloodletting tonight. Or your blood will flow like rivers in the sand!"

The flames in her eyes intensified.

He shapeshifted, and let the Valkyrie and the slayer mount and grasp his mane, then he was flying, Pighead the Magnificent, against the twilight, a dark, beautiful Pegasus.

With the two lovers on his back riding hell for leather across the sky.

24.

As he landed on a bit of beach, Pighead's hooves imprinted the sand next to the small waves lapping at the inlet shore. James and Daelyn climbed from his back and he quickly shadowed and became himself. "It's almost dawn," he said, looking around the shady inlet desperately for a place to daysleep. "I do not relish burying myself in the sand."

"Come on, we'll find you an outbuilding or something once we reach the plantation," Daelyn said.

Two hundred year-old trees formed a canopied, cathedral aisle driveway leading in a straight-away to the columned porch of a coastal plantation that could have rivaled the immortal Tara from *Gone With The Wind.*

Greek pillars ascended to the second story, supporting galleries that spanned across the front of the house and wrapped around all four sides to offer an encompassing view of the acreage from every balcony. No matter which of the upper story French shuttered doors a person stepped from, they had a pillared alcove from which to view the sunrise or sunset with tea and brandy.

Or view the foreman's smaller wood and brick house sitting back in the trees, and the indigent housing reserved for slaves.

The remains of the graying cabins were grim reminders of how dark the heart could bleed.

From all appearances, this plantation had been built on the backs of the sweat of servitude. Slavery.

But—

Something was wrong.

"Odd," James murmured, as though to himself, "This land is scarred, and I should be sensing a silence of suffering, and the wounds, feeling it in every drop of mist clinging to the magnolia trees and giant oaks." His eyes narrowed, darted over the grounds. "But I don't."

Daelyn's eyes became cloudy, deep with thought. "Are your slayer's perceptions diminished because you have become intimate with a vampyre who is not yet proven mettle? With—me?" she asked, her head lowered slightly, barely able to look into his velvety, chocolate eyes. "Did my enhancement—hurt—you, James?"

He put his hand under her chin, lifted her face to his, and flashed his curvy smile. "Having sex with my Valkyrie would not put my perceptive powers at risk." His eyes traveled to the shacks, and turned inward like muddy water rushing backward. "Something else is going on here."

James studied the disturbing currents within him. Perhaps the lack of sensory contact had to do with the present resident evil more than the past.

The new slavery was to scar the land with every race on the face of the earth. Descendents of a new legacy of arrogance and self-imagined royalty had risen from the ground to walk these porches, swilling blood in their brandy glasses as they would gaze down from their balconies at the spate of slave cabins.

"If it was deep night, I guess we would be headed for the house through the trees and shadows, but it's about to become broad daylight," Daelyn's soft voice nudged him, interrupting his thoughts. "What's the plan, pardner? Just walk right in, guns blazing?"

"My butt will be blazing and I'll become broad daylight if I don't find a place to daysleep, and soon," Pighead said tensely, skittish about being here in the first place.

"We'll hide you in one of the cabins," Daelyn offered.

At the first decaying row of housing, Daelyn ran her hand across the rotting door frame of a "cabin" and a puzzled look furrowed her brow. She stepped inside and rested her hand against a destitute wall, then touched a splintery window sill. The puzzlement deepened into short, startled breaths.

She turned to James with a look of panic. "I feel—nothing."

"You, too? The Roses might be in the big house then," he said, glancing back through the open door toward the mansion.

"No, you don't understand," she said with scarcely a breath. "I don't feel—anything. It's as though no one, living or undead, ever walked across this threshold. The door, the window, the walls—this place should be shedding tears. Instead, it's a void, a vacuum."

"Like the plantation grounds," James murmured. "These Southern Belle gardens are not the beauties they seem."

"Then I have not—lost—my talent?" she said shakily.

"Hardly think so," he smiled, lacing his fingers in hers reassuringly. "I think we'll find a reason. There has to be a logical basis for this pervasive blank in time we seem to have fallen into."

"James the Practical," she said, her lips curving onto his in a crushing kiss.

"Smooch later. I'm going to fry here," Pighead expounded, literally trembling.

A pale glow announcing a new day filled a broken window. Daelyn pulled up a couple of the cabin floorboards, Pighead slid into the crawl space. "See you tonight, if you live," he said as she replaced the flooring.

"I never figured Pighead for shapeshifting into a winged horse," James remarked as they left the shack and slipped through the gardens.

"That kind of shapeshifting takes a depth of concentrated power most of us do not have," Daelyn said. "But he is an old one, and in his hatred for his own face, he spent centuries searching for the trigger to tap in to that power. When he shapes into what he feels is something magnificent, something beautiful, for awhile he escapes his stigma of plainness. In those moments, he is free."

James made no comment. While he might have been tempted to feel a drop of pity for the vampyre—he didn't. The vampyre had spent those centuries taking the blood of innocents, mortals, to enhance that power.

And his puny, half-assed agreement with the Shadow envoys did not erase those years.

James and Daelyn scouted the cabins but found no sensory trace of female occupancy—or any occupancy past or present.

The sun rose, spilling reams of golden light across the stones of the garden walkways. Beside the path, rose bushes full of the last blooms of the season encircled a stone fountain, and several plots had been hoed to ready the soil for fall plantings.

But in spite of the meticulous attempts at beauty, a pervasive gloominess prevailed.

James' eyes swept the dormers and French windows, and balconies of "the big house," searching for signs of the Roses, for signs of Katrien.

Daelyn was intent on the garden. In particular, one corner of the garden.

The wooden pickle barrel planter next to a stone bench seemed out of place in the midst of Roman style stone statuary, elegant fountains and ceramic planters. She touched the pickle barrel, ran her hand across the wood planks that formed it.

"This particular plantation had also had another view from its balconies, of the sea," she said slowly as James moved beside her. "One terrible, fateful night."

She pressed the palm of her hand to the wood and gasped. "Screams. Cries. Carried over the waves. Helplessness, shouts for help, a horror of cries lost on the waves, from mortals."

James yanked her hand away. She was collapsing from the mental onslaught of terror and fear traveling through the wood.

He held her gently in his arms and lowered her to the stone bench. "Easy, Daelyn. Take a moment to recover."

"Over one hundred people drowned, others died from being burned," she continued to relate in floating gasps. "A shipwreck. A terrible shipwreck, James, in a terrible storm that swept in just as they were celebrating because they could see the shoreline. So— close to home."

A lightning bolt had struck the stern as an unforgiving sea storm clawed at the ship with tenacity.

In the aftermath, the barrel had rolled in on the tide, drifting onto the beach, along with a flotsam of luggage, burnt wood, and bits of cloth, the only eulogy the dead would receive.

She pressed her fingertips against a knothole in the planter. "The groundskeepers who tended this garden believed the house and the grounds were haunted by the ghosts of the ship's passengers," she breathed. "There were stories that a passerby would sometimes appear walking on the road to the house, holding out his ticket, trying to hitch a ride. Another would present his passport, a desperate look on his dead face as he would insist he was just trying to get home."

But the only ghost James saw coming up the road today toward them was the Victorian apparition twirling his cane, whistling his melancholy tune, and sauntering nonchalantly toward the garden and the bench.

"Who was tending the garden, Daelyn?" James asked urgently, one eye on the ghost. "Slaves?"

She pressed her cheek against his. "No slaves tended that barrel. A paid gardener's hand tended these grounds." She paused. "But there was something—something about him. He wasn't just a gardener."

Her hand dropped away, weakened from precog contact.

"Come on back to the present slowly, Daelyn," James whispered, cradling her in his arms. "Take your time. No Realm newbie is going to attack us in full sun."

As Daelyn rested in his arms, James smoothed the lines of distress that had appeared on her forehead. "Looks like you got an emotional double whammy." She was experiencing the intensity of the past through the emotions of a Valkyrie, far more intense than the pencil shavings she had felt as a vampyre.

And it was a rough crossing.

"We need to find your sister," she said imperatively. "I'll be all right."

Hand in hand, clinging hard as though even the slice of a sunray might separate them, James and Daelyn ran through the gardens and across the lawn toward the megalithic house.

The ghost sat on the bench, legs crossed, and watched them.

All may not be as it seems, he sent on a frosty gust of breath, and faded.

"We need to head for the English basement," James directed Daelyn. "We can enter the house from beneath the main floors through the basement entrance."

A wing had been added recently on the west side of the mansion. The boards were different, wider, and not as weathered. On the east, however, the edge of a narrow horizontal window close to the ground indicated the older English basement.

"English basements, known as garden apartments, are partially above and partially below ground," James said. "The basements served as kitchens, or servants' dining rooms, or wood storage. Or often, as quarters for working class tenants. They had their own entrance separate from the rest of the house."

"I like your daddy's Texas alfalfa farm a hell of a lot better than these southern antique doll houses," Daelyn said as she ran with him from the garden.

But just as suddenly, she was grabbing his arm, pulling him to a stop.

"There's someone in that basement." She froze. "And opening the door."

James' hand swept to his belt pack.

An ankle-length blue cape appeared on the steps in the basement doorway alcove, and a young woman began making her way across the lawn toward the garden, a basket on her arm.

A mass of black-brown curls fell across the back of the cape.

"Katie?" Daelyn called out in surprise.

She gasped, and fled back into the house.

"She's put on a little weight," Daelyn remarked. James yanked her behind the corner of the house to hide. They kept their backs to the brick until Daelyn felt assured no one had been warned of their presence.

James entered the lower level of the house carefully, stakes drawn.

The basement appeared to be empty, one of those no-longer-used Civil War era oversized cellars with an oversized kitchen fireplace and one of those brick-lined sub-floor pits that no one knew exactly what the hell they were ever really used for.

Just a big hole in the floor.

Except that this one had hardwood boards forming the bottom instead of dirt.

The pit was about six feet deep. Bracing his hands on the edge of one of the rectangular sides, James eased down to the bottom of the pit, then took a Maglite from his pack. Kneeling on one knee, he worked a corner of a floor board free, and shined the light's tiny but powerful beam in under the slit.

"Don't tell me, more friggin' tunnels," Daelyn moaned down to him.

"A deep shaft," James said. "And ..."

Quickly replacing the board, James reached up, grasped the edge of the pit, and leaped out. "We need to hurry," he said, breathing hard.

25.

"Elaborate, mahogany, gilt edged caskets all over the place on granite slabs, and six-sided coffins stacked on stone shelving at least three high from wall to wall," James said.

A living morgue.

"We could grab the girls and then torch the place, but the pit and the cave room underneath are deep enough that the fire would simply pass over the sub-floor pit and they would be untouched," he continued.

"I'm not a real big fan of fire anyway," Daelyn shuddered. "How about we just grab and go?"

Her voice was pleading, begging him to leave, and leave before the New Royals awakened—

The blue mist forming a pale cloud in her eyes betrayed she would not be able to bear seeing him tortured …

James shone the Maglite around the basement service room, toward a recessed door beside a shelf of canned goods.

All may not be as it seems.

He continued shining the light around the room.

Another set of door hinges glinted in the Maglite's beam from behind the shelves.

"I suppose we're choosing door number two?" Daelyn sighed as he began clearing cans and jars from the shelves.

In flashing, almost invisible movements, she whipped back and forth in a burst of wind that tussled his hair, and emptied the shelves.

Then she slid the heavy shelving to the side with a single push, exposing a door bolted with multiple locks. Daelyn crushed the bolts, broke the locks.

"Well, that was easy," James grinned, as he stood more than a little in awe of her.

"So if I need any renovations, can I call on you?" he teased.

"You don't need any renovations," she smiled coyly, drawing her forefinger with a light upward stroke along his zipper.

"A kiss for luck?" She crushed against him, and poured her heart into her kiss. So he would know how deeply she loved him—and wanted him to live. "I don't want to have to take you to Valhalla tonight," she whispered. "This Valkyrie doesn't want to hold a dead warrior in her arms. I plan to keep you alive, James Lauren."

Fire was still racing through James' veins from her kiss as he pushed the door open and they leaped through to the other side, stakes blazing.

"Well, gee, what do you know? Tunnels," Daelyn said. They stopped dead, enveloped by a stone and dirt corridor running under the length of the house.

A sparse scattering of lanterns mounted to the walls at intervals offered shadow-filled bits of dim light through the dank passage-way, creating a ghostly semi-dark that outlined the rough cut of the arched roofing and a couple of side rooms.

The cobwebby lanterns were old, rusty, dating back to the plantation's younger years, dating back to the Civil War.

James took one of the lanterns from an iron wall hanger, and lengthened the wick to shed stronger light while he took a few guarded steps to get a closer look at the strange tunnel.

"We get to go spelunking again," Daelyn said in a falsely bright tone, rolling her eyes.

They ventured a little farther.

And discovered puzzling oddities—a couple of dusty, crumbling apple crates, an old trunk with a lid falling off the hinges, a moth-eaten afghan of unidentifiable origin.

And a dirt encrusted corn cob doll.

Had this been a secret play room?

Daelyn picked up a bit cloth, rubbed it gingerly between her fingers. Then drew her hand across the lid of the trunk, and held the doll.

"There was a little girl sitting on this trunk," she said. "A fright-ened little girl. Scared to even breathe as she listened to the silence around her, a horror of absolute silence in a pitch black world. She was listening for hard, angry boot steps, boots that would reveal the railroad had been betrayed." Her eyes searched the depths of the tunnel, puzzled. "Railroad? I see no signs rails were ever here." She drew her hand across the earthen tunnel wall. "Yet I feel beings moving past these walls of unrest, clinging to them as though to a lifeline."

"Things are not as they seem," James murmured, his eyes busy. Then he knew. The lantern lit corridor had been hewn for a single purpose.

"The underground railroad. This was part of the underground railroad to help runaway slaves escape to the north."

"That's why I didn't feel anything in the cabins," Daelyn said. "They were part of a façade. No one ever lived in them. This plantation was loyal to the confederacy in appearances only. In reality, southern unionists."

"How would they have hid the fact they had no slaves living here?" James exclaimed in genuine surprise.

"There's no time for a history tour of the artifacts to find out," she said. "The day is waning, James."

"Do you feel Katie in anything?" James asked urgently. The name seemed so easy to say now, comfortable, as though he had been saying it all his life. The young woman in the cape had made that name a reality. And she was somewhere above them in this house. Speaking her name sealed the reality of her presence for him. It felt so natural for him to speak of her.

"I don't sense that she's been anywhere near this dark hall," Daelyn said. "Only in the basement. I also felt the pickle barrel gardener's touch in the basement, on the canning shelves and the hidden door. His touch was in the dust, the Civil War was in the dust."

"Speaking of dust," James said. Every fiber of his being was suddenly warming as thought hit with hot spots. His muscles tensed, a singular warning as all his senses blended. A vampyre was near. A familiar vampyre.

"I sense him also," Daelyn said in a lowered voice.

James lifted the lantern high, throwing light into the darker depths of the tunnel. "Show yourself, Nicholai."

The almost invisible brush of a wing along a wall, and the Russian vampyre materialized.

He was dressed totally in black, right down to his boots, except for the imperial gold braided, deep purple cape he flaunted, normally reserved for select Realm rulers.

James briefly wondered who he had killed for it.

His black satin shirt was unbuttoned all the way to his waist.

"The gardener was the plantation's only groundskeeper, by the way," he directed at Daelyn as he came toward them.

Catching a golden edge of the cape in his hand, he carried himself with the demeanor of one who believed himself a god.

Roman Caesars had nothing on the proud Nicholai.

"A sympathizer was hired as a groundskeeper," he continued. "By day he tended the gardens and lawn, by night he was a lookout while the Jamaican refugees were being brought in across the grounds."

Nicholai leaned against the wall and smiled at them as though by his very presence he was bestowing benevolence on them—or malevolence.

That twisted, secretive smile told James clearly the Russian had the upper hand in something godawful and was about to share it with them.

Sweeping the cape to cover his right shoulder, Nicholai let his eyes travel over Daelyn's lithe body. "The so-called gardener also took them food and water while they were in this tunnel waiting for their guide. Some of them, however, chose to stay and help keep up the pretense of oh-so-genteel southern living so others could ride the 'rails' to freedom. They lived in the west wing of the house, appearing as needed for the faux "slave owner," when company came calling. They would work the fields, and keep up appearances by making like house maids and cooks ..."

"How do you know all this?" Daelyn asked, perpetually suspicious, and rightly so, of anything that came out of the Vanguard's mouth.

"I used to live down the road," he said. "I know every secret passageway in this house. The owner thought I was the perfect neighbor. Never nosy. Little did he know how often I was in the walls. The house I owned, buried in a thick woods only a fool would enter, was also perfect. The perfect hiding place, unnoticed, as I was unnoticed. A few friends and I could come and go, travel and return as we pleased. Or visit the war, see who was winning and who was losing the battle. Battlefields are rich in nutrients, an overflowing source of vitamins A, K, C, D and platelets."

James' hatred of the arrogant vampyre flared, his breathing became hard, and as his anger swept through his eyes, they became fiery brown chasms.

"Don't get your bolts all twisted in your crossbow string, Van Helsing. I didn't prick the healthy 'Damn Yankees' or 'Johnny Rebs'. Only the wounded. They were dying anyway." Nicholai shrugged. His emotions were as lackluster dead as his soul when it came to mortals. "But we were very fair in our selections. We made no distinction between North and South. We did not influence the outcome of the war either way. The present conflict, however, is needing a little outside intervention."

Here it comes, James thought. *He's about to place his chips on the table.*

"Your little sister is on the second story, and the second story is protected by a bevy of minions."

"What are you wanting, Nicholai?" James demanded, his fingers itching to grasp a stake and lunge.

"Dracula's head on a platter."

Nicholai shifted his weight against the wall, crossed his arms on his half-bare chest. As his eyes moved from Daelyn to James, he arched an eyebrow. Their affection was unconcealed. "Does she kiss pretty good, Crossbow?" he grinned, with a sly sideways glance at Daelyn.

James was silent.

Nicholai laughed, a guttural dry laugh that seemed to come from a hollow hole in the ground. "Pretty good, ha! She's a hell fire kisser, and you want to be with her. You want to thread with her. You want to be a part of her innermost being. Rather dangerous thoughts for a slayer of your caliber."

He leaned his chin on his hand and his eyes narrowed into two amber points as he zeroed in on James' gaze. "And do you want to share blood with her, James Lauren, son of Van Helsing?"

James was silent.

Every word flowing from the master vampyre's lips was melting the walls, deepening the temptation James already struggled with. And Nicholai sliced into his damaged will like Excalibur into stone. By playing on James' weakness for the sable-haired beauty, he was weakening his slayer's strength. The harsh words of truth struck at

James' heart.

Nicholai released his power to penetrate the hot, warm tunnel air.

And penetrate James's thoughts.

"Stop it, Nicholai!" Daelyn demanded angrily, knowing the spell he was trying to cast.

James exhaled deeply, slowly. "I'm all right."

"Are you thinking you could just sort of share a small, insignificant exchange with her, and you could survive the blood blow and only become sort of a vampyre?" Nicholai continued relentlessly. "Think again. A blood union with this one would be the beginning and end of your desire. She is a vampyre queen. The beginning of dead desire." His eyes filled with laughter. "But look on the bright side. We could all be gloriously wicked killers together!"

The laughter spilled out raucously past his lips in a harsh, brittle sound. "She's taken that control you're so wickedly proud of and smashed and spattered you like roadkill." He paused and inhaled a deep amused breath. "You want to have your Daelyn cake and eat it, too."

James glanced at Daelyn. Hurt shone in her eyes.

"You could be assigned to another envoy where you would be invaluable and not have to worry about me becoming a fatal attraction," James said softly, turning to her.

"Am I the one who's worried?" she popped back.

Nicholai's laughter filled the entire earthen tunnel.

26.

Fifty-two hundred square feet of southern living was filled with secret passageways and hidden rooms. Nicholai shared knowledge of only one.

"Past the second door in the basement there's a breakfast nook off the main kitchen," he said. "The high bench that appears built into the wall conceals a passageway. The spring latch is under the seat in the back and appears to be nothing more than a corner brace. The bench will move to the side. Behind the panel, a set of stairs leads straight to her room. It's not a journey for everyone. The steps are steep, and the passageway black as your desire for Gypsy Rose there." He picked a bit of lint from his cape. "Don't use it."

Both James and Daelyn looked at him in shock—and open suspicion.

"You tell us how to find my sister, then tell us not to go that way," James said drily. "Are you toying with us, sitting here chewing the fat, buying time till dusk when the Royals will awaken?"

"The count didn't buy this place sight unseen," Nicholai warned him sharply, harshly. "He knows every crevice and knothole. And he knows you would probably find that passageway. He'll have guards stationed at every one of those crevices and knotholes. He'll trap you on those stairs and drink you into oblivion and you'll never have your Daelyn dream. You start looking for secret passageways, slayer, and the only passageway you'll find is a permanent one out."

And Dracula will also die, James thought. As he looked at Daelyn, he knew she was thinking the same thought.

"I guess you're about to suggest an alternative?" Daelyn said.

"Straight up the main staircase," he responded soberly, his tone resolute.

"Storm the castle," Daelyn laughed, then her lips pursed and her eyes settled on him in two hard blue points as she realized he was serious. "You may think yourself a god and invincible, Nicholai, but we are not quite so omnipotent."

"You are vampyre," he smiled, and held out his cape-draped hand. "Join me, Daelyn. I have plans."

"Do your plans include Jane Weston? Yes, I thought so."

His eyes had betrayed him. Jane was his reason for every step he took, every plan, every scheme he plotted.

"There's always room for one more," he grinned.

"Not on Jane's bed," she retorted.

Nicholai turned his attention to James. "Your little Katie's room is at the end of the west wing. All the Roses are in the west wing. Odd irony for this house, isn't it? Dracula has twisted its purity to fit his purpose. Where there were no slaves, he enslaves. The house dedicated to Heaven is now being redesigned—for Hell."

James bit his lip to keep from leaping and grabbing the vampyre by the throat and demanding he stop fart-assing around and get to the crux of the plan. His heart was rampant to save the Rose who was of his blood. She was his only link to the birth mother who had traveled time to save him.

Nicholai was enjoyably taking his own sweet time, knowing he was prolonging James' heart's agony. Having the famed cross-bow slayer totally at his mercy inordinately pleased him. Begrudgingly, James admitted to himself Nicholai was right about the hidden construction within the plantation home. As soon as Dracula sensed Katrien was being rescued, he would have every New Royal awake and cordoning off the entire structure.

Katie could only be rescued by stealth. What in hell was Nicholai thinking? Straight up the staircase? He was a soldier, he should be well-versed in military tactics.

"Daelyn will storm the castle, and create a breach in their security," Nicholai smiled, with a glance toward her. "A beautiful breach, wouldn't you say?"

"I'd say you were insane," she countered.

"*Au contraire*," Nicholai said. "You can walk right in sporting a sexy little outfit and announce you have returned, victorious with your human trophy, and every minionhead will spin one hundred, eighty degrees just to glimpse you, victory be damned. You will be dragging your trophy with you, the son of Van Helsing, torn and bleeding and punctured and appearing to be half-dead." He paused and grinned. "Actually, we do have a betting pool going on you, Daelyn, on when you will completely lose it and leap on him. Considering your history, I put a few dollars on two days from now."

"You're making sport of me?" she threw at him in an angry, indignant cry, and she would have flown at him and scratched him with her nails if James had not stepped in front of her.

"Forget it, Blues. It's Nicholai, remember? Rotten to the core?"

The vampyre only laughed. Then his eyes became deadly sober and narrowed in on him like a missile. "You would be wise to stick to business, slayer. They can kill you in an instant if they discover your weakness. Not to mention what their phantoms could do to you. Surely you remember your last run-in with one?"

James remembered his last encounter with a phantom. Not much fun, and a hell of a lot of terror. A fire phantom.

"Now. While you have the minions' attention otherwise engaged," Nicholai continued, "I would like to say a few of my friends and I would arrive in a visit that appears to incidentally coincide with your entrance, act like we're going to arrest you and slit their throats instead. But—we're not. We're simply going to arrive in the nick of time to really arrest you."

"The hell you say," James said flatly.

"Well, that's not a big plus for us, is it?" Daelyn said smartly, still stinging from knowing the vanguards had made sport of her. They had probably laughed and made her the brunt of table jokes. Too bad they hadn't laughed their heads off.

"You'll have to trust me," he said. "And the rest—will be history." Briefly, he described the details of a plan that sounded incredulous, but just might work to free the Roses and give him what he wanted—a dead Dracula.

"The rub is your face looks too smooth, slayer boy," Nicholai said. "That one bruise won't cut it. Your vamp there needs to smash you up a bit. Or I can do the honors."

James held out his hand to halt his advance. "I want to talk to her. In private."

The vampyre shrugged, but as he receded into the darker reaches of the tunnel, he warned, "Don't take too long. Twilight is breaking."

James pulled Daelyn aside into a low ceilinged recess. "Can you block him so he can't hear us?"

"Somewhat. He's powerful, James. You can't imagine."

"You have the power of the Valkyries, Daelyn. Look within you."

She sealed them into the recess in a shade of shadowy privacy.

"About those things he said," James began.

"Is that what you want, James? Vampirism? With me? Was he telling the truth? You did not deny his words." She began wringing her hands, being pulled in directions that left her agonizing. Was she going to have to choose between her newfound life of redemptive light that had just begun to flower, and James?

He took her hand, as though reading her thoughts, and gazed calmly into the face of pale perfect dawn he had grown to love, but now creased with too many lines of misgiving. "There is always temptation to taste the darkness, Daelyn. It comes with the territory. But I will never ask you, or let you, exchange life for life's blood with me."

"Why? Because you do not want me to lose my life?" she asked, confused by him, by his words.

He smoothed her hair away from her cheeks, and held her face in the warmth of his hands. "Because I don't want you to lose your dance in the sunlight."

She placed her hand over his, immersing her fingertips in the deep warmth. "Am I the torment of your heart, James?"

"That you are, partner," he said. He pressed his cheek to her hair, close to her ear, and his voice became whispery. "I won't deny I'm captured by you, Daelyn. I knew I would be the moment you invited me into those eyes and I accepted. But we are not imprisoned, only in union. We have not exchanged blood vows."

"You're part of my being," she returned, melting into the strong, hard muscles of his chest. "What do we do?"

He leaned back slightly, and grinned his curvy grin. "A room at the Luxor with a lovely buffet and champagne after we escape sounds nice."

She kissed him, and he felt a slight touch of wet on his cheek, as though a raindrop had fallen there then smeared as her face touched his.

A single tear.

"If we don't hit them where it hurts soon," Nicholai's stern voice echoed through the tunnel, "we won't have a leg to stand on—literally. And little sister will be gone with the wind in Dracula's wings." He was suddenly in front of the little alcove. He could move like lightning when he flashed. "That's a dramatization, of course. He doesn't have any. Doesn't need them. I don't either, but I like 'em. They have a—movieland—effect, don't you think?"

They turned to him, to nine feet of ink black wingspan.

"Now I need to hit you where it hurts," Nicholai grinned at James as he folded his wings.

"Go for it," James said coldly, tightening.

Nicholai's fist curled into a hard ball. "You don't know how long I've wanted to do this," he said, slamming him with a painful jab to the jaw.

James reeled back, but held his stance. Nicholai gave him two more blows, careful, enough to make him bleed and bruise but not break.

"That's enough!" Daelyn said, stepping between them as he raised his fist to deliver another blow.

"Damn! I enjoyed that!" Nicholai laughed as he moved back, rubbed his knuckles in satisfaction and appraised his handiwork.

James eyes were hardened brown rocks. He hated this vampyre, but he hated not being able to rescue his sister more.

"We can't fake punctures in your neck," Nicholai said. "For that you'll need your lovely neck pricker there."

Daelyn's eyes darted to James. "I—can't," she said, barely above a whisper.

"Oh, hell. A small prick won't kill him," Nicholai said, then his lips formed a twisted smile. "Unless, of course, you mean you would lose control. Or would—he?" He laughed scornfully.

Her eyes wordlessly pleaded with James to tell her what to do.

"Well, I sure as hell can prick the prick," Nicholai finally said, impatient. He stepped forward and let his fangs drop.

"You can't, either," James said. "As much as I would like to let you."

The vampyre reared back, his eyes flaming into brittle bricks as he comprehended James' words.

"But I can," a voice said behind them.

Pighead stood just inside the basement doorway, and as he

nodded knowingly to James, James knew he was remembering the night club incident.

He knew he would die.

"Couldn't sleep," Pighead said, coming full into the tunnel. "Even the sleep of the dead, knowing those damned Royals were in caskets somewhere on the grounds. Every whistle of the wind through those drafty walls and creak in the floor boards disturbed me."

"They are below us," Daelyn said.

"Figures," Pighead shuddered, then he turned to James. "I'm a coward. Everyone knows that. I've always been a coward. Maybe this is my chance. I can be a hero. I can be—brave, or at least remembered. Who knows? Maybe I will even find redemption."

He let his fangs drop. Nicholai stepped aside, but a flicker of pain crossed through his eyes. He had remembered, though only for a short space of time, what it was like.

To be holy.

James gritted his teeth, pulled down the collar of his shirt and held on for one hell of a painful ride. No vamp could mesmerize him forcefully, so he knew he would feel the full impact of the pain and the force of the draw, not counting the joining of being to being, and the loss of life force.

"Cry God for Harry, England, and whatever the hell the rest of that phrase is," Pighead said, his power rising as he took James by the shoulders. "Once more unto the breach. No one is immortal."

The punctures were two sharp drills but not enough blood taken to deeply weaken him.

"Wow," Pighead said as he released him. His eyes were glowing from the impact of slayer's blood in his veins. Especially the slayer who was the son of Abraham Van Helsing. "Wow. Incredible. Who knew? It's like …"

He succumbed, collapsing to the floor with barely a life glow left in his eyes.

Nicholai stared at James, or rather at his blood-stained collar and the holes in his neck still pulsing with seepage that trickled down his neck.

He wiped his hand across his mouth, wiping away the drool. His fangs were out. His eyes bulged. He was wanting what the outcast vampyre had experienced, wanting, but knowing he could not, would not. He was now affirmed in his suspicions that Van Helsing's son carried tainted blood. He visibly fought for control, tightening his muscles as he hissed and groaned, a wail from the soulless abyss within him.

The scent of spilled slayer blood was too strong. He swept forward as instincts ruled. Lifted his hands, but dropped back as his gaze again fell on Pighead, dying in the dirt—cold, hard dirt and rocks.

He backed off.

"What? You don't want a taste?" James scoffed.

"If I die at all, it will be more glorious than that," Nicholai said, pointing at Pighead. "I don't intend to die a cold, uncelebrated death in the dirt. In fact, I don't intend to die at all. Ever. Remember that."

"I'll remember," James said drily.

Pushing her hair out of the way, from her shoulder to her back, Daelyn knelt tenderly beside Pighead and tears spilled from her eyes. "Don't be afraid," she whispered. "Tonight you will be in the halls of Valhalla. The dark angels cannot take you. You belong to Heaven now."

As he heard her words, Nicholai shrank from her in shock, horrified, his eyes filling with instinctive fear at even being near her. His face contorted with the agonies of his own soul. "You're a Valkyrie!" He could barely utter the word.

She looked up at him, and a slight aura, like pale light through a cloud, touched her wings. "There is still hope for you, Nicholai. I sense your battle with your own demons."

"I do not want your hope. Or your pity," he retorted, slinging his cape across his chest defensively, proudly.

Daelyn felt Pighead's hand touch hers, and she turned her attention back to him, holding his gaze in her own, to ease his suffering.

"Will I be—magnificent?" he asked. "Not quite—so ugly?"

"You are magnificent."

"You made me feel—special, a part of the fun," he said. "You—danced—with me when no one else would." He gave her a weak smile, then his eyes turned inward.

Daelyn's breath released in a silent sob of agony, untold grips of sorrow. She looked up helplessly at James, and held her hands outward in a hopeless gesture, her cheeks streaming with wet tributaries. "Is this what it will be like? This pain? This agony in my heart? I don't think I can bear it."

"It's been awhile since you felt mortal emotion. And you were just hit with a double dose because of what you are becoming." He held out his hand to her and lifted her from the floor, then placed his fingertips tenderly under her chin. "There are great rewards as well as pain, Daelyn, but you have a debt to the dead you must also pay."

She clung to him, trembling.

A glistening, beads of shimmer, floated suddenly into their vision, ribboning toward them through the tunnel. Daelyn drew away and gazed in awe as the beads became golden streams and surrounded Pighead's body.

Then he was gone.

It was as though he had never been. No sign, no trace of his existence was left on the tunnel floor.

"Who was he?" James asked as the last of the light streams faded. "Do you know anything about him at all?"

Both Nicholai and Daelyn shrugged. They knew nothing of his mortal past. Or of his vampyre past.

The being who had just given his life to save a slayer's sister and a Valkyrie and possibly the whole mortal world, had died the unknown soldier.

27.

Dragging James by the hair of his head, Daelyn smacked open the massive, oak double doors of the plantation house, and hauled him inside the foyer.

The plantation home had been handsomely refurbished by its new owner. A ballroom with chandeliers draped in teardrop crystals led off to the right, and red velvet curtains draped the windows from floor to ceiling. The floor was black, to give the illusion of stepping into a well as you stepped into the room.

The grand staircase was carpeted in a rich red, and becoming quite busy. Minions who had heard Daelyn's rowdy entrance had come running along the upper story banister to form ranks on the stairs.

"I've returned. With a prize. The mortal world sucks. Where's the Count?" she announced loudly, confidently, in a commanding voice toward them.

She dropped the slayer feigning unconsciousness with a "plop" on the floor. "And this mortal is mine to claim when the Count has no further use for him. So don't get any ideas of selling him to the highest bidder."

These vampyre minions were not the trance-eyed, knock-kneed crab walkers usually seen catching flies as they trudged behind their vampyre masters. These serviles were sharp-eyed, trained defenders of the Realm. But they were rather trance-eyed as they enjoyed her short, ripped skirt and scrap of blouse barely covering her assets.

"Looks like he gave you a run for your money," one of them laughed, ogling her.

He wasn't much taller than herself, with sunken eyes, but his jawline was square, his face clean shaven. She doubted he ate bugs.

"Yeah, well, looks like my money was well spent," she bounced back.

Keep their attention, keep their eyes on you, Daelyn thought. *Just for a few more minutes.*

She gasped. Katrien was making her way to the second story balustrade, edging between the minions to peer over the banister rail.

This was not a good idea, Daelyn thought desperately. *Where are you?* she threaded angrily across the silent telepathic portals toward Nicholai.

Saving your dammed Roses! He threaded back, just as angry. *We're in their rooms and herding them into the wall passageways. Keep those minions busy! I haven't found Van Helsing's sister yet!*

You can't find her because she's—here! On the damned, friggin' landing!

Daelyn glanced quickly at the floor, to see if James had seen his sister.

He was faced away from the stairs, with his knees curled to his chest, his eyes closed. He was playing his role, unmoving, immobile.

Katrien's long, loose black curls fell past her shoulders and to the waist of her forest green gown as she leaned farther over the rail. She was looking at James, distressed, then her blue eyes shot to Daelyn—and darkened in abject hatred.

"Get back to your room!" the ogling minion ordered harshly.

Yes, go back to your room, Daelyn thought hopelessly. This plan was falling apart faster than cracking ice.

The minion suddenly grabbed the young girl by the upper arm and whisked her away, forcing her down the hallway.

She tried to wrench free, fighting her captor's grasp, looking back, distraught.

Her small form disappeared into the midst of a group of vampyres who were suddenly filling the halls and stairway.

The Vanguards.

Loyal to Nicholai, they stood aside as he walked through them, flaunting his garishly beautiful cape. His steps were hard, and directed toward Daelyn.

With only a slight downward glance of scorn thrown at James, lying prostrate on the floor, he stood in front of her. "You and your mortal paramour are confiscated. By order of the Realm."

"You—can't be serious," she sputtered.

He waved a hand of command toward two of his soldiers. "Take them to the south room at the end of the upstairs hallway and double bolt the door."

A tall minion, bald and surly, with a large bone structure, and ample muscles covering those bones, marched down the stairs and stood defiantly before the Captain of the Vanguards. "She is to be killed. I have received no orders that she was to be detained."

"You just did," Nicholai said in a controlled, cold voice.

With a short bow, the minion guard turned and ordered his men to return to their posts outside the Roses' rooms. Minions did not dare question this vampyre's orders. He killed at will.

Fools, Nicholai threaded to Daelyn, watching them with contempt. *It will be hours before they know the ladies of the court have gone.*

And in the meantime? Daelyn asked.

You're detained. He grinned. *And when the Roses are discovered missing, you and Crossbow there are going to get blamed with the whole thing. The Count will be screaming at the top of his lungs, and everyone will be running all over the plantation in abject terror of him looking for the Roses and your accomplices. The Count will be demanding of Van Helsing to know where his Shadow troupe has taken them. There will be an inquisition, a public trial, the Count will be attendance ... and, oh yes, I will have a place of honor in his court and be hailed as a hero for arriving in the nick of time to take the famed slayer "prince" prisoner. Good times, you and I, yes, Daelyn? If the Count is true to form, he will offer Crossbow to Andre DuPre in exchange for the return of his Rose garden, what do you think?*

I think you're mad.

He laughed, raucously, and they ascended the stairs.

Two vanguards picked up a limp James and took up the rear.

Once in the room, the two guards tossed him to the floor and left. Nicholai alone remained, and closed the door firmly.

"Damn. I've been slammed, rammed and slung like a rag," James said, rubbing his neck and shoulders as he got up from the floor. "Not to mention my face being a battering ram and I had the hell bit out of me."

"Or the hell bit into you," Nicholai smirked, lingering in the room only long enough to thread quickly with the Valkyrie. *Do not tell your mortal lover we were unable to include his sister in the exodus. He will no doubt jump the gun and indulge his hero complex by trying to rescue her. We need him to stay put until I figure out how to get her out without raising suspicion that I'm in any way involved. Besides the fact if he goes running around all over the house dripping blood from the punctures in his neck, someone's bound to get hungry.*

He swept from the room, and the sound of heavy bolts locking into place followed his departure.

"Not even a warm cookie or chocolate mint in Hotel Dracula before we're secured for the night?"

Daelyn looked around the room. "Typical jail cell fare. Sparse. Conventional iron décor. A bed with an iron bedstead, a chair with iron grillwork on the back and iron legs, a padded iron bench, an open, iron shelf—and iron bars on the windows."

"I don't have to ask why there's no wood," James said. "I guess they wouldn't want anyone whittling to pass the time while incarcerated."

James rubbed the back of his neck, then gingerly touched the punctures in his neck.

Daelyn gazed at them, wondering how deeply Pighead had touched him with fire before he released him. "How do you feel?"

"A little hazy. Like I'm walking two worlds. The corridor was a fog."

The venom had seeped. "Are you becoming a vampyre?" she asked, feeling a little panicky.

"I needed the wounds burned clean, but he didn't sink long enough to do major damage. The haze will fade." He paused. "Splashing some cold water on my face would probably help."

Daelyn opened a door in the room she thought might be a bathroom. It was. Simple but functional with a plain white cabinet sink and toilet, and an old-fashioned clawfoot tub. No fresh smelling shower gels or soft towels draped over the edge of the tub, just a bar of plain soap on the sink.

The walls were painted pantyhose beige and the paint was peeling. She closed the door with a sigh. There was nothing of beauty here, not even anything that could pass for pretty. Just—functional. Sitting on the edge of the bed, she put her hands in her lap, remembered her beautiful home, and her shoulders slumped unhappily.

"I just want to go home," she sobbed suddenly, her eyes wells of blue water. "I was a college student, and working, and making a life for myself." She put her head in her hands and sobbed openly.

James sat down beside her, to comfort her.

"I want to go back to my apartment," she continued sobbing, leaning against his shoulder, "with lots of oak and windows, and George …"

"George?" James asked, an eyebrow raised. She had never mentioned a boyfriend.

"My—cat."

"You had a cat?"

"Until he disappeared," she said between sobs.

"I'll get you another one," James promised. He rubbed the wet from her cheeks. She had lost everything. She could damn well at least have a cat, if he had anything to say about it. Somebody should know of a feline that needed a home.

"You could probably use some warm water on your face and sore muscles," Daelyn said, forcing a small smile for him as she drew her fingertips across the bruises on his jawline.

"You're right, I could. Doesn't look like we're going anywhere for awhile, anyway. There's going to be one hell of a commotion in the hallway when it's discovered all those rooms are empty."

All but one, Daelyn thought darkly.

The one room we came here to empty.

Torn with guilt at keeping Katrien's presence a secret, Daelyn wrestled with whether to tell him or remain silent as Nicholai had warned her. He deserved to know …

"Try to thread to me, Blues," James said unexpectedly, interrupting the thoughts kick boxing her heart.

"Thread?" she asked in surprise.

"I think Pighead may have left me a temporary gift."

"What do you want me to thread?"

"Anything. The weather. Nicholai has a fat ass."

She giggled, her tears dissipated, then her eyebrows came together as she thought hard. When she looked up, her thoughts were in her eyes.

Do you still—want me, James?

He took her hands in his. "I want you, Daelyn."

"Whoa," she murmured. He had caught her thread. Easily. "How long do you think it will last?"

He shrugged. "Hard to say. But maybe we can make good use of it while we're being strung along by that damned master of the night until he gets what he wants and we can get Katrien and get out of here."

At the mention of his sister's name, said with so much affection, Daelyn swallowed hard. *Will James still want me when he discovers the secret I'm keeping?* she wondered helplessly.

"I'll get a quick wash down. You should probably get daysleep," James said. "You look like this whole barrel of pig crap has been a drain on you, and it's been hours since you slept. If you go off routine, you could fall out in the middle of a battle. Everyone will be fighting like hell while you're out cold on the ground taking a snooze." He laughed lightly and lifted her spirits.

She climbed in under the beige bed covers while James headed for the bathroom, hoping the faucet actually worked and there might be some water in the groaning pipes.

There was. A warm stream was soon flowing into the sink. James took off his shirt, soaked the wash cloth and let the liquid penetrate his face wounds and overworked, aching shoulder muscles. Then he rubbed the bar of soap into a lather, gritted his teeth, and scraped the raw wounds in his neck.

A slight sound, like a quick bump, emitted from within the wall next him, but he sensed no threat.

A mouse possibly, or a skunk or opossum that had found its way into one of the secret passages and was now lost in the walls.

The crossbow slayer could not know that there was indeed a secret passage on the other side of that beige painted wall, a walkway in the walls leading to the bolted bedroom—from the room housing Katrien.

She had made her way through the walls—to kill.

28.

The watery soak cleared the lingering webs from Pighead's bite, and James felt the haze dissipating from being in blood union with a vampyre longer than was safe mentally.

His thoughts now clearing, he hurriedly dried off with a rough towel that felt like it had never known fabric softener, and smelled of strong bleach. He wanted to return to the bedroom quickly, to keep vigil over his Valkyrie. He didn't like the way Nicholai looked at her now, knowing what she was.

The Vanguard wanted to taste her, have Valkyrie blood in his veins. James had sensed his dark desire to force her to submit to him as plain as Saturday rain. Somehow in this unholy alliance, he had a feeling Nicholai was going to try to find a way to make her submission to him part of the bargain to give him Katrien.

Nicholai just wouldn't let an opportunity like that go by.

It was his nature.

James pushed the bathroom door open and stepped out to watch over the sleeping beauty who had grand slammed her way into his life.

His gaze fell on the bed—in horror.

Agony tore through James' heart, ripping at his very soul. The stake hovered no more than a few inches over the Valkyrie's heart as she lie in daysleep, and was about to descend. A point like a needle was going to erase Daelyn's existence. And the polished hand grip was notched to allow the small, determined fingers that held it to have a firm, unflinching grasp that would send it to its destination without error.

The young woman gripping the stake with both hands was staring intently down into the vampyre's face.

James was fearful to speak, fearful the sudden distraction would startle her and she would drop the stake. If it fell, it would fall straight down. Point down.

He also knew he could not make the far leap across the room that he would need to knock it from her grasp in time.

But he knew he could wake his Valkyrie.

Daelyn, wake up, but don't move, he threaded, reaching deep into the corridors of her death sleep. *Not even a centimeter. And open your eyes slowly. You have a stake over your heart and you don't want to startle the bearer of the weapon. Moan a little so she will be warned you are waking.*

Daelyn moaned, just slightly, then carefully, slowly opened her eyes.

And gasped.

"James!" she called in a helpless, terrified choke.

Easy, he threaded, taking a careful step away from the bathroom doorway and moving into the room.

The stake wavered, trembled. But Katrien, although terrified, did not look away from the vampyre, afraid she would strike if she even dared to blink. She tightened her grip on the stake. "Prince James? Are you here, in the room?" she voiced.

"Katrien. She is not the enemy. Release her. Please."

"She tried to kill you," she said, her tone vehement. "They tell me I have a brother. I have family. And she was going to take that away from me. Bleed you day by day, bleed your life from you drink by drink."

The needle broke skin. Daelyn's breath caught as a tiny splotch of red appeared on her blouse.

James! she screamed in a heart rending thread.

She could send nothing else. Her thoughts were numbed with fear.

As fast as he dared, James began moving toward his sister. "Let me have the stake, Katie. She's your friend. Trust me. Take away the stake and I'll explain. I want to get to know you. You're my sister. Let me be your brother. But not this way. I love her."

She dared to look away for a tiny second, and whipped a quick, stinging, dark glance toward him. "Are you bewitched? She's notorious!"

"Notoriously mine," he said with a weak smile, and held out his hand toward the stake.

"She bit you!" she cried, her attention rocketing back to the vampira, the stake poised once more to strike. And strike hard.

"No, she didn't. Another vampyre did this."

"I—don't understand."

"Give me the stake, Katie. We'll talk."

The needle lifted slightly.

Daelyn was breathing so hard and her chest rising and falling so rapidly it appeared her heart would burst even without being staked.

James eased the stake from his sister's hand as she turned her wounded, uncertain, sapphire eyes to his.

Daelyn rolled and leaped away from the wicked wood, tumbling out of the bed, her eyes wide, wild, as she backed flat against the wall and stared disbelievingly at the Black Rose who had almost killed her.

James rushed to her side, and gathering her into his embrace, held her tight against him. "It's all right. It's all right, Daelyn," he kept repeating in tender whispers.

She clung to him, her body trembling violently.

He stroked her back, his fingers soothing her through her hair as he kept her in the warmth of his strong arms until her terrors finally subsided. But his own terror was still sharp. He had almost lost the creature he loved so deeply to the hand of the sister he had sought so hard to find.

Katrien sank into the seat of the iron bench, miserably glum. "I saw you on the floor, Prince James. All beat up and bleeding. I thought—"

"You saw me?" he exclaimed. His eyes darted into Daelyn's, splintering with unspoken questions.

Daelyn suddenly felt miserably glum herself. The man who had just said he loved her had just discovered she was keeping things from him. The day was turning into a latrine minute by minute.

"It's a long Nicholai story," Daelyn said, with a sigh. "But to make a long story short, he botched her rescue."

"Botched?"

Daelyn watched an angry frown settle in on James' face. The Vanguard "botching" Katrien's escape from the clutches of the New Royals was, if the taut jawline on that perfect face was any indication, filling him with fury.

It was only seeing his sister, seeing her for the first time, deject-edly sitting on the plain, ugly bench, that smoothed the tightness from the face muscles and gentled his eyes.

Go to her, Daelyn threaded, easing out of his arms. *She looks like a little abandoned bird.*

He sat down beside her on the bench. "How did you get in here, Katie?"

Yeah. That's comforting, Daelyn sent in a smirky thread.

"Through the passageways in the walls," Katrien answered. She turned her eyes upward to him, and the deep blue softened with touches of trust. "It's how I get around the whole house. No one is ever any the wiser."

Daelyn slowly eased to the edge of the bed. She was still sting-ing with a few lingering shreds of terror, the sharp point of a stake still chasing around in her eyes. She never wanted that, that thing, close to her unblemished skin again. "You've found every passage in the house?"

"Most."

"How have you been able to come and go without being noticed or missed?"

"I—have my own room. And I—take most of my meals there."

Isolation. It was the way the "special" ones were handled, the ones who had conceived.

Well, that explains those pounds she's put on, Daelyn thought, but she said nothing to James of her suspicions his sister was with child. Probably not a good idea yet, considering how he had re-acted to the Nicholai mishap.

"Katie, how old are you?" Daelyn asked.

"Almost twenty-four," she said, puzzled. "Why?"

Twenty-four, James threaded to Daelyn. *My—our mother could have been pregnant when she crossed through the mirror. And might not have known yet.*

"Do you know where our mother is, Katie?" he asked, his voice barely hiding the emotion rocking his heart. "Is she alive?"

"I know nothing of her," Katrien said quickly, her eyes darting to the darker corners of the room, and traveling in spurts to the window and ceiling, and the doors.

She's not telling the truth, Daelyn threaded. *Don't ask her any-*

thing else, James. She's not going to give you a truthful answer as long as she's afraid vampyres could be listening.

"We need to get you out of here, Katie," James said, rising from the bench and swiftly holding his hand out to her. "There has to be a passageway through the house we—"

"No!" she cried, jumping up, and backing away from them. She waved her hands frantically. "No! I—can't! I can't go with you! I—can't leave!"

She darted for the door.

"It's bolted, Katie," James said, moving to her side. "Why do you feel you can't leave?"

"I—I just can't."

"You're pregnant," Daelyn said knowingly.

"It isn't like that," the girl returned defensively, lifting her chin and pursing her lip. "I love him."

"Who?"

"Therin."

Therin! One of the Count's descendent nephews! Daelyn glued her eyes to the girl, avoiding James' glance. She didn't have the heart to tell him. She wasn't sure how James would react. Would he cry in sorrow and combust in fiery anger at the same time? Bad enough to finally find his sister then find out she was preggers by a mortal destined for vampirism. But to find out that the mortal was the nephew of the Count?

Lordy, lordy. All hell and tears both might break loose in those chocolate eyes she loved. And she would be unable to comfort him.

"Who's Therin?" James demanded to know.

"Her lover, obviously," Daelyn said quickly, before Katrien could open her mouth and maybe make James go berserk.

"How can you think you love him?" Daelyn probed. "He's a puppet in the puppet master's hands, just like you."

"Therin's different," Katie defended. "He doesn't want to be like them. The first night he just sat on the bed, talking. The next night, we both talked. And every night after that. He was a gentleman, and we—fell in love."

She averted her gaze to the floor, and two big tears fell from her rain blue eyes.

"No offense, but you don't at the moment look like a woman happily, madly in love," Daelyn remarked.

"They separated us after they discovered I was carrying his child. I'm not allowed to see him again until after I give birth. It's the law."

"The law," James scoffed scornfully under his breath. "Their law. Anti-law."

Please, James. She's a little emotional right now. And so are you. Be quiet and calm down. And be patient. She's terrified. Of us, of them, of everything.

"What were you doing when we saw you on your way to the garden, Katie?" Daelyn asked gently.

"The Roses are always talking about escaping, but they're afraid to try. They said it was rumored the house had been a way station for slaves on the run. I searched my room, found the portal. Whenever the minions were occupied, stuffing their faces mostly, I explored the secret fissures in the walls, found a hallway in the older part of the house, and found the back stairs that lead to the basement. I would slip out through the basement and take a basket to the garden to get bouquets of flowers for my room."

"And meet Therin," Daelyn guessed.

She sighed and nodded. "Therin meets me in the garden behind the walls, where we can't be seen by those minion monkeys." She breathed in deeply as though smelling fragrant scents in breeze-cooled air. "So different in the garden."

James looked down at the bedroom door threshold suddenly. Shadows were sweeping back and forth through the hallway light.

"The New Realm is awake," he said tensely.

More shadows.

The sound of doors opening, followed by doors closing with hard slams that shook the house.

Then a bevy of angry shouts and calls.

"I hope to hell Nicholai can keep things under control," James said.

"Katie, if you can make it through the walls, go to Therin. Now!" Daelyn urged her. "You don't want to be found with us!"

"Take the tunnel and get off the property," a voice said from the window.

A curl of smoke through the iron bars like a fog, then across the floor, and Nicholai was standing before them. "Go to my house. Therin shouldn't have any trouble finding a place to hide there. He's good at that. A master of nothing except hiding from his ancestral uncle."

The girl ran to the wall next to the bed, pushed a large picture of a shadowy forest to the side, hoisted herself up and disappeared into a round hole behind it. The painting slid perfectly back into place.

James took Daelyn's hand and she held it tightly while they waited for the door to the shabby bedroom to open.

Nicholai drew his sword from its scabbard. "Damn near perfect plan," he smiled thinly. "Perfect if the little wench doesn't make stupid and not do what I said."

Daelyn frowned at the sword that was rising to present its pointed nose no more than half a foot from her midriff, and reacted. "I am tired of having sharp objects pointed at me," she said, and reaching out, crushed the blade into bits of steel beading that fell to the floor in a silvery rain.

"I'll be damned," Nicholai said, staring dumbfounded at the hilt in his hand, sans the blade. "I might even fall in love with you myself, Valkyrie," he laughed in singular admiration, his brown orbs glinting like brown diamonds.

James's eyes hardened like mud under a hot desert sun. "Not hardly," he said.

A sound of bolts on the bedroom door loosening …

"Well, since the absence of a weapon will now make it appear I'm in league with you instead of collaring you for setting the Roses free to scatter all over the woods," Nicholai said, tossing the sword handle into the silver beads on the floor, "I'd say we should follow little sister there and get the hell out of this room."

Daelyn shot a long look toward him, but James figured the Vanguard Royal must have clipped the threads short she was sending because he hissed, "And don't give me that lecture again about 'there's good in you, Nicholai.'"

They leaped for the picture, shoved it aside, and dove through the hole in the wall.

The painting slid placidly, perfectly, back into place.

The door blew open, and the Count stepped into the empty room, his eyes torches of neon red.

Spying the hilt with the emerald inlay in the oval pommel, he picked it up then stared hard at the beads of steel swirling across the floor in the draft from the open door.

"They've taken the Captain of the Vanguards captive," he said in an even, emotionless tone.

He studied every corner of the room, corners silent as hardened cement, and turned to his troop of New Royals.

"The vampira has become a Valkyrie. Kill her."

29.

Slapping at yet another curtain of cobwebs that kept wrapping his face in a sticky cocoon, James tackled a stairwell passage so narrow his broad shoulders broom-brushed the sides of the walls. Not a pleasant run. Nicholai navigated through the crimped space like lightning, and Daelyn was whisking right behind him, with James as wing man, covering the rear. And catching the webs.

"The Count just threaded me that he has my prized hilt and 'knows' I'm your prisoner," Nicholai said with throaty laughter as they began swiftly descending a tight stairwell. "He thinks I'm your hostage. Me. Nicholai Petronovich. The Realm's Second Life Vanguard. A slayer's hostage. As if that would ever happen."

His boots slowed suddenly and his laughter died in his throat. "Apparently, that's not all he's thinking. He wants our castle coquet dead on sight, Crossbow. That little meltdown she had in the room back there with my sword alerted him she's a Valkyrie. No one can destroy a haunted blade but a master slayer or a Vampyre of Light, a Valkyrie. And her essence was all over the handle's crossguard."

"Stay close in front of me, Blues," James said urgently. "In minutes, there will be vampyres swarming these fissures like termites on new wood."

"I don't care for your analogy," Nicholai hissed.

"The Count will have the New Royals blocking these stairs and the stairwell exit," Daelyn said shakily, her words sticking in her throat like sand.

"In a moment, we won't be on these stairs," Nicholai responded calmly.

Within minutes, he had stopped and was pulling up the top board of one of the steps. "I made a few adjustments to the Count's escape route renovations," he said. "It's a tight fit, but you should be able to squeeze through, Crossbow."

"Another friggin' hole," Daelyn sighed as she stared into the pitch black under the step.

"It's about a six to seven foot drop," Nicholai said, "into a new tunnel that connects to the original. At the end, we'll be climbing out into the woods away from the plantation, next to a road where hay wagons used to pick up the runners waiting in the trees." He sniffed the air. "Go! They're closing in!"

He shadowed and shapeshifted into a bat. Daelyn shadowed and became a sparrow, sat on the edge of the open step for a moment peering in, then flew reluctantly into the dark void.

James took a deep breath, wished to hell he could shapeshift, sucked in his gut and twisted his body through the stair top opening. He felt his feet dangle momentarily in thin air, then he was free falling in pitch dark. The short six feet felt like a sky fall. But as his shoes made contact with solid ground, his training kicked in instinctively. He bent his knees, and rolled to recoil from the impact. A bat's claws clutched, jerked him roughly up. Nicholai. Enjoyably hurrying him along.

He heard Daelyn's soft voice pierce the dark.

"Hold my hand, James. We cannot use a torch."

"Can't see a damned thing," he said.

He felt her soft, cool hand encircle his, felt their fingers link together tightly so she would not lose him in the dark. Felt her breath close to his cheek.

Felt her sudden kiss. Slightly warm, moist lips brushing his own, trembling a little, not wanting it to be their last. He let his mouth memorize hers, keeping the memory close against his heart. No way was he going to let the Count kill her. The plan Nicholai had conjured to pursue his own selfish gains had to work, had to succeed.

It just had to. Even though nothing so far had gone very much according to the Vanguard's plan …

They ran. A Valkyrie racing with a bat's radar, a mortal with nothing to guide him but the Valkyrie's hand as she followed the Vanguard. And the Vanguard was a scary thought.

As they raced, James discovered a newfound appreciation for the blind who must live in a sightless world—full of things to stumble into.

Craggy extensions from the walls jabbed and poked at him. Large rocks tripped him. Dirt and pebbles fell at whim from the loose-ceilinged earth. He swore he felt the edge of a bat's wing as it flew back and forth in a whiff of wind.

Nicholai. Or at least he hoped it was Nicholai.

"Get your butt in higher gear," a demanding voice hissed next to his ear.

Yeah, it was Nicholai.

He ran harder, harder, until his lungs ached for want of breath. He ran through the dark and finally they connected to the underground railroad tunnel.

A bit of light. A lantern had been left hanging in a distant stony curve for them, its wick weak but steady.

An understanding encompassed James, for Daelyn, for what she must have felt and been through, running and running, cold and alone through tunnels of uncertainty, willing to run and keep running, and fight to the death to be free, because even death was preferable to returning to her enslavement.

He squeezed her hand tightly, felt her return crush and saw the shadow of her smile in the tiny bit of light now mingling with the dark.

The tunnel ended and Nicholai rolled away a boulder hiding a secret entrance to—somewhere. God only knew where. They crawled through—and ran again. James felt the floor begin to slope upward.

A bit of stronger, hazy, dusty light began to filter into the inclining tunnel from up ahead.

Nicholai heaved at a covering of sod. The tunnel opened into a night full of moon—they were in a deep ditch.

They clambered out, checked to the right and the left, then rushed across an asphalt road that had once been dirt and rutted by apprehensive hay wagon wheels.

Beyond the tangle of trees and brush that created a short stitching of woods, Nicholai led them down a pithy drive to a sepulcher of house, nothing more than wood and brick bones in the moonlight. No glory of the old South here. Grayed with age, the house was bent, crooked and just plain old—a habitat for ghosts and not much else in its barnacled halls.

"Place looks like a pit," Daelyn remarked as she stared at porch pillars with missing bricks and crumbling mortar.

"Well, hell, I haven't lived here in almost two hundred years," Nicholai clipped. "You'd have to expect it to be run down a little."

He rushed inside and they could hear him rumble around looking for the Count's nephew.

"Run over would be a better description," Daelyn said as her eyes traveled from broken, busted out windows to cracks in a collapsing gallery, and a leaning porch ready to give up what little life was left in its roof and collapse.

James hesitated as he placed a boot on a weak porch step. The board creaked and gave way under his weight. He grabbed a pillar for support and leaped over the steps to the porch.

"I know you want your sister in safety," Daelyn said as she glided to his side. "But Therin will be ready to defend her for that same reason, to keep her safe—with him. She's carrying his child, James. Don't kill him."

Shock and anger raced across his eyes.

Then he forced his blood to run calm. *You know*, he threaded as they entered the house, *you imagine and practice all the things you'll say and do and feel in that first meeting with the sister you've never met, a meeting that should be a banana split in an ice cream parlor, or the comfortable atmosphere of a cozy little Italian restaurant, a get-to-know-you place like normal people. Then you realize your sister was conceived in another century, her mother took a mirror instead of a train to get here. She may not have been raised by wolves, but she may have been raised by vampyres and mush brained minions. So why should I be surprised she would be pregnant by the nephew of the most infamous vampyre on the face of the earth?* He paused, then muttered in his thoughts. *But I am, damn it to hell.*

He headed down the main hallway, checking every door, searching as they made their way to the kitchen. He continued, *It was not totally unexpected, considering the Count's fierce hatred for the Van Helsing name. In his mind, he'd planned the perfect revenge. A child of his bloodline in the Van Helsing legacy. A legacy of slayers. He could wake every night enjoying the irony.*

James, Daelyn sent softly in her thoughts, *the child was conceived—in love. Perhaps the Count's perfect revenge is not so per-*

fect. Love can change the course of a century like the power of rain against a river bank.

She smiled deeply into his eyes. "Like rain against a river bank?"

"I love you, Valkyrie," he said, his gaze tender.

"Hold that thought," she said, nodding toward a darkened corner in the kitchen where Nicholai was shrunken against a wall. His eyes were a horror of pain and he was staring starkly at a closet-like pantry door underneath the back of a staircase.

A white cross was painted on the decaying wood from top to bottom.

"They're in there," Nicholai said, pointing from his secure corner.

Daelyn ran her hand over the frame. "They definitely went through this door."

James jerked the door open.

The pantry was empty. Only a set of bare shelves met their gaze.

"They aren't here," James said, disheartened.

"But the door does not reveal they left," Daelyn said in puzzlement.

"Press the top right hand corner of the shelves inward," Nicholai instructed them from his haven across from the painted door.

James pushed at the edge of the shelf, and felt it budge. The entire shelf was a door to a smaller, deeper hiding place. He pushed it open carefully.

The frightened couple were huddled on the floor wrapped in a blanket and each other's arms, crosses hanging from their necks that could have fit a steeple.

James scrutinized the skinny, blond kid holding his sister. Pushing his glasses up his nose, he tried bravely, "Are you Van Helsing? You gonna get us the hell out of this mess?"

They crawled out of the pantry and he stood up, then helped Katrien to her feet. James saw that the muscles of the lean arms were ropey. The sinew was strong.

James had no doubt but that the legs that appeared to be "skinny" were also well honed and could pummel steel to protect the woman he loved.

"Get them out of there," Nicholai commanded from the shadows. "The ship won't be in the harbor long." He shaded his eyes and face with his hand, his body bent and his head turned to the side as he moved out of the corner.

"He's not real fond of religious symbols," James explained to Daelyn's questioning gaze.

"I thought nothing frightened him."

"That does," he said, nodding toward the painted cross. "He's forced to remember, in living color, what he abandoned on a bridge one night."

"Give her a history lesson later, slayer," Nicholai said, gathering his cloak around him and whirling away down the crumbling excuse for a hall. "There's a small inlet to the south. Pirates used to use it to hide their ships. We have to get them to the ship before Henri sails with the Roses."

They entered the woods watchfully, their senses acutely on the alert for vamps as they made their way toward the beach.

There were no sounds beyond the hoot of an owl, and an occasional whirl of fall wind rustling the trees.

A gibbous moon shone full and sweet and James was more than thankful for the woods with moonbeams splintering down through a multitude of branches to light the way.

Of course, it also made them visible to anyone who would want to kill them.

He decided they should run like hell. Sweeping his sister into his arms, he zipped through the trees, knowing he was betraying his slayer speed and skill to a Vanguard vampyre, to Nicholai.

And he knew the Vanguard would not forget the secret training he was witnessing.

But his sister's life, and Daelyn's, hung in the balance.

And not only from the New Royals, he soon realized.

Nicholai was beginning to look at his sister with hunger in his eyes. James knew the vampyre was hearing human hearts beating like timpani drums and pulses throbbing with rivers of blood rushing in overflow under the adrenalin push, and it was driving him to kill. The red pits in his eyes were drowning the corneas.

James was not so foolish to think he could run interference quickly enough if the powerful vampyre made up his mind to leap on Katrien if she was left alone and unprotected, even for a moment.

It would take only that one swing of the pendulum for a skilled vampyre to kill her, and Nicholai was skilled. Strike, and vanish into the night.

Daelyn flashed defensively to his side. She had also seen the eyes of lightless night light up with fire.

James was sweating heavily as they emerged from the woods and stepped onto a sandy expanse of shoreline. A ship sat expectantly some distance out, and a boat waited at the edge of the waves lapping the beach.

Two figures waited by the boat, dressed in black to blend with the night, their faces hidden in jacket hoods. Angie and Henri.

"Hurry!" Angie called, waving them over.

James carried Katrien to them. "Don't leave her alone. Not for a minute. Not even once you're at sea."

One glance toward Nicholai and the mystic nodded in understanding.

Henri helped Katrien on the boat. Therin climbed in beside her and drew her close to keep her warm under a blanket on the seat. "There doesn't seem to be enough room on this boat," she said, looking around in the small row boat as Henri and Angie climbed in front and picked up the oars.

She waved at James, waving her brother over to sit beside her. "Come on, James, we can make room," she said, scooting closer to Therin.

James and Daelyn didn't move, but stood at the edge of the sandy beach, holding hands as Henri began to back the boat away.

"Hurry!" Katrien cried, her big blue eyes suddenly lost, confused. "Get in!"

"We—can't go, Katie. I love you, little sister," James called, then ordered the vampyre in black, "Get them out of here, Henri!"

"No!" Katrien cried, dissolving in tears. "You're coming with us!" She made a movement as if to try to rise in the boat now moving swiftly across the inlet.

Therin pulled her close and kept her in his grasp. "They made a bargain, Katie. They have to keep it."

30.

Silently but swiftly, the tiny rowboat crossed the inlet and the last two passengers were soon on board the ship, and headed into open and what was hoped would be a safe sea.

"The New Royals will not go near bodies of water," Nicholai said. "If they have to travel the oceans, they travel in their caskets, and in daysleep."

"And you?" James asked coldly, turning from the ship that was becoming an ink blot on a white-capped sea under the half-moon.

"I can travel anywhere," Nicholai responded with a challenging arch of his eyebrow.

He began ripping his beautiful white cape and smearing sand on his face and arms. "I'm not about to let you happily get even with me for nearly breaking your jaw," he said, "so this will have to do."

He starting watching the sky, his eyes searching every stray wisp of cloud, every star. "It won't be long," he said. He hurried into the woods to warn those who were loyal to him to stay alert. What few there were. New Royals had not been invited to the party to "arrest" the slayer and the renegade vamp, but that didn't mean they might not show up. He had had to tell them why he had formed a posse.

Daelyn had not moved from gazing out at the ocean. "They were clinging to each other under the blanket so tightly, their sole hope in each other and a little boat, both of them so vulnerable. James, I feel a crush against my heart, but I don't know what it is."

He smoothed his warm hand across the back of her shoulder. "It's called the human experience," he said.

"Dance with me, James," she said suddenly, turning to him and clinging to him as hard as Katie had been clinging to Therin. "I can hear the faint shirring of wings in the far sky. Nicholai's troops are in the woods. Which means it's not vanguards flying across that sky to the beach party. It's the Count's cutthroats. Distant, but distinct." She paused. "I want to dance on the warm sand before the fog rolls in and sucks away the warmth."

"To what song, Blues?" he asked, his lips curling upward slightly in a sad smile.

"Kryptonite," she said with a winsome tone. "Take me around the moon one last time, James, before it's gone?"

She began dancing in the sand, humming and swaying her hips to the song beating in her mind, and traveling through her body. She murmured the lyrics, pretended Dracula's forces were not coming to block out the moon and the night. And her life.

She closed her eyes, and let go of the North Carolina shore. They were dancing on warm Santa Monica sand and the night was filled with bright voices along the pier and street musicians. The beach glistened in the moonlight, and she could taste the salt in the sea breeze, hear the ocean as its waves lapped the shore. And she was mortal.

Closer. The wings were closer. James stroked her arms to warm away the chill on them.

"Is it okay for a rookie Valkyrie to be scared all the way down to her shoe tops?" Daelyn murmured.

"Yeah. Yeah, it's okay, Blues," he said. He could also now clearly hear the malicious wing whips. The muscles in his shoulders and arms tensed, tightened as he danced close, not wanting to let go of her.

A sound, a sound like many bats, a veritable storm of bats. Not just closer, but closing in.

They stopped dancing.

"You give a girl one hell of a date night, Van Helsing," she whispered in a trembling smile.

His eyes were full of pain, regret for bringing her back to this world.

"It's all right, James," she said, reading the remorse in his gaze. "We both know I had to come."

"He doesn't have any more time for an episode of 'romancing the vampyre,'" Nicholai commanded sharply as he came running out of the woods. "Start fighting me, Crossbow. At least try to look a little like you're interested in resisting arrest. The whole damned Realm is about to descend on us, from the sounds of it!"

They fought, slinging sand and punches.

"Who would've thought they would actually show up?" Nicholai said.

Daelyn looked into the sky and felt a sting of panic. What was that silvery, glittering mesh she could see in the descending black midst?

Odd, it was as though silvery threads were thrown across the sky. The silver glitter fell toward her. She kept gazing upward, mesmerized.

"Daelyn! Leap away!" she heard James shout.

His warning came too late. Daelyn cried out as a net of heavy, silvery mesh fell over her, trapping her. The New Royals landing next to her moved swiftly, viciously tightening the net around her body. She could not extend her wings or move her arms.

She collapsed to the sand in the shining horrible cocoon, but Nicholai ordered the vanguard runners to pick her up and carry her into the woods. He ordered the New Royals, who had decided to show up and "help," not to touch her.

She could hear the clash of metal behind her, a sword blade meeting sword blades. She could hear the sword singing, parting the air. Vampyres hissed, and then something strange—cries, angry, then gurgles of panic, of terror.

James! she cried in a thread. *What's happening?*

Nicholai was flashing to her side, taking up stride with the vampyre runners.

Two more runners ran past them, hauling an unconscious James.

His clothes were ripped and bloodied far more than Nicholai would have done.

Fools, Nicholai threaded to her. *Fifty of them tried to bite him. Dead all over the beach. He killed ten, his blood killed forty.*

Is James all right? she cried in a silent sob.

How would you feel if forty idiots had glutted you wherever they could land a fang? he grumped. *I need him strong and healthy and they just sucked half the life out of him!*

She struggled violently against the silvery netting.

Stop it! Don't try! he warned. *We both know if that Valkyrie power surges, you'll break the net, but the New Royals don't know what you are. You're being carried by my arresting vanguards. Let them. You fight and get free and I can't guarantee your safety with that ass-dumb, bastard army back there if they figure you out.*

Were the attackers all New Royals?

New Royals and jackasses.

He flashed ahead to join the vanguards carrying James.

So far, your plan to kill the Count—sucks, she threaded.

"Well, you're awake," she heard him say. "A little orange juice and a cookie and a transfusion and you'll be just fine."

James, can you hear me? Daelyn quickly threaded.

Hell, yes. I've got more venom in me than a rat-eyed sidewinder. But I'm feeling awfully ... kind of ...

The threading trailed off.

What? I didn't catch your threads, my love, she sent in sobs, straining to turn her head to the side and upward, to see up ahead, see if he still lived.

All she could see was a bunch of running butts.

New Royals in garments that looked like they came straight out of a Medieval costume movie appeared to accompany the vanguards and Royals. Unsure of the extent of their power as they swarmed around her, she stopped threading.

All the king's men, she thought.

And Humpty's about to fall.

We hope.

She was carried up marble steps to a long front porch, heavily pillared, then through a hall to a kitchen and down steps to a wine cellar where she was hoisted through the entrance of a room with metal walls carved out of an old coal mine tunnel.

The door to the room was lead, and thick—a Cold War era bomb shelter door.

A cylindrical iron cage hung from the ceiling by thick chains.

The vanguards cut away the netting, then flew upward with her, and locked her in the cage.

As the door to the room closed with a solid, heavy roll behind them, she sat on cold metal in a darkness that could have stolen a mortal's sanity within minutes.

But she was not mortal.

And the mortal she loved and desired had been separated from her. "Idiots," she muttered as she crushed the lock on the cage door, threw it open, and flew out. "Did they think a cage would hold me?"

She pushed at the leaden door to the room and felt it budge. "I will not be treated this way," she said aloud, her teeth clenched together as she pressed harder. The door gave way bit by bit slowly until she had room to fog and escape.

She ran along the edge of the cellar wall, searching, sniffing.

James, she threaded trying to feel his essence in the stone, listening to the walls' stories to see where he had been taken.

Following the past stored in the walls, she raced deeper into the recesses until she felt him behind a wood door.

The door opened from within and Nicholai stood in front of her. "I didn't think their monkey cage would hold you, but—why spoil their fun?"

Standing aside, he motioned her into the room with a slow sweep of his arm.

He crossed the room to stand next to a glass-door cabinet full of cotton balls, bottles of unidentifiable liquids, bandages of various sizes, and alcohol.

His eyes closed, James was lying on a gurney under a thin, white cotton blanket. Blood was traveling through tubing from a plastic bag hanging from a pole into the back of his hand. The needle's entry point was deeply bruised, and the taping over the needle was amateurish.

Drops of blood seeped out from under the wrinkled tape and down his hand. Daelyn went to the cabinet and filled her hands with white cloths, gauge, tape and antiseptic ointment.

James came to with a moan, his hand and arm aching from the slipshod IV job. Blinking through blurry vision, he gazed at the soft hand holding a white cloth and wiping away the drops of blood.

His shirt had been stripped away, and lay in red and black shreds on the floor. "I hear you took a few with you," she smiled.

His eyes focused, the pupils cleared. "Hey Blues," he said, a little raspy. "Your face is pretty beautiful framed in an aura of cave light. Not quite oval, not quite round. The face of a Roman goddess. Bright blue eyes, soft sable hair brushing across my chest, masses of silk a man could wrap his fingers into."

"They must have drugged you," she said with a light, lilting laugh.

Her molten sky eyes pierced his with glimmering, golden flecks. She was ecstatic he was alive.

"Is this heaven?" he said, forcing a weak smile.

"Not hardly, pardner," she smiled back tenderly. "It's North Carolina. And here we are together again in a friggin' hole in the ground."

31.

Daelyn dabbed antibiotic ointment to the bites on James' chest, slow and careful.

I love your chest, she threaded with a smile. *Especially when the muscles quiver and tighten when you sense I want you.*

Her eyes cut to the "medic" vampyre and her smile dissolved. He was staring hungrily at the seepage on the cloth laying to the side of the sheet on the gurney. His eyes devoured the IV pumping blood into James, then became riveted on the red liquid traveling the tube. He wiped at a bit of new seepage running down James' hand with his finger and stared at the blood on his fingertips with open thirst

"It's not exactly finger licking good," James said in a force of breath. "I don't think you'd like it very much. Quite a few others didn't find it very tasty tonight."

The vampyre took a tissue from a box on the bed table next to the gurney and wiped it carefully away.

Unable to turn on his side, James shifted his gaze to try to look around the room.

Bags of blood were stacked on a counter next to the cabinet and Nicholai kept moving his eyes over them with the same red, hungry pits in the pupils James had seen flaring on the beach as he gazed at his sister.

Daelyn was also having control issues. She kept stealing glances toward the bags of blood on the counter the way a dry drunk steals a glance at bootleg whiskey. The backpack she had hung onto like a lifeline had become lost somewhere in the beach melee.

Vampyres in a room full of blood was not exactly a controlled environment, and James could see a glistening of pleasure enveloping the Vanguard's gaze as he watched Daelyn rippling with craving. James was sure Nicholai would like nothing better than to see the Valkyrie fall and fail, return to the dark, to the castles bathed in human blood.

James sighed. This was not going to be a good night if she wasn't fed.

"If she's not satiated, she'll be of no use to either one of us," Nicholai said.

"Feed her," James relented.

Nicholai tossed her a full bag.

She took it, but held it away, her heart's conflict in her eyes as she viewed the red, sloshing liquid.

"It was donated, not taken by force," Nicholai said in response to her hesitation. "Nobody died for the Van Helsing cause."

"The son of Van Helsing," Daelyn murmured thoughtfully, her gaze moving back to James, the sexy slayer with switch-hitter pecs and dark brown eyes of mystery.

The "medic" and his assistant, less hesitantly, were also gaping at the bags on the counter. As Daelyn's fangs dropped and she ripped the bag open and downed the contents, their tongues were practically dangling.

When Nicholai helped himself to a bag of the extra blood as well, they exchanged glances, shrugged and gulped a couple themselves.

The room became a blood bag fest.

James felt light-headed, and closed his eyes.

A bad feeling spread through him, and he wished he could slip through the metal table he was strapped to, grab Daelyn on the way, and sink through the ground to the other side of the world far from the vampyres in this "friggin' hole."

The sinking feeling deepened, spreading through his body rather oddly.

A strange, wild heat traveled straight into his brain and made every muscle in his body spasm with an unholy strength. His eyes saw every color in the room three shades brighter, could almost smell them. His body stiffened straight as a board and jerked upward, almost up and off the bed.

Daelyn quickly moved to restrain him.

He could hear Nicholai snickering under his breath.

Hear him rather loudly.

"Hell of a ride, isn't it?" the vampyre goaded, his white teeth gleaming as he walked coolly to the side of the bed.

"What did you put in the blood?" James demanded in a gasp as the firestorm continued rushing through him.

A purely wicked, thoroughly satisfied grin played around Nicholai's mouth. "Just a little something to kick you up a notch."

"You bastard."

"I'm the universal donor," Nicholai said with resplendent laughter. Then his tone sobered and became stern. "Enjoy the ride, slayer. It won't last long. Just long enough to give you the power to help me kill the Count."

James wanted to rip the IV from his hand, rip away the vampyre's blood drops riding side saddle with the human transfusion coursing through his veins, stampeding his heart, his lungs, his senses. His soul.

Calming him with her touch, Daelyn drew her hand from his cheek down the side of his neck, where two bright circles of red still warred for possession of his soul, then she checked the myriad of punctures lightly with her fingertips. "He's right, James. You would recover too slowly on your own. The—trial—is at twilight. The Count likes to defy the dawn."

"First crack of light, and he retreats," Nicholai added, urgency edging his tone. "So we'll have to move fast."

"There are New Royals coming down through the caves," Daelyn said, tilting her head toward the door.

"Took them long enough to discover you were gone," Nicholai said.

The door burst open and she was unceremoniously escorted back to her room by four grotesquely mesmerizing beings, beautiful, powerful and completely naïve to the world they wanted to conquer.

Damn stupid, these New Royals were.

She was washed and dressed by four female vampyres who were almost terrified to touch her, but she gave them no trouble except to slap them across the room once in awhile when they touched her where she didn't want to be touched.

For James' sake, and only for his, she controlled her power.

They brought in a black satin bridal gown, but hesitated to

pull it over her head, quaking in the face of her open anger as she looked at it.

Daelyn forced herself to remember James needed her, she acquiesced, letting them clasp a multi-strand necklace of black pearls around her neck. They fastened the satin buttons on her dress with trembling fingers, then cloistered her face in a black veil garishly sprinkled with obsidian seed pearls. The gown's train trailed behind her at least twenty-five feet under the veil.

Her death dress.

She tripped. Purposely. To rip it.

The vamps gasped, their eyes filled with horror.

"She cannot enter the grand council chamber like this!" they cried in unison. "The Count will have our heads!"

There was suddenly a flurry to mend it. Or at least try.

Female vampyres were not seamstresses. Their business was blood.

By the time they reached the "grand council chamber," Daelyn had made sure the ensemble was disassembled, and in shreds around her.

And her hair was a tangled mess. She pulled the veil to a crooked slant, and as she stepped into the aisle of the high ceilinged cave, she held her chin proudly, and broke the strands of black pearls from her neck—spilling them from her hands into the aisle in front of the Count.

She began walking slowly down the aisle, the bride of death, her steps proud, defiant as she glided between rows of vampyres dressed as though they were attending an evening at the opera. The aisle stopped at the steps to a platform. A highback white padded throne embellished with gold gargoyles at the sides sat square in the middle.

The Count was sitting square in the middle of the seat, all in black. Black pants, black high collar shirt, and a black ankle-length trench coat draping the chair legs.

Not a single flutter of an eyelash disturbed his eyes as he viewed Daelyn's disheveled appearance.

"They were to dress you in white," he said.

His voice may have reflected no emotion, but his eyes were filled with calm fury.

"Guess they didn't get that email," she retorted.

He raised his hand palm outward, his eyes glowed with red heat—

The female vampyres fled, screaming down a side aisle toward an entrance to the outside of the cave. He had given the signal they were to be killed. They ran wildly, fleeing his presence toward the sprinkling of stars, a night that could hide them if they could reach it.

The wall next to the entrance seemed to move slightly. A shadowy presence stepped out from the dark.

The New Royal had snapped their necks and staked them into dust before they could lift a wing to freedom.

Nodding briefly toward the Count, the vampyre stepped back into the shadows of stone, becoming a part of them once more.

This is insane! We cannot survive this! Daelyn thought frantically as she sought to spot James and Nicholai.

A red drape that ran from the ceiling to the floor of the platform parted, and Nicholai, in full regalia of gold braid and shimmering white cape, stepped through escorting the "slayer prince." Gripping the arm of his collar, he stood slightly behind and to the right of the Count.

The Count curled his hand inward, motioning Daelyn wordlessly toward him. She took a step forward in a gesture of obedience, but she was determined to go down hard if need be to save the mortal she loved.

Walk slowly, Daelyn, James threaded toward her. *We still have three minutes to daylight.*

Two and a half, Nicholai popped toward him.

I can hear both of you! Daelyn threaded in astonishment.

The three-way will last only for a few minutes he tells me, James responded, then he sent a soft, *I love you, Daelyn.*

Let's not waste the sand in our hourglass, shall we? Nicholai careened toward them both with expediency.

In the precious seconds that followed, Daelyn, at their instruction, vied for time by halting and ripping her dress deliberately as though in defiance, then she glided forward. Just a bit. Out of the corner of her eye, she could see Nicholai nodding to the vanguards closest to the marble platform steps.

She pretended her knees were weak, made a half-fall to the floor, gathered herself up. One more step. The vanguards' hands eased in under their capes.

Nicholai turned, faced James, and slid his hand in under his cape.

Daelyn could see the glint of the crossguard as Nicholai slipped the sword into his waiting grasp, unnoticed by the gawking crowd salivating at the shreds of black gossamer and satin sliding around Daelyn's bare, creamy smooth legs and thighs.

It's a broadsword, Nicholai threaded to James. *It takes two hands to wield it. Think you can handle it, Crossbow?*

I can handle it.

Swing it high, Daelyn added. *It will pick up energy from the very air around it. We call it Earth force.*

Two more sliding, sensual steps.

The bare tree branches beyond the side cave entrance filled with hundreds of shadows. Silent as ravens.

Vanguards.

Realizing she was standing in the best spot in the house to get caught in the crossfire—and killed—in the beginnings of a war. Daelyn felt fear become her magistrate, but she channeled the quaking within her, and made it appear to the Count that he, and her impending doom, were the cause of her sharp breathing.

"I don't want to die," she suddenly cried, as though humbling herself before the cruel, self-proclaimed ruler of the undead who had made himself her book of judgment. "I can—return to you," she implored, casting her eyes at him from under her spell of long, black lashes.

For a moment his gaze wavered, as even he became lost in her sensuous countenance.

Her voice swirled like sweet syrup toward him—

But as she approached the steps to the platform, her thoughts were focused on the threading between the two beings now counting every second with the precision of a pendulum.

This has nothing to do with Roses and Royals, does it? James threaded at Nicholai as he pressed the bright sword to his side out of sight. *It's personal isn't it? Because of Jane?*

He took her, knowing she was my life mate, he answered bitterly.

The perfect full mouth that had kissed Jane's for centuries turned down, unhappy, pursed tight with a hatred barely concealed.

The Count was taking his typical Caesar-like, half-step down the marble stairs to deliver sentence.

And kill the Valkyrie himself.

Three, two, one, Nicholai threaded in a nod toward the trees.

The vanguards descended like black snow into the cave, startling the New Royals.

The vanguards who were within the council chamber turned and drew their swords, and the New Royals, taken by surprise, could only stare numbly as they were surrounded.

But not for long.

With snarls, like cornered dogs, they bared their fangs, and steel flashed. They attacked, fighting viciously rather than face defeat by Nicholai and his crew or be pulled into the sun by the slayer's hand. But James was focused on the one vampyre he was to pull into the sun.

The Count stepped backward up the stairs. He could not shapeshift into a bat and fly to his escape hole high above him because the fighting now extended to the cave roof. He swept toward the back of the council platform to escape behind the heavy drapes.

Just a single, James told himself as he stepped out toward the vampyre. *All you need is a single*. Gripping the hilt of the broadsword, James swung it back and above his head. *Oh, hell, let's make it a grand slam.* Forward and down, and the blade sang through the air, lighting up the cave like a bolt of lightning.

The Count's hand reached out to grasp the drapery pulls.

His body slumped against the folds.

Headless.

The icy, pale blue fingers slid down the cloth, entwined in the ropes.

Blood trailed, pooled, soaked the crimson folds of the drapes that seemed to float to the floor of the platform, broken from their rungs high overhead by the fingers still gripping the pulls.

Beyond the cave, the sun spilled across a placid, foamy ocean.

Pull him outside! Nicholai commanded. *Then get the hell out! I will be expected to kill you. And I just might.*

Daelyn and James grabbed the head and the body and hauled them out the side entrance and into the autumn sun now a full golden globe above the shoreline.

The vampyre remains became dust and ash on the ground, then

sparked into a fiery end.

Briefly, James looked back inside the cave. The vanguards were mopping up. The battle had been swift, an intense attack. How many, if any, New Royals and New Realm vanguards might have escaped, could not be known. Not many, from the looks of it. They had scattered from the cave and been caught in the sun, or shimmied back into the passageway depths.

Nicholai draped his cape victoriously around him and walked to the center of the platform to stand in front of the throne.

Turning and sweeping his arm upward and toward the drapes still hanging to his left, he announced, "Behold! Your queen!"

With a dramatic parting of the drapes, the Lady Jane Weston glided onto the platform in a mint green, floor-length gown draped in layers of chiffon. Swirls of mint and white chiffon flowers held her raven curls in place on the sides, and long lengths of the pale green chiffon cascaded from them to the floor.

She raised her arm and took the Vanguard's hand.

The assemblage of vanguards cheered.

With her free hand, she gave him a golden goblet.

He tilted his head back and drank from it deeply, letting the blood pour from around the bowl and down his chin.

The crowd cheered loudly, wildly, lifting their blood-bathed swords in honor to the new Ruler of the Realm and his Lady. They lifted their interlocked hands high above them into in the air to royally acknowledge their subjects.

Amid the din and cheers, Nicholai's eyes traveled to James, with one last thread.

When next we meet, there will be no bargain.

Then they and the vanguards were gone, flashing deep into the caves before any New Royals who might have escaped could tail them or James could alert the Shadows to their whereabouts.

James turned to Daelyn. "We need to be out of this state before nightfall. Just in case any New Royals decide a vendetta is in order."

But as they started to run, she glanced back at the evil ashes on the ground dissolving in smoke under a scathing, purging sun. "We do not know where he sequestered the mirror." Lines of worry creased her forehead. "James, what if Nicholai knew about the mirror? What if they escaped into the mirror?"

"The mirror. My mother had been running toward a window—

the mirror," James murmured. "And the man who ran beside her was a slayer, a professor who led a double life.

"The secret hunter was sending her away to protect her, fearing his hidden profession was placing her in peril. A rage of vampyres was seeking to know who was destroying them, quite possibly incited by the vampyre who himself did not want to be unearthed by the elusive hunter."

Had his father kept an eye out early on for a vampyre spoken of only in hushed whispers and alley rumors—in case he was real? In his later years, the hunter had, of course, discovered the vampyre of rumor to be truth …

Epilogue

A jacket of wind outside the mullioned windows was wrapping the trees in chilly gusts. Andre tossed another log on the fire crackling in the fireplace.

"Looks like we might get an early snow," he said as he glanced out at the heavy cloud cover. He offered Katrien Van Helsing a sweater, which she accepted gratefully.

James walked across the library and embraced his sister without speaking. There was so much to say, so much he was feeling. He did not know where to start, how to start, where to end.

So he started with the ending. "The Count is dead."

Well, that's gotta be the best howdy do I've ever heard! Daelyn laughed in a thread behind him. *You could tell her she's safe now, and you're glad she's your sister, then welcome the nephew into the family. He looks like a scared skinny rabbit all sunken into the couch like that. Like he thinks you might slay him where he sits for getting her pregnant. Or because he's from the Count's side of town.*

James held out his hand to Therin. "Thanks for taking care of her. You're all right."

Therin relaxed and rose from the couch to shake hands.

The kid has a strong grasp. Always a good thing in our business, James threaded to Daelyn.

Conversation flowed easier after that. They hadn't picked a name for the baby yet, but they were looking through a baby name book with five thousand names to choose from. Katie was craving ice cream and peanut butter biscuits. The Roses were hidden safely away until they could be assimilated into the middle of millions of Americans, with new identities and new lives. The Shadows were on the alert for New Royals and turncoat vanguards who might have survived and might want to continue the vampyre skirmishes now dubbed, "The Cave Wars."

The mirror was officially declared missing.

Neither Katrien or Therin could shed any light on the dilemma, not having seen it at the plantation.

A thorough sweep of the grounds had also revealed nothing. Even Daelyn's precog touch had not sensed it had ever been present in the house or on the grounds. It was as though it had fallen off the face of the earth—or into the hands of Nicholai Petronovich.

"Speaking of the mirror," James said, clearing his throat. "Is our mother still alive, Katie? Do you know?"

"She's in the northeastern United States, James. But to protect her, we cannot ever acknowledge or see her. You must promise me. If it was ever known where she is, what she does ... Therin alone has managed to get messages to her so she would know I was all right after I was—stolen. She's a research analyst." She paused and drew in a deep breath. "In time travel."

"And she's cracked a few secrets," James said, reading her face, filled with the expression of words she could not say.

The girl nodded.

"Is she working for the government?"

"Oh, God no!" Katie exclaimed. "No way would the institute let the government stick their bureaucratic noses in time travel. What a mess that would be."

The smell of Colombian coffee filled the halls of the house, and a plate of key lime pie Andre brought in with coffee from the kitchen was soon demolished. Mostly by the mother-to-be.

"I was thinking," she said in a small voice, "that the baby might be, you know, the turnaround for Therin's family—mark the end of evil and the beginning of a new day, a past founded on love, and grounded in redemption."

"Well said," Andre commented. "May the future make it so."

"We'd better go, James," Daelyn said softly, touching James on the shoulder and handing him his Giants baseball cap. "Mama Pistola said she's going to make breakfast for you. Something she said you liked as a kid. Spam and eggs?"

"Maybe we better pick up some oatmeal on the way," he laughed.

As they heard a limousine pull up in front of the house, James turned to Andre and for a few moments their gazes locked, filled with the knowledge of who and what they were. And James knew Andre was damned glad he was back in one piece with his soul intact. "See you at the farm for Thanksgiving," he said.

James nodded, and smiled. He was damned glad he was back in one piece, too.

Katie leaped into his arms to say goodbye. "You'll come see us? When the baby's born? So she can meet her uncle?"

James shot a glance at Therin. "It's a girl?"

"We had the ultrasound done as soon as we docked in Boston," he grinned.

"She's going to have quite a childhood," Daelyn said with a silvery laugh. "One grandma is an ex-sheriff who keeps her shotgun loaded with silver bullets, and the other one loves to travel—in time."

Gathering up her back pack and the long cashmere and wool coat James had given her, she started for the door of the study … "Whoa," she murmured as a dizzy feeling gripped her and she was thrown slightly off balance. The walls of the room had seemed to weave.

"What's happening?" Katie said in a small, panicky voice from the couch as she stared wide-eyed at the melting walls and reached for Therin.

The windows swayed, the fire became cold ashes, the room blurred and lost its color. A rolling sensation rumbled across the floor under their feet.

"An earthquake!" Daelyn cried.

"It's a time rift," Andre said, grabbing the edge of the desk to keep his balance. "Hold on!"

Katie clutched Therin, James and Daelyn grabbed a door frame. The rest of the Shadow troupe clung to the rolling bookcases, but they were tossed to the floor as the jolts intensified.

The knickknacks and books on the shelves rattled. The house itself seemed to move off its foundation …

Stillness.

The fire crackled tranquilly, the wind whistled in under the sill.

Whistled in under the sill.

James looked up at the windows. They were dual-paned. There shouldn't be any whistling.

Correction. They *had* been dual-paned.

Daelyn straightened her back and smoothed her hair. "Not much light in here," she murmured. Then she stared dumbfounded at the coal oil lamps on the tables and desk, the bookcases with far fewer books, and the skirt extending from her waist, a waist that was now corseted. The skirt seemed to have no less than fifteen petticoats under it, fifteen uncomfortable petticoats.

"What the ...?"

"That's a beautiful set!" the Shadows' other Valkyrie, Kathryn, said. She crossed the room to admire her gray traveling cloak and matching gloves, and apparently unperturbed by the time rifts that continued to rock the house.

But then time meant very little to vampyres. It did not matter what decade, or century passed before them.

Kathryn was wearing a dress with bubble sleeves and her breasts bubbled above a low neckline.

"Oh, my God! Do we have to fight him again?" Daelyn cried toward James, suddenly realizing what era they were in.

James stroked the beard on his chin ...

His hand bumped something sticking out of his mouth. His fingers felt the object, the curve of a pipe. Pulling it from between his lips, he stared at the bowl in awe, then at the deerstalker cap in his hand.

Walking to the window, he opened the drapes and looked down at the drive—where the limo should have been.

The horses neighed. The driver of the carriage looked up and nodded from under his cap.

At that moment in time, only one phrase seemed appropriate.

"I need a brandy," he said.

He walked past the coal oil lamp on the end table to a sideboard.

"But we don't have ..." Daelyn began.

"We do now," he said.

"You don't drink brandy."

"I do now."

The paneled wall next to the fireplace seemed to weave again slightly, causing everyone to draw in a sharp breath and dash for something solid to grab onto again.

The room did not rock. The ghost materialized out of the weaving wood and stood in front of the fireplace.

The Shadows could see the fire's red and yellow flames flickering through him.

Within the mirror is the ghost from the past who will write the future in the present.

The apparition's words floated through the glow of the oil lamps, causing the flames to waver.

When he dissipated, the room rolled again, the furniture quaked, the house returned to normal.

Almost.

The coal oil lamps remained.

"Well, this is—interesting," Andre said as he looked around and realized there also were no plug-ins for electrical cords.

"That was a damned good pipe," James murmured, staring at his empty hand. Then he looked up and spotted the oil lamps. "Double damn. You don't think this is our mother's doing, do you, Katie? An experiment?"

"Or Nicholai found the mirror," Daelyn said with a shudder. "And something's gone terribly wrong."

"Either that or an innocent found the mirror, doesn't know what it is, and they are intrigued with the runes," Andre said pensively.

"And your educated guess?" James queried.

His jawline twitched. "Someone found the mirror."

Another roll.

The room returned to normal.

"I hope whoever it is finishes dusting their attic find pretty soon," Dailyn said.

"We, and the other envoys feel the time rifts because of what we are," Andre said. "The rest of the world will not even have remembered the tilts in time."

Andre's cell phone vibrated on the desk. He read the text, and his jaw began to twitch. "Someone bought the plantation. The furniture, including a cheval mirror found in a sealed casket under a basement floor pit, was part of the package deal."

"Easy fix," James said, an excitement starting to light up his eyes. "We just go steal it, right?"

Daelyn grabbed his arm and began pulling him toward the foyer. "Andre can steal it. We're expected for breakfast."

She piled him into the back of the limo and directed the driver to, "Make haste, my good man, before this limousine turns into a pumpkin. And I have to wear those damned horrid petticoats again!"

He nodded and sped out of the drive toward the freeway to the airport.

Daelyn slipped off her shoes and curled up on the seat under the softness of the cashmere coat.

"Petticoats," James murmured. "Henri said once he retained somewhat of a fondness for the eras of petticoats. A lot easier, he said, to, umm, maneuver than skinny jeans and tight, zippered pants. Just slide them down and slip them off and, 'Voilá!'"

"Hmm," she responded. "My voila has never been maneuvered out from under petticoats or tight jeans in a limo. Have you ever—done it in a limousine, James? Yes, of course you have. I can tell by that sheepish grin on your face."

Snow began to fall softly outside the car, and before long they were stopped in a traffic jam until the highway could be cleared.

From under her coat, Daelyn slipped discreetly out of her jeans and panties, then unbuttoned her sweater a little, just enough to offer him a glimpse of pink nub.

"Never in a limo in the snow," he said, yearning filling his voice.

"Voilá, Van Helsing," she murmured, sinking with him into the plush leather seat under the warm luxury of cashmere.

"Voilá, my beautiful Valkyrie." Then he smiled with his curvy smile.

• • •

ELIZABETH BROCKIE

A native of Oklahoma, Elizabeth Brockie graduated from the University of Oklahoma with a bachelor's degree in English Literature. After graduation, she relocated to Southern California, became a college instructor, and began a career in writing.

When she isn't at her laptop, she works for a grant program at the local high school district, enjoys cooking and trying new foods with her husband, and spending time with their golden retriever, Summer, and cat, Taffy. Her two children, presently residing in California, are her best critics and loyal supporters of her writing.

He is a Royal.
And a vampyre.

She is a mystic.
And mortal.

Their combination is forbidden.

ISBN: 978-1-934912-49-2
Price: $16.95 paperback

ELIZABETH BROCKIE

He is a Royal. And a vampyre.
She is a mystic. And mortal.
Their combination is forbidden.

MASTERS OF THE NIGHT